The creatures knew she was there...

There was nowhere near enough flesh on the emaciated corpse to satisfy them. Nothing was left now but stained dust and pink bones. One by one the bloody-mouthed creatures left the gruesome pile and began to slither toward her, their beady eyes fixed on the warm sleek flesh of her body. Her nerve broke; she turned and fled toward the house she had seen, the only possible place of refuge on these barren plains...

At last the building loomed darkly in her blurring vision. She staggered up the steps and sagged against it, turning to look back. The creatures had fallen behind in the remaining few hundred yards, but they were coming, they were coming! Slowly, but inexorably they drew near, yammering with insatiable hunger. Adelinda turned back to the building, searching for an entrance. There was none...

◀ ◀ ◀   ▶ ▶ ▶

Also by Claudia J. Edwards

Taming the Forest King

Published by
POPULAR LIBRARY

A HORSEWOMAN IN GODSLAND

CLAUDIA J. EDWARDS

POPULAR LIBRARY

An Imprint of Warner Books, Inc.

A Warner Communications Company

POPULAR LIBRARY EDITION

Popular Library®, the fanciful P design, and Questar® are
registered trademarks of Warner Books, Inc.

Cover design by Don Puckey
Cover illustration by Kinuko Craft

Popular Library books are published by
Warner Books, Inc.
666 Fifth Avenue
New York, N.Y. 10103

 A Warner Communications Company

Printed in the United States of America

First Printing: July, 1987

10 9 8 7 6 5 4 3 2 1

CHAPTER 1

An-Shai, hierarch of the Quadrate God, leaned on the railing of the balcony of the Bishop's Palace and lusted with all his soul and being for the position and power of the man before him. The initiate Tsu-Linn was gazing peacefully out over the Vale of Misty Waters, a half-smile upon his lips. He did not have the appearance of a man to be envied; Bishop An-Shai, tall, elegant, with long, tapered fingers and fiery dark eyes was far more the picture of dread and power than the moon-faced little man quietly absorbing the beauty of the Vale.

An-Shai had been filled with hope when he found out that one of the usually aloof initiates was coming to inspect his diocese. He had done well here and he knew it. His rise through the ranks of the priesthood had been meteoric. He had scrupulously adhered to the rules of dress, diet, and conduct appropriate to each level of attainment. Why, then, why was the summons to join the last and most exalted brotherhood denied him?

"You've done well here, Bishop. The Vale is peaceful and productive, the peasants are docile, and the heresy that was spreading among the village priests when you came here has been eradicated."

"Thank you, sir."

The initiate turned back to the Vale, which lay spread before him like a delicate watercolor painting. "I think this Vale is the most beautiful spot in Godsland," he said. "You are fortunate to have been allowed to stay here so long."

An-Shai just managed not to grind his teeth together in

frustration. "Yes, indeed, sir." It was true that the Vale was a lovely place, a misty green valley nestled among stark crags. The Hall of the Initiates was in a barren, forbidding place, so rumor said, where nothing could live and no color flourished. An-Shai longed to forsake the beauty for the harshness.

"How many peasants and other laity are there in the Vale?"

An-Shai told him. Keeping an exact and detailed census of his diocese was one of the most important functions of a bishop, just as keeping precise parish registers was the responsibility of the village priests. Only the clergy was literate; the written word was one of the most powerful tools the servants of the Quadrate God had for maintaining their absolute power over the populace of Godsland.

"H'mm. And what percentage are productive workers?"

"Sixteen percent work in the cloth industry. Twenty-nine percent are farmers."

"Forty-five percent productive—you must have a high percentage of aged and children."

"Yes, sir. Life is easier here than in some parts of Godsland. People live longer and more infants survive."

"You aren't sending the food exports out of the Vale that you used to. Has productivity declined?"

"No, sir, but it takes more to feed our own people. I have found that individual productivity increases when the workers are allowed a better diet. Cloth exports have increased."

Tsu-Linn ignored the cloth. "That food is needed. I will arrange for a raid of slavers after young girls. That will reduce the number of breeders. And I think...yes...night stalkers prey upon the young, the old and the weak. Is there a colony of them nearby?"

"Yes, sir, in the hills," said An-Shai, unenthusiastically. He disliked letting the cannibalistic semihumans in among the people he thought of as his own. They created a desolation of fear and suffering.

"Good. They should cut down your excess population in just the right areas. What's the matter?"

"I don't like to let the night stalkers in, sir. They cause so much economic chaos."

"Would you rather I send a coven of Fire Priests?"

An-Shai suppressed a shudder. The priests of the Fire God were worse than the night stalkers. They encouraged corruption and brutality, and their rites of human sacrifice and uncontrolled licentiousness left a stain of evil that sometimes lasted for generations.

"Well, what then?" inquired the initiate, with some irritation.

An-Shai hesitated. Was it this that kept the elusive summons from arriving, that he was too soft with his people? Would thinning them mercilessly impress the initiate? Yet death and suffering were distasteful to An-Shai. Once, long ago, he had joined the priesthood mainly because it was the only route to advancement for a village boy, but partly because it had seemed to the child he was then that the priesthood was a way to relieve human suffering. That, of course, was before he understood that it was actually to the benefit of the peasants to have their numbers managed and to weed out the unfit breeders. "Let me try to improve our agricultural production and to thin a little by less drastic methods first, sir. I can improve agricultural techniques and extend the land under cultivation."

Once again the initiate turned to gaze out over the Vale. Perched as it was upon an outjutting shoulder of the eastern cliff, the Bishop's Palace afforded a magnificent view, although of course the northern and southern reaches were invisible in the distance and the western edge of the Vale was only a thin blue line. "There certainly seems to be plenty of water and many stretches of unused land. Very well, see what you can do. I'll send the slave raiders along." The initiate turned and peered keenly at An-Shai. "Tell me, Bishop, have you managed to overcome your crisis of faith?" he asked abruptly.

"Yes, sir," An-Shai replied promptly, striving to the utmost to put every last bit of sincerity he could muster into the reply, without seeming to be too eager. "I have come through the experience cleansed of doubt and rededicated to the Fourfold God more strongly than ever before." How had the old busybody found out about that? An-Shai wondered. And then it occurred to him that perhaps the old busybody had not known about it and had been fishing for a response. His eyes flickered; the initiate must have noticed. Even a hierarch was trained to see such physical reflections of the internal mental climate. An-Shai cursed to himself.

"You're an intelligent man, Bishop An-Shai. Surely the thought has occurred to you that if the animistic spirits we teach the peasants about are a fraud, and if God the Father that we teach the upper classes about is a construct, that perhaps the Fourfold God is equally false and just a tool that we initiates use to control the hierarchs?"

By a sheer effort of will, An-Shai kept himself from squirming. The thought had occurred to him, often and with increasing conviction. What answer would satisfy the initiate, who was looking at him with the intensity of a cat about to pounce on a bird? "I prefer to think of the spirits and God the Father as a simpler form of truth, more suited to the primitive and unschooled minds of the laity and the village priests. If I am ever summoned to join the initiates, and I find that the Fourfold God is a simpler truth than the reality, I'm prepared to accept that. For now, I am content in the strength lent me by my simple faith in the power of the Fourfold God." There, he thought, that ought to either satisfy you or at least confuse you enough to get by.

"Well put, Bishop," Tsu-Linn said, but there was no real approbation in his tone.

An-Shai spent the night in his private chapel, praying—trying to pray—before the four-branched tree that was the visible symbol of the Fourfold God. "Please, Unseen One, let the summons come," he repeated a thousand times that night. "Should I be harsher to my people? Would that please your initiates?" But no answer came, either to supplication or question. Not for the first time, An-Shai wondered in his despair if his prayers were heard. And not for the first time, he struggled to banish the heretical thoughts from his mind.

The next morning, having seen the initiate off, An-Shai ordered his chariot hitched. His driver whipped up the on-agers that drew the chariot. "North," An-Shai told him tersely. He intended to look at the fields and see what might be improved as he traveled. He found himself wondering, though, as he stared at the onagers' mousy backsides, if he had agreed to the night stalkers and the Fire Priests, if he might not have received the summons. The hard part about attaining elevation to initiate was that no one in the lower ranks had any idea what the requirements for admission were. The summons arrived or it didn't, and no pattern or reason was apparent.

It was the season for preparing the fields and gardens for planting. An-Shai halted in the fields which surrounded Bishopstown, the nearest of the fourteen villages of the Vale to his palace. He walked through the fields and among the workers, causing considerable disruption of the work. The village priest of Bishopstown was not far behind his bishop, panting, since he was not entitled to a chariot.

"Put your workers back to work, Father Neh-tu. I want to see what they're doing."

After the deference he had had to show Tsu-Linn, the eagerness these laymen and the humble priest showed to please him was a draft of fresh air, refreshing and invigorating. An-Shai watched as the peasants picked up their spades and forks and began to prepare the earth for planting. Clod by clod they turned over the rich dark soil, crumbling it up and mixing it with rotted goat droppings. They followed the long furrows made by the plow pulled by two patient and elderly donkeys, but progress was slow. An-Shai watched for an hour, and in that time only a few yards of soil were made ready for seed.

"What these people need is a bigger plow, one that covers more area and breaks the clod up better," said An-Shai suddenly.

Neh-tu jumped. "The donkeys couldn't pull a larger plow, Your Grace."

"I can see that. They also need larger and stronger draft animals." An-Shai returned to his chariot, much to the relief of the peasants and the worried priest.

In the afternoon he returned to his palace and went to his library, a pleasant, shaded room where he spent much of his time. After pulling out several of the scroll-books from the cubbyholes on the wall, he went to his desk. The germ of an idea was beginning to take form in his mind, but he needed to refresh his memory on a few points before making a decision.

The scrolls he had taken down were the journals of a bishop of the Vale of Misty Waters from nearly a century ago. An-Shai liked to read, and he had plenty of time on his hands. He had read all the journals of his predecessors from the library for nearly a thousand years back, until the bark paper was so brittle with age that opening the scroll would cause it to disintegrate. And even some of these he had caused to be carefully flattened and glued upon a backing of the fine soft cloth for which the Vale was famous throughout Godsland.

But of all the journals he had read, this one was the most interesting. That long-dead bishop had had a way with words, and apparently had enjoyed writing in his journals; far more than the usual facts and reports was included. Especially vivid were the anecdotes of unusual happenings that had occurred during the sixty years the man had served as Bishop of the Vale. He had died in office—An-Shai shook off that thought and opened the scroll.

There it was, the watercolor that had stuck in his memory. An-Shai wondered if the man had been a gifted artist as well as a writer of rare talent, for the scrolls he had filled during his life were lavishly and vividly illustrated. There before him was a painting of a man, dressed in strange and ragged clothing, fair in coloring where all the people Al-Shai had ever seen were dark. But the man himself, singular though he might be, was not what the bishop wanted to look at. The man was holding three horses.

An-Shai knew what horses were; the troops of the military arm of the hierarchy used horses to pull the war chariots, because they were faster and more biddable than either onagers or donkeys. They were too rare and expensive for anyone else to own, and they were really no larger than a big onager, certainly too small to be ridden as was sometimes done with donkeys. They were dun creatures with a blackish stripe down their spines and short, upstanding manes.

But these horses! They were truly enormous! The reddish one's back was as tall as the man's shoulder. It was saddled and bridled. In the painting, it nuzzled the hand of the man. An-Shai wished the long-gone bishop had seen fit to paint, or have painted, the man mounted upon his strange steed. One of the other horses was obviously a young one, gangly and long-legged, though it was nearly as tall as the reddish horse. But the third one, that was amazing! Its back was higher than the heads of the men around it. It was a shining black color, which the artist had cleverly highlighted in pale blue. Its huge head towered over the people around it. Its legs were like trees, its buttocks like hills. It wore a docile expression, and seemed to incline its ear toward the man who held its halter.

An-Shai turned to the text, reading the slightly archaic syllabic symbols again. "The man came, he said, from a continent to the east, to which he longed to return, so that he stayed in the Vale for only a few days, whilst recovering from the clawing he had gotten from a tiger. He said that in the land he came from there were many of the giant horses, if I understood him rightly, for his speech was barbaric and strangely accented. He had given the one he rode a name as if it were a rational being, a word that he said meant 'friend' in the language of his own land. He said that he had crossed from the Eastern Continent by ship, far to the north, and was now intending to travel down the coast, hoping that the land would curve around to the east and join with his home continent. I did not tell him that I thought such was not possible, for I was glad to have him gone. He was not a follower of either the spirits nor God the Father and denied the priests and myself any right to guide his life as is proper. I feared that his example would infect the peasants."

There was no more. An-Shai wished that the bishop had questioned the man a little more closely about his origins, although he thought he knew where the man must have been from. He took up a second scroll, this one new and fresh, its syllabary the modern, gracefully accented kind that An-Shai himself wrote so well. This was "Accounts of Explorations of the Eastern Seas," copied that year from an original only a few months old at the time. In it was mentioned a great city placed upon the delta of a mighty river, the capital of a large kingdom. The hierarch who led the expedition had felt that there must be some commerce that could be opened with these people, and he had mentioned that they had a fast and convenient means of hauling freight over the land.

That had to be the giant horses, An-Shai thought. Some peoples used oxen for the purpose, he knew, but they could by no means be described as fast. If he could only bring some of the giant horses here, as well as some of the people who knew how to raise and train them, not only could he solve the problem of increasing production, but he could improve the freighting of the Vale's wonderful cloth, perhaps even ultimately the commerce of all of Godsland. Then, surely the summons would arrive at long last and he would be called to join the mysterious rulers of the land, those servants of the Quadrate God who had been initiated in the final and most secret rites. His plans spun themselves into daydreams of power and respect.

While the hierarch An-Shai planned and dreamed in his lovely Vale, far away upon the eastern continent another dreamed. It has been said that a stranger is only a friend we haven't met, and often it is true. But sometimes a stranger can be a bitter enemy with whom we have not yet crossed daggers.

Adelinda rested her chin on the forearms which were crossed on the rail of the arena and watched the young stallion kick his heels into the air with the exuberance of his youth and sex. Squealing, the bay wheeled on his quarters and reared, tossing his mane into the air.

"You'll never win with him," her brother's cool voice came from behind her.

Adelinda, jerked abruptly out of her dream of trophies and admiring crowds, jumped. "I know," she snapped. "The judges aren't looking for anything but warmbloods. It's not right."

Felim shrugged, careless of the hang of his elegant suit. "Right or not, no stallion of the old pure blood is even going to get a second glance. You might as well geld him and sell him for a pony. It isn't any sort of a hobby for a lady anyway, breeding horses."

Adelinda turned away from the arena. Kinship was very

clear in the sandy blond hair, the height, the gray eyes of brother and sister. "I thought you were glad when I took up a hobby."

"I was glad when you quit chasing—and catching— every male from here to the Black Mountain. I didn't expect you to take up horse-breeding. Mother gets one of her attacks whenever it's mentioned in her presence."

"She'll get used to it." Adelinda scrubbed her hands through her heavy hair. "I have to have something to do."

Felim snorted. "Great wealth does have its disadvantages, doesn't it? If you were a woman of the farmer folk, you'd have seven or eight children to take care of."

Adelinda shuddered. "It's boring enough being rich without being trapped. Anyway, horse-breeding is a fine old tradition in our family. If the first Mara hadn't been a horse breeder and the first one to discover the greathorses, we wouldn't be rich today."

"Yes, but then it was a necessary occupation. They had to get out and get all grubby. You don't." Felim wrinkled his nose. "You smell like a horse."

"There are worse things to smell like."

"Maybe. But how are you going to make a suitable match smelling like that? You can't go on living here forever, you know. When the baby is born, Iona and I are going to need your room."

"Then I guess I'll have to move out, but you had better face the fact that I'm not going to make a suitable match. Your high-toned friends won't give me the time of day. I wouldn't go so far as to say my heart is broken. Your friends are dull."

"If you hadn't ruined your reputation playing around . . ." Felim caught himself. "I'm sorry, sis. I didn't mean that you weren't welcome here as long as you need to stay. But do be thinking about what you want to do with the rest of your life, please?"

"All right." Adelinda inclined her cheek for a brotherly peck and turned back to the magnificent stallion still playing in the arena. What did she want to do with the rest of her life? Marriage was not a possibility. Felim was right; she had ruined her chances when she was younger. Why, once she

had even had an affair with a farmer lad! That had scanda-
lized the society ladies and their dutiful sons, right enough.
Never mind that Dep had been kind and gentle and merry.
She missed him yet.

Perhaps she could take her horses—besides the stallion,
she had four mares and two of last year's weanlings—and
set up her own breeding farm. But how was she to support
her hobby? Her mother would doubtless give her an allow-
ance, but would balk at the expenses of a separate ranch.
There was little market for the old warhorse stock. The
buyers wanted warmbloods that could win races or ribbons
at the shows, or they wanted greathorses for draft. Only a
few dedicated fanciers kept the old lines pure, and they were
a clannish lot who would laugh at the idea of buying from a
newcomer, especially one with (whisper it) a reputation.

"I have as much courage and strength and ability as any of
those old-time people. Why wasn't I born then so I could
use them?" Adelinda cried to the bay stallion, which came
over and offered some slobbery sympathy. She slipped
through the fence and buried her face in his coarse black
mane.

There was a quiet footstep nearby. "Shall I take the horse
in now, miss? He'll be wanting his feed and I've mucked out
his stall."

Adelinda had been daydreaming of an adventurous trip,
just she and Red Hawk, the stallion, traveling as her ancestors had done into unknown lands, dependent only on her
brains and his speed and stamina for survival. They could do
it, she knew they could. But where could they go? And
why? There was no need for such a trip, certainly no such
desperate need as had driven her great-grandmother to ride
out into the unknown, and not alone, at that, but with five
companions and a whole herd of horses.

Life had certainly been simpler in the old days, before
prosperity had struck the folk of the Black Mountains. There
had been work to do for everybody, necessary work that
meant the difference between survival and starvation. Things
were so superficial now. The proper clothes, the right kind
of house, correctly given parties, and most of all, the right
match—these were what her contemporaries thought about.

"Orvet! You startled me. Yes, take the horse and put him away. He's had his exercise." She clipped the lead rope to the stallion's halter and gave it to the man. The horse greeted his groom good-naturedly and followed him into the stables.

Distracted for the moment from her daydreams, Adelinda wondered for the thousandth time about Orvet. He had the manner of a city man, and was obviously educated, probably, she thought, in one of the great universities in King's City. He had simply appeared, asking for a job with the horses, one day, driving a battered and worn farm wagon pulled by six chunky draft horses. He was good with animals, clearly liked them, and by contrast with the usual run of groom they had been able to hire, dependable and sober. He had soon been promoted to the family stables, rather than the huge horse factory that was the main commercial enterprise of her family.

Orvet cared competently and kindly for the family's riding horses, carriage team, and now Adelinda's pets. He lived in a little cottage alone, almost never went into the nearby village, much less the city of Black Mountain two hundred miles away, where the family went for shopping and business two or three times a year. He spent his money on books, refused all promotions to assistant coachman or even stud manager, almost never spoke unless spoken to, and was a complete enigma as to origins and previous life. He was also completely immune to feminine temptations, or at least her temptations, Adelinda thought wryly, for she had tried to engage his attentions, even though he was no taller than she and rather roly-poly.

Dismissing the man from her mind, for she had wondered about him many times before with no profit, Adelinda returned to the house for a bath and a change before dinner.

"Is that you, dear?" her mother called from her sitting room as she came in the door and tossed her jacket to the maid, a pretty farmer girl.

"Yes, Mother. I'm just on my way for a bath," she called back.

"Could you come in here and sit with me for a moment? I want to talk to you."

Adelinda sighed. Another lecture, no doubt. "Yes,

Mother." She went into the sitting room and slumped into a chair.

"Adelinda, dear, you know that I worry about you," Marith said.

"I wish you wouldn't."

"It's time you were married and settled in a place of your own," Marith pressed on.

"There isn't anyone for me to marry."

"No, there isn't," Marith agreed surprisingly. "Not here, anyway. If only you hadn't . . . But that's all water under the bridge now," she added hastily, surmising from the way her daughter's face clouded up that her son had been at the girl again on the same subject. Adelinda, with her freethinking ways and her constant rebellion against the restrictions she had been born to, was a thorn in her conservative brother's side and a particular irritation to his lovely, empty-headed wife, Iona. "There really isn't anyone for you to marry here, or even in Black Mountain. What I think you should do is go down to King's City. You could rent an apartment, get yourself a boat, go to the parties and festivals, and surely meet someone there you could fall in love with."

Adelinda stared at her mother in amazement. "King's City? Mother, you know I hate cities. I don't even like to go into Black Mountain. If I married someone there I'd have to stay there the rest of my life. Where would I keep my horses? King's City is all canals. There'd be no place to ride."

"Horses aren't everything, dear," said Marith. "You should marry and have a family of your own."

"Marriage doesn't interest me, Mother. You'll have to admit that I've had enough experience with men to know that I don't want to be tied to one of them forever. I want to do something useful with my life, not just produce more little brats to do the same futile things."

"But you have so much love to give, dear. Look at the affection you lavish on those horses of yours. All that love should be going to a man and some babies, not animals."

"Animals are a lot more reliable and responsive than men. If you take good care of a horse, you get back faithful service. If you come to depend on a man, he dumps you for the next pretty face."

"Not all men are like that. Look at your brother. In any case, I think you should consider very carefully what I'm saying. To be frank, dear, I think you realize that you and Iona don't get along and that you can't stay here forever." Marith picked up a portfolio from the table beside her. "I've made all your arrangements. Here is your letter of credit with the Guild of Beast Merchants—that should be plenty for the first year. I've included enough for a new wardrobe and one of those painted boats. This is your ticket for the coach to Eastend and here's the ticket for the steamboat south. You'll need servants in King's City so here are two third-class tickets so that you can take a maid and a butler from here. You can hire the rest there, with a good butler to help you."

Adelinda stared bewilderedly at the papers in her hands. "But, Mother, these are for next week! I can't go so soon. I'll miss summer in the mountains!"

"Nevertheless, my dear, I think you must go. Your brother will dispose of your horses for you. You'll find a new set of luggage in your room. You'll be interviewing servants tomorrow morning. Now, you must be wanting a bath, dear, so run along."

Adelinda looked at her mother's loving, implacable face and turned. Blindly she walked out of the room and up to her bedroom, where she laid the papers on her dressing table, stumbling over the pile of new wicker luggage as she crossed the floor. Breathing very carefully, she stood for a while, trying to think what to do.

Instinctively, she walked back down the stairs and out the door, crossing to the stables. She went to Red Hawk's stall, as so often before she had turned to one of her horses for comfort in her distress. The young stallion was occupied with his evening meal, and in no mood to offer sympathy, but she leaned against his stall door and listened to the regular, soothing sound of hay being munched.

Orvet, finishing up his evening's chores, came down the aisle of the stable carrying a bucket and a broken halter.

When he saw the utter desolation on the woman's face he halted.

"Is there anything I can do?" he asked.

"They're sending me to King's City to find a husband." She said it quietly, with little inflection, but the bleakness of her face didn't change.

"King's City is a marvelous place."

"They're going to sell my horses."

"I see." Orvet was aware of the ill will her sister-in-law bore for Adelinda, and also of her rather shocking reputation. He also had seen her with her horses often since his promotion to the family stables and knew how much she cared for them, and how important they were to her.

"What will you do?" he asked.

Adelinda made a sudden sharp motion, a gesture eloquent of despair and helplessness, and a huge tear oozed from her eye and tracked its way through the dust on her cheek. She turned away; she detested having anyone see her cry.

Orvet, knowing that sympathy would only make it worse, went on about his chores, staying near enough to keep an eye on her but not so near as to intrude.

Felim came striding into the stable. "Where have you been?" he shouted furiously. "Dinner's getting cold and here you are mooning about the stables."

"Go ahead without me. I'm not hungry."

"What's the matter with you? You should be grateful. We're giving up most of last year's profits to see you started well in King's City, which doesn't thrill Iona, I assure you, and you act as if you're being sent into exile."

"I'm not going."

"What? You have to go."

"I'm not."

Felim crossed to her. "Sis, you can't stay here. Iona gets so upset. We just want you to be happy."

"I'll never be happy away from the horses."

"Yes, you will, once you find some nice man to marry."

"Felim, listen to me very carefully, and deliver this message to Mother and your poor upset little wife. I do not want to get married. I do not want to live in King's City. I do not want to sell my horses. I am going to take my share of the greathorses and mountain horses and I am going to find somewhere where I can raise them in peace."

"But where? There isn't anywhere for you to go."

"For now, up into the mountains, to let the horses graze on the pastures up there, as they used to do in the old days. When fall comes—well, I'll worry about it then."

"What will everyone think?"

"They'll think that I'm not just a slut, I'm a crazy slut. Know what? I don't care."

"You can't go alone."

"If you'll be here tomorrow morning at dawn you can watch me."

"I'll go with you," Orvet offered hastily. For the wrong reasons, her brother was right. She couldn't go alone.

Adelinda looked at him, surprised. "I can't pay you."

"I'll pay you," Felim said, "until she gets this mad idea out of her head. And some of the farmer folk, too, for herders and cooks and whatnot."

"I don't want your help."

"Don't be silly, sis, it's cheaper than King's City."

"It could be the difference betweens success and failure," Orvet said softly.

Adelinda considered. "Yes, all right. We'll leave in three days. Mother's already got a bunch of interviews lined up. Maybe some of those will want to come." Her step was jaunty and her eyes bright with excitement as she left to begin packing.

Chapter 2

There was a lot of preparation needed for Adelinda's venture. She and Orvet plunged into it the next morning. Choosing people from among the applicants for the jobs was Adelinda's chore. Orvet was sorting tack and equipment when they were interrupted. Felim had been talking to a potential customer; now he led the man and his entourage to the barn office, where Adelinda and Orvet were working.

Felim's companions were quite the strangest men she had ever seen. They were dressed in robes of soft, silky cloth, with the designs woven in. Their hair and eyes were uniformly dark, and they were...sleek was the only word Adelinda could find to describe them, as if their features and figures were less well defined than other folks'. Of medium height and medium build, they were narrow at the shoulders and hips, while at the same time they were thicker in the waist than was usual among the mountain folk.

"Sis, this is Li-Mun, from the Western Continent. He's come all this way to buy greathorses and take them back. Li-Mun, this is my sister Adelinda," Felim introduced. "Let's go have a look at the horses I was telling you about and you can talk to Adelinda as we go."

Li-Mun was utterly appalled. His command of the language was far from perfect; he had not understood that the noun "sister" was feminine. He stood before a lithe, tanned, smiling woman as tall as he, who took his hand and offered him some conventional words of welcome, while his mind reeled.

Li-Mun was about at the end of his tether. Neither in

King's City nor along the River Groan, up which he had sailed with his little fleet of horse transports, had he been able to find the number or quality of horses An-Shai had sent him after, nor anyone willing to come with him. High summer had come and gone, and he knew that if he did not return soon, he might better not return at all than face his bishop's extreme displeasure. At last, in the Black Mountains, he had found horses available for purchase, but these folk were even more adamant in their refusal to go with him than the lowland people.

Then at last he met Felim, who seemed to think his "sister" might be willing to go with him. His sister, he had said, was as skilled as anybody in the care, breeding, and training of horses, and had always longed for adventure. For a suitable fee, and if Li-Mun bought horses from them both, perhaps . . . Li-Mun had allowed himself to hope.

But a woman! In Godsland, women were baby-incubators and stoop labor. They were considered to be at best semi-intelligent. They were strictly controlled from birth, through their breeding careers, and into their graves so that they might not learn enough to disprove that opinion. They were a valuable commodity; some men actually allowed themselves to become fond of their assigned wives and to enjoy the performance of their fertilizing duty, so that the life that the women led was not as restricted as the theory would have it. But to bring a woman in the role of expert mentor! Li-Mun quailed at the thought of what An-Shai would do and say.

But wait. Maybe there were some advantages to bringing a woman. A man might be missed if he never returned, but this was obviously an excess woman, one that no man claimed as his own, and therefore one that would not be missed. And if she were as expert as her brother claimed, she would certainly be better than nothing. An-Shai could either get used to the idea, or he could think of a better solution himself.

Smiling internally behind an impassive face, Li-Mun described the Vale and all of its beauties. He was careful to leave the impression that the term of employment would be a year or less, and he offered a handsome fee. And for good measure, he truthfully described the need of the people of the Vale for heavy draft horses. Adelinda's questions were intelligent and pointed; Li-Mun completely forgot that this was a mere woman he was talking to. Orvet, too, contributed some excellent questions, and Li-Mun, instinctively scenting in him one with whom he had much in common, offered him too a generous salary and wages for whatever peasants they required.

"It certainly sounds interesting," Adelinda said at last. "We'll talk it over and give you our decision tomorrow."

Li-Mun bowed graciously. Felim, Orvet, and Adelinda retired to the barn office.

"Well, what do you think?" Felim asked.

"It would solve the problem of where to go, for this year, anyway," Adelinda said thoughtfully. "The money would come in handy, too. How many horses does he want?"

"Fifty, some work stock and some breeding stock. I thought thirty trained geldings, two good young stallions, and eighteen mares in foal to different stallions might just about suit his purposes."

"How does he intend to get them to the Western Continent?"

"He's got three little ships rigged up as horse transports. Each one can take about twenty horses, so there's plenty of room. I think it must be really important to him to hire someone who knows about horses. He hardly looked at the horses I showed him, but he kept asking about someone to go with him."

"Don't they have horses over there?"

"Not like greathorses. When I asked him he showed me how big their horses were, no bigger than a pony. He said they were too small to ride."

Adelinda paused thoughtfully. "What do you think, Orvet?"

"I think there's something decidedly fishy about the man. He isn't telling us everything. And he almost fainted when he saw you. I don't think he was expecting a woman."

"Do you think that might be a problem, Adelinda's being a woman?" Felim asked.

"It could be. Not all peoples let their women do as they like the way you horse folk do."

"Do as they like! After all the pressure that's been put on me to marry! I wouldn't like to see your idea of a repressive society!"

"Nobody made you marry," Orvet pointed out mildly. "Nor sold you to your prospective husband, will-you-nill-you. You were let to go to school, and to take up a business venture of your own, and if you're successful at it you'll be just as respected as your brother, and just as laughed at if you fail. There are many places where such freedom for a woman would be unthinkable."

"Ah, sis, we weren't trying to force you into anything you didn't want to do. You've got to admit, you used to give the impression of a girl whose main interest in life was men. We all just thought you ought to have one of your own."

"All right, all right. What are we going to do about this fellow's offer?"

Felim said, "I'm beginning to think Orvet's right. It would be foolish to go off with him who-knows-where."

"I didn't say that. I think it might be quite interesting to go with him. There's a feeling about him—or something. If you want to go, I'm ready to go with you. But I don't think we should go unprepared. We should take someone who understands war."

"War?" Adelinda and Felim chorused.

"Yes, war. I know that you can ride with any man in the Midsummer Games, light-horsed or heavy. But just because you can handle games weapons doesn't mean you're mentally ready to kill, even to avoid being killed. We need a real soldier—just in case. And we'll need to take trained war-horses for ourselves and teach the farmer folk we take to use weapons and to ride a warhorse."

"Farmer folk?" objected Felim. "Everybody knows they haven't the courage to fight . . ." He trailed off as he saw the look exchanged between Orvet and his sister.

"I know who understands war," said Adelinda. "Karel."

"Perfect," said Orvet. "If he'll come."

"We can ask. He certainly doesn't seem too happy here."
Many of the horse folk were recruited into government ser-

vice, since they had had for many years the reputation of being honest and dependable. Most joined the civil service, but one occasionally chose the King's Army. Karel was such a one. He had returned, scarred, limping, and bitter, to live on his pension, two years ago. But he was restless and unhappy. He was a few years older than Adelinda, and had left when she was still a gawky child, but they had been good friends before he went and after his return she had been one of the few of his old associates he had been comfortable with. Adelinda could not think of anyone she would rather have at her side in a sticky spot, crippled or not.

"Then you'll try it?" Felim asked.

"Yes. Will you keep my breeding stock for me until I get back?"

"Sure. I'll have plenty of room, selling fifty horses at one shot."

Orvet summoned the farmer folk Adelinda had chosen. They accepted the offered jobs with alacrity; work was not so easily come by, and the wage, with Li-Mun's offered addition, was princely compared to what they could expect if they stayed. There were two young men: handsome, sullen Len and fair-haired, lazy Tobin, who gave promise of being the jokester of the crew. The third member was Ina, a plain, sensible girl who had hoped to become Adelinda's personal maid. All three could ride and handle horses, Len having been employed as a plowman, Tobin as a groom, and Ina as a driver for the children of another family.

The next morning, Felim and Orvet devoted themselves to picking the horses to be sold, including several of Adelinda's, and getting the young geldings at least minimally broken to harness, saddle, and pack. Adelinda began the training of the farmer folk to the use and management of weapons and warhorses. Even Ina, somewhat to her indignation, was given lance and bow and mounted on one of the lightning-quick mountain horses.

"Why do we have to ride these horses?" asked Tobin, picking himself up out of the dust of the big schooling arena and rubbing his posterior. The mare snorted. "Look at that, the beast is laughing at me."

"You signaled her to turn that sharply. I told you to go

easy with kicking her in the sides. She's just wondering why you jumped off like that," Adelinda said, patiently. "You'll get a chance to learn to ride a greathorse. But they're not nearly as comfortable to ride nor as easy to maneuver as the mountain horses. When someone's coming at you with a big nasty sword intending to do you bodily harm, you'll be glad your horse can jump out of the way."

"If I don't fall off at the fellow's feet." Tobin gathered up the reins and struggled back into the saddle.

They had had a difficult time finding enough trained warhorses to mount the whole crew. Adelinda insisted upon taking Red Hawk.

"Oh, sis, you know nobody rides a stallion to war. They're too noisy, always yelling at other horses," expostulated Felim. "I'll let you take my old Games horse Dusty if you like."

"Even taking Red Hawk, we're having a hard time mounting everybody on a trained warhorse. There's the chestnut gelding, and your old gray, thank you. I don't know if we ought to take him; he is fifteen years old, after all. Then if we take three of the mares, even though they're in foal, that's just barely enough. I know Red Hawk and trust him. I've been riding him all summer and he's bold enough to try anything."

"Taking a mixed bunch of mares and geldings is bad enough, but a stallion? They'll be fighting all the time."

"Maybe not. Red Hawk and Blackie didn't fight. They threatened and cursed at each other, but they kept their herds apart and minded their own business."

"Maybe so, although I suspect that Red Hawk had better sense than to tackle Blackie—he's twice as big. Maybe we'd better make Blackie one of the greathorse stallions we send."

That afternoon, Adelinda saddled Red Hawk and rode down to the village to talk to Karel, leaving Felim to teach the farmer folk and Orvet how to use a lance—his favorite events at the Midsummer Games were the ring-spearing and other contests that depended upon accuracy with the lance.

Karel was where he was usually to be found, sitting on a bench in the shade of a cottonwood tree near his cottage, lame leg stretched out before him. He was staring somberly into space when Adelinda rode up and double-tied Red Hawk.

Karel brightened a little when he saw Adelinda. "Hello, Nubbin!" he called, almost smiling. The scars on his face pulled grotesquely when he smiled broadly, so he tended to avoid it. "I thought you were going up to the mountains for the summer."

"I was, but something came up. How's the leg?"

"Better." The leg was not better, and it wasn't ever going to be better, but that was Karel's stock answer when anyone asked about it; he loathed whiners. "How about a glass of beer? I've got a keg draped in wet towels, so it ought to be cool."

"Sounds great." Adelinda watched while he struggled to his feet with the aid of his cane, and went to get the beer; Karel resented being waited on.

Adelinda drained her glass and set it aside. "Buster, I didn't come just to visit. I came because I need help."

Karel looked up at her with his crooked grin. "I thought there might be something wrong."

Adelinda told him about Li-Mun and his offer. "I'm going to go, Buster, but I don't want to go alone. I need someone who knows about war and fighting. I don't know what I'm getting into on the other continent and I might need someone I can trust on my side. Will you come?"

"Surely you aren't going alone."

"Well, Orvet and some of the farmer folk are coming, but they . . . they aren't horse folk. I don't know how far I can trust them."

"Orvet seems pretty reliable."

"Yes, but he's a flatlander, and he doesn't even know as much as I do about fighting. I really need you, Buster."

Karel gestured helplessly at his leg. "I'm not much of a fighter anymore, Nubbin."

"But you know about fighting. Most of the traveling will be on a ship, and I've got Felim's old gray gelding Dusty for you to ride. He's the easiest-gaited horse I've ever ridden. I know it would be hard for you, and you deserve your retirement, and if you don't think you can do it, I'll understand. But I'm asking you to come."

Karel sighed. Adelinda waited quietly; there was no point rushing Karel. It only made him stubborn. "Well, I've got to admit that retirement has been pretty boring. All right, I'll go. Hey!"

Adelinda had flung herself at him and given him a rough hug, at once delighting him and rather shocking him. All the horse folk tended to be a little reserved, and Karel more than most, especially since his return. He ruffled her thatch of hair as he used to do when he was a twelve-year-old dare-devil and she a nuisancy tagalong tomboy. "Well, all right, then. When do we leave?"

"We're still breaking horses and teaching the farmer folk to handle a warhorse. You'll want to help with teaching them about weapons. Li-Mun is in a terrific hurry. Say, two weeks?"

"All right. I'll need the time to get back in some kind of shape for riding, too. I haven't been on a horse since I got back. You say you convinced Felim to lend me Dusty?"

"Yes, if you want him. Unless you think he's too old?"

"What is he, fifteen? That's not so old. You've fallen into the flatlanders' way of thinking. They break their warm-bloods at two and burn them out by the time they're ten. I've known purebreds of either breed to be as useful and active when they were twenty-five as they ever were."

"You're right, I've seen it too. I'll bring him over in the morning and you can ride back with me and get us all started on real weapons. So far we've just used Games lances."

"All right, Nubbin, I'll see you in the morning." He hob-bled with her to where Red Hawk was tied and held his head for her while she mounted—not that it was necessary; the stallion stood like a statue. "And, Nubbin, thanks for think-ing of me."

"Who else would I think of? Thanks for accepting!" She wheeled the stallion and rode down the street, riding, Karel noticed as he watched her out of sight, with an unconscious grace that he knew he could never again match.

Chapter 3

An-Shai stood looking sadly down at the mangled, half-eaten body of the frail old woman.

"You see, Your Grace," babbled the peasant, nearly incoherent with fear and grief, "it's night stalkers, all right, Your Grace, poor old Granny, she liked to take a walk in the evenings. She never thought of coming to harm!"

"Hush, you fool, you're disturbing His Grace. He can see that it was night stalkers that killed your old granny," the village priest hissed. Abashed, the peasant subsided. At a little distance, the rest of the family grieved noisily.

An-Shai turned to the priest and the family. "You're not to tell anyone about this, any of you. I'll see to the night stalkers." He turned on his heel and marched briskly to his chariot.

He should be pleased, he told himself grimly. His plan to reduce the population of the old and the very young was succeeding admirably. This was the third death in as many days, and so far he had managed to keep the news of it from getting out. The other old folks would be less cautious if they didn't know about it. He really should be celebrating. Instead he felt angry, and sick, and sorry for the victim. Poor old woman, she liked to take a walk in the evening, and her bishop wanted to be an initiate, and for these two crimes she had died horribly. Her family, too, seemed to be genuinely sorry for her death; in spite of being old and useless, she was evidently loved.

The chariot lurched into motion and An-Shai managed, with difficulty, not to disgrace himself by vomiting all over his driver. A great rage was welling up in him. He longed to take all the men at his disposal and clean out the night stalker nest. He knew where it was, oh yes, indeed he did. It was, if not by his permission, at least without his interference, that they came raiding by night into the Vale.

He managed to contain himself in white-faced and stony dignity until he got back to the palace and into his private library, where he slammed the door so forcefully behind himself that none of his staff would have dared to disturb him to announce the end of the world.

"When I become an initiate," he said through clenched teeth to the silence of the books, "I shall have every night stalker in Godsland hunted down and destroyed. And Li-Mun, if he isn't back by fall."

Adelinda leaned on the salt-gritty rail of the ship, breathing great gulps of the damp sea air. The little vessel heaved itself groaning up the back of a long ocean roller, poised shuddering on the crest, and swooped down the wave's face as if intending to drive itself right into the bottom of the sea. Adelinda swallowed and fixed her gaze on the horizon.

She had been uncomfortable since they had sailed past King's City and into the open ocean. These foreign ships with their strange high poops and what seemed to Adelinda's eyes to be dangerously high masts and heavy top-hamper were fast. They had passed several of the King's crack packets coming downriver. But they bobbed in the water like corks and struggled with wind and wave instead of yielding smoothly to them. Tobin, who shared the flagship of the small fleet with her, was below in his bunk, completely incapacitated. He alternated between semiconsciousness and heaving fit to bring up his socks.

"Are you ready for another lesson?" Li-Mun asked from behind her. Adelinda had asked him to give her lessons in the language of Godsland. Owing to the fact that she was surrounded by the language, and Tobin was in no condition to bear her company, she was making excellent progress. One of Li-Mun's soldiers on the second ship, the one with blue sails that Orvet and Ina were on, and another on the last one with the rosy sails, where Karel and Len were, had been delegated to teach the language. But whether anyone was in a condition to take advantage of the instruction, Adelinda didn't know, nor whether the horses on the other ships were being properly cared for.

"I think we should begin on the written language today," Adelinda said.

Li-Mun was nonplussed. "You will not learn the written language!" he protested.

"Why not?"

"Women don't learn to read and write. It's forbidden by God the Father," Li-Mun said indignantly.

"Li-Mun, I want to learn. The prohibitions of your Father-God don't impress me. I can read and write perfectly well in my own language, and if I'm going to teach your people how to care for, breed, and train horses all within a year, there are lots of things I'm going to have to write down. Unless, of course, you intend to follow me around and write for me, or assign one of your secretaries to do it."

The thought of assigning a priest to follow a woman about and transcribe her words was even more appalling. "I don't think . . ."

"Probably not. Here, these are the symbols I've figured out already," Adelinda said, holding out a piece of the thin, crisp white paper her people used, much superior to the heavy bark paper in use in Godsland.

Li-Mun took the paper and gaped at a list of the fifty or so most common syllabic symbols in use. "How did you get these?"

"It's very obliging of you to label everything. Once I knew the words for them, it was clear that each symbol stands for a syllable. Very awkward; there must be a million different symbols to memorize."

"Only about three hundred," Li-Mun said incautiously.

"I wasn't sure of this one. Is this 'ba' or 'bi'?"

"That's 'ba.' And this one here is 'ke,' not 'ge.'" Before he quite knew what was happening, Li-Mun was showing her the basic syllables and helping her to write the complex shapes that represented them.

It wasn't until later that night that Li-Mun woke up in a perfect sweat, realizing that he was breaking two of the most fundamental taboos of his religion—that no lay person could ever be taught to read and write and that no woman should ever be taught anything. It was fortunate, he mused, that An-Shai was so much superior to him in controlling the laity. He would have to worry about domesticating Adelinda.

Adelinda, for her part, found Li-Mun something of an enigma, too. The Black Mountains horse folk had always prided themselves on their freedom from superstition, and their schools were organized around strictly rational lines. The poor farmer folk, on the other hand, were afflicted with a wide variety of superstitions and almost as many cultish religions. Adelinda had the full measure of contempt for the preachers and priests of these cults, who were either self-deluded or outright frauds. At first she had tended to lump Li-Mun in with those social parasites.

Somewhat to her surprise, she found that she liked him, and that he was an intelligent and articulate man. They spent many hours talking of Godsland, ostensibly practicing the language. But Adelinda was keenly aware that she was also getting an education in the attitudes and customs of his country. Li-Mun no doubt told her far more than he intended; he liked to talk and Adelinda was a good listener. Even so, she was aware that there was still more that he could have told that he did not. To inquire into certain areas meant an immediate change of subject, and she could not help but wonder why he was being less than honest with her. This knowledge kept her a little wary.

At last the blue coast of Godsland appeared over the horizon; the ships docked in a quiet bay, and the wan, staggering victims of seasickness made their appearance, gazing about them as those raised from the dead might peer about the precincts of their tombs. The horses, too, were glad to be unloaded and given a chance to stretch their stiffened limbs and roll away the itches of many days in their confining shipboard stalls.

The visitors from the Kingdom were amazed at the lush greenness of the land through which they rode. The incredible variety of plants, the many lakes and ponds, the hazy, heavy-scented atmosphere were as different from their own clear-aired mountains and canyons as if they had crossed a great gulf of space, rather than a mere few thousand miles of ocean. There were no tangled forests, but only open parklike woods. The hills were as gently rounded as a girl's breast, and their greenness as muted a shade as twilight's own dimness. Even the flowers that drifted in banks over the sloping flanks of the hills or nestled in the dells were delicate and subdued in hue.

The greathorses with their huge thudding hooves and the fiery mountain horses were somehow out of place in this tame and gentle landscape, and Adelinda felt herself to be alien here, made on a different scale, bold in a subtle land. But she could not deny that it was very beautiful.

In the late afternoon, Adelinda and Orvet turned their horses to where Li-Mun rode, clinging grimly to the pommel of his saddle.

"I think we'd better think about stopping for the night soon," Adelinda called up to him. "The horses will need to graze."

"We'll stop in the next village," Lin-Mun jolted out. "The priest there has room enough for all of us."

"Oh, we don't mind camping," Adelinda returned.

"We can't camp here; this area is infested with succubi and incubi."

"What are those?" Adelinda asked. The words Li-Mun had used were unknown to her.

"Supernatural beings which approach their victims in the form of lovely girls or handsome young men of irresistible physical attractiveness. They feed upon the life force of their victims while seeming to make love to them."

Orvet straightened in his saddle and looked keenly at Li-Mun, clearly startled and alerted. Adelinda wondered, but Li-Mun, absorbed in trying to ease his aching bones in the saddle, failed to notice.

The rectory of the lovely little village was almost a small hotel, with accommodations for all of them, though the horses had to be picketed. Sleeping arrangements were simple benches around the walls of the communal sleeping chambers, made of the same pale rough stone as the walls from which they projected. The food they were offered consisted of crisp vegetables, very lightly cooked in hot oil, and bland boiled grains. Nothing was seasoned, even with salt. The drink they were given was a thin, colorless, very sour wine.

Supper over, Orvet disappeared. Karel laid out the weapons they had brought and began to test them for corrosion from the sea air. Len helped him, and Ina and Tobin began to unpack and prepare their room for the night. Adelinda strolled out in the last fading twilight to check on the horses and found Orvet walking briskly about. He checked, hearing her step, and seemed to peer into the gathering darkness. He raised his head as if smelling the air, as a hound will do when it scents a wisp of odor. Then he moved quickly on. Adelinda got the definite impression that he was searching for something that was not readily discoverable by sight alone.

Adelinda double-checked the security of the picket lines, untangling those horses that had gotten their legs over the ropes, and gave Red Hawk a last pat. Then she sought out Orvet. He was still scouting restlessly about.

"What are you doing?" Adelinda asked. Orvet jumped; Adelinda customarily moved as quietly and as gracefully as a cat, and he had been intent upon a pillar of stone set in the midst of an open meadow, intricately and meaningfully carved.

"I'm looking for succubi and incubi," he answered crisply.

Adelinda looked sharply at him; she had taken the hierarch's words to be more mythological nonsense. But Orvet seemed perfectly serious. "Have you found any?" she asked, cautiously.

"No. But there are supernaturals of some sort about. Look at this." He pointed to the pillar. "This is a guardian stone, set to ward off creatures of the night. And I can feel them, not very near. Not quite what I'm used to, though. Perhaps the supernaturals are different here."

Adelinda regarded her employee with astonishment. This was a facet of the sober, hardworking, taciturn man she had never seen. He seemed to vibrate with intensity. "What sort of supernaturals are you used to?"

"Vampires, mostly, although I have tangled with a few others in my day." Orvet sighed. "I expect I had better tell you a few things about myself that you don't know. It's a very good thing for you that I happened to come along."

Adelinda goggled. Until this minute, "modest" and "unassuming" would have seemed too strong to describe Orvet. He glanced at her dumbfounded expression and grinned wryly. "You see, this whole land absolutely reeks of supernaturals, of every kind I'm familiar with and many I can't identify. Not Karel, with all his warlike skill, nor you with your courage, and certainly not the farmer folk, handicapped with superstition as they are, could prevail against any of them."

"But you can?"

"I am an exorcist."

Adelinda had passed beyond surprise. She looked at her employee with new eyes, and found that she could believe the preposterous claim without any difficulty. "Let's sit down on that log and you can tell me how you came to be cleaning out stalls on my brother's farm."

"Not that one; it's outside the ring of guardian stones. I don't want to be warding werewolves and night stalkers off as we talk. Come over here."

As they crossed the meadow to the log Orvet indicated, Adelinda considered his position. The exorcists were a small and elite group, seven in number, whose purpose was to battle the supernatural. Most of the time they lived in King's City, studying and preparing themselves, but when any part of the Kingdom was threatened by infestations of supernatural beings, they could be summoned to deal with the problem. Legend had it that in the early days of the Kingdom, after the fall of the First Civilization, hundreds of kinds of malign creatures had run riot over the lands, feeding off its miserable inhabitants. The exorcists had struggled for centuries to overcome them, at great cost to themselves. They had succeeded so well that most kinds of supernaturals were just legends in the Kingdom now, and many were extinct and forgotten.

"I left the exorcists several years ago when I was sent out on my first call. A village in the Clearwater sheep country was being plagued with vampires, and they sent for an exorcist. When I left King's City, I was pretty well convinced that the whole thing was a fraud.

"But it was not so. There were vampires there, three of them. They were a male and his mate and baby, pitiful creatures, lost and alone and on the verge of starvation. A crippled goatherd had taken them in, providing milk from her goats for the baby—the mother was unable to provide enough—and acting as host to the male. The vampires had been searching desperately for others of their species, and at last had come to believe that they were the last of their kind."

Adelinda had been following the story with amazement. "How did you find all this out?"

"They told me." Orvet grinned at Adelinda's startled reaction. "Oh, yes, they can speak, and they use our language. I don't doubt that if there are vampires here they use the local language. Of all the supernaturals, vampires have the closest relationship with human beings. They are parasites, not predators as so many of the other supernaturals are. It's very much in their interest to keep their hosts alive and well. In fact, in the bad old days they often protected whole villages from other, more destructive supernaturals. A colony of vampires was associated with a particular village for generations, each with his or her host among the villagers, and if 'their' village was threatened, they fought off the attackers. Many gave their lives in defense of their hosts."

"I always heard stories that vampires were the undead human victims of other vampires."

"Superstition. You wouldn't think so if you had ever seen one. They're human only in general outline. I believe that they're more closely allied to the bats than to humankind. They even have enormous mobile ears and little vestigial flaps of skin that once may have been wings. But they are certainly semiintelligent, perhaps not much less intelligent than we are. I came to know those three well."

"You seem to have liked them."

"Not liked, exactly, but pitied. I couldn't kill them, as was my clear duty. The goatherd gave me their baby to hold, poor tiny starveling creature, and it trusted me." Orvet paused, face somber, lost in the memory. "I had read an account of a journey into the wild lands to the east of the Republics. The travelers had met vampires and even been saved by them from the attack of a predator that would have undoubtedly destroyed the whole party."

"East of the Republics? That sounds like the journey of my ancestress Mara."

"The very same. I sought your family out for that reason, and because I thought you might have more complete records of the journey."

"We haven't kept any written records, and the stories that have come down from that time are unreliable. They claim, for example, that Mara brought a slave with her from the Republics and that this slave was our ancestor."

Orvet regarded her and the corner of his mouth twitched. Fortunately, the gathering darkness hid his amusement from Adelinda. "That happens to be true. Mara did rescue a man from slavery in the Republics and later married him. I think you can trace your blond hair right back to the slave-breeding farms of the Republics."

"I don't believe it. All our family has always loathed slavery."

"Who should loathe slavery more than a slave? And teach his descendants to loathe it, too?"

"It can't be true," Adelinda said hotly. "We're pure mountain folk stock. Everybody knows that." She paused and took a rein on her temper. "What did you do about the vampires?"

"I took them to the place mentioned in the account. There were remnants of a once numerous colony of vampires there, and they were very happy indeed to have the three I brought from the Kingdom join them. But I couldn't go back to the exorcists then. I would have been accounted a renegade—as I am, by their standards. So I wandered east, and then south, and met many strange peoples and many different species of supernaturals, and studied with those who deal with the supernatural in other ways than the exorcists use. But at last I had to come back to the Kingdom, though of course I dared not return to King's City. I was tormented by the thought that although we—the exorcists—are skilled at destroying supernatural beings, so skilled in fact that we have completely wiped out several species, we really know very little about them. Some are benign and some are harmless. The vampires I knew healed my wounds on several occasions. We shouldn't destroy whole species without knowing more about them."

"Did you become the host of one of the vampires?"

"Of course not!" Orvet snapped, shocked. "The rest of the College of exorcists might not say so, but I am still an exorcist, and I follow the rules of conduct as much as I can. I don't wear the robes, of course, but I have kept my virginity."

"So that's why you weren't interested in me."

"I was interested," said Orvet wryly, "but I've had a lot of practice at resisting temptation. And also some very good reasons for doing so. For example, if there are succubi here, they will have no power over me. I can meet and study them without fear. You, on the other hand, I'm afraid, would be in deadly danger if approached by an incubus."

The next day they took their time and arrived at the head of the trail down into the Vale in midafternoon, just as the sun gilded the land in an aura of hazy golden light. Adelinda and Karel left the horses bunched on the rich grass with the soldiers to watch them and rode ahead with Li-Mun to inspect the trail down into the valley.

Adelinda had never seen, never imagined anything so lovely as the Vale of Misty Waters. If a superlatively talented artist had taken a palette of ethereally delicate colors and had painted an earthly paradise, he might have counted himself fortunate if his canvas were half so beautiful as the view which lay before them.

The Vale of Misty Waters was a ribbon of land perhaps five miles wide, stretching out of sight to the north and south. The farther, west boundary of the Vale was bordered by low cliffs, shaded and blue now as the sun began its descent toward night. The eastern boundary, upon which they sat and gazed in wonder, was a line of sheer bluffs, illuminated and gleaming, a creamy white in the full light of the afternoon sun. The floor of the Vale was all clothed in soft green velvet, laid out into an irregularly divided but harmonious pattern of fields and pastures. Within view were half a dozen exquisite jewel boxes of villages. Every tidy cottage, every barn and fold and shop and temple was a separately sculpted little gem, unique and yet a harmonious part of the whole village. Even from the heights it could be seen that each village was itself unique and still belonging as comfortably to the landscape around it as if it had grown there of its own accord.

The Vale of Misty Waters it was indeed, for waterfalls, brooks, streams, and (most astonishing to these children of the arid eastern continent) gushing artesian fountains were everywhere.

There were many lacy waterfalls visible on both cliffs, as well as the spouting natural fountains, frothing with some great pressure from far below. The travelers were to discover later that the water from these artesian fountains had a different flavor from the surface water, a back-of-the-tongue, crystalline, mineral flavor, that brought to mind deep caverns filled with scintillating jewels far down in the cold granite heart of the earth. There were a multitude of more ordinary springs, too, bubbling up through sandy bottoms, their water pure and tasteless, but these were not visible from the heights.

The Vale was filled with the music of the waters, a symphony of the rush of the falls, the singing of the little brooks, the rhythmical lapping of the streams, and the chiming of the fountains.

The air of the Vale was rich and sweet, spicy with the smoke of the cooking fires; the people of the Vale burned the wood of the dark spicewood trees that grew in orderly groves everywhere. The hazy atmosphere seemed as hard to breathe as syrup to the travelers, used as they were to the thin, crisp air of home. Balmy—neither too warm nor too cool—the very air of the Vale was as enervating as a drug, bathing the visitors in sweet luxurious languor.

Besides the dark spicewoods, the Vale was dotted with pale featherleaf trees, their plumelike leaves trembling with every breath of breeze. Fruit trees lined the fields and pastures, and the hedges were berry brambles. Whenever the peasants cut down one tree, for firewood or lumber or to clear a field, they planted three more like it; they were taught by their priests that if they did not offer the spirit of the tree a choice of new homes, she would be angered and turn their luck against them.

To the travelers' left, sited commandingly on a low shoulder of the cliff below them, was the Bishop's Palace. An undecorated, rectilinear building constructed of the same creamy stone that protected its back, the palace was a rambling, one-storied structure with several wings and many rooms. In that place of gardens, there was no plant to mar its purity. The full light of the afternoon sun shone uncompromisingly upon it and only the soft, sweet air of the Vale transformed its severity into dignity.

Adelinda and Karel gazed into the Vale for many minutes, and Li-Mun enjoyed their amazement. At last he suggested, "If you think the horses can get down the trail, we'd better go and meet the bishop. He's been waiting since spring."

It was like the first clash of swords in a duel to the death. Adelinda sat her bay stallion and An-Shai stood on the low balcony of the Bishop's Palace; their eyes were on a level. An-Shai was rigid with shock and anger; Adelinda was proud and bold. That they were enemies by birth and breeding glanced forth as the sun glitters on polished steel. Will thrust against stubborn will. Neither dropped an eye or flinched. There was no hatred between them—not yet. As yet there were only two people, equally matched, dark and light, courage set against courage, pride against pride, mind against mind. If the one was older and more subtle, the other was bolder and less hampered by convention; and which would emerge from the conflict triumphant and which would go down to defeat, the canniest of seers could not have foretold.

It would have seemed that only An-Shai realized how deep the animosity between them was doomed to run, for he knew that he planned virtually to enslave these strangers; but Adelinda felt the more strongly of the two that this man before her was her enemy. Causes she could not have given, but in the instant of confrontation, she realized that there were only two possible outcomes for her: victory or destruction. An-Shai as yet underestimated his adversary.

The hierarch chose to loose the opening volley of the war. "Woman, you will not ride into my presence."

"Hierarch, this is my horse and I ride him wherever I please."

"You are the servant of God the Father and you will obey His bishop or suffer His wrath."

Adelinda laughed. A woman's laugh in the presence of the bishop was as unlikely a sound as if the stones had begun to play sweet music. "I respect your feelings for your religion, Hierarch, but it has nothing to do with me. Your secretary there hired my services for a year to help your people learn to manage the horses he bought from me and my family. The salary does not include adherence to outlandish cults."

An-Shai was no fool. He sensed that to bluster and threaten further would not serve his purpose. His most potent weapon, superstitious fear, was ineffective with this outrageous woman. He measured his next words carefully. "Very well, then. I bid you welcome to the Vale. Quarters will be made available for your people in the villages. You may begin to instruct the farmers in the use of the horses." Without waiting for a reply, which he felt certain would be impertinent, An-Shai turned with dignity and went into the palace. "Li-Mun," he said ominously, "I'll see you in my library immediately." The secretary battened down his mental hatches in preparation for the storm and followed.

"Your Grace," Li-Mun said as soon as the library door closed on his heels, "I know that bringing a woman to teach us was a surprise to you. But no one else would come."

An-Shai rounded on him. "You would have done better to have brought no one. But if you had to have brought a woman, you certainly should have indoctrinated her in the proper place and behavior of women in Godsland. You should have taught her to fear God the Father."

"I don't think she fears anything. Women on the Eastern Continent are different from ours."

"I can see that. How did you expect us to control her?"

"Well, Your Grace, knowing how skilled you are at establishing respect and fear in the hearts of even the most recalcitrant lay people, I felt quite confident that you would be able to reduce the outlanders to submission in short order."

An-Shai snorted. "However confident you may be, the fact remains that you've brought an uncivilized woman among our well-behaved people. What effect will these people have on our own folk? Aren't they likely to see them defying us with impunity and decide to try it themselves?"

"Then, sir, may I respectfully suggest that they ought not to be allowed to defy us? They, and especially the woman Adelinda, must be brought under control. The means to do it lie ready to your hand. The supernatural has been virtually eliminated in their own land. They should be frightened to death and eager to turn to you for protection at the first manifestation."

An-Shai looked thoughtfully at Li-Mun. "I hope you're right. I certainly do hope you're right. What about the rest of the group?"

"They're of little account. One is a cripple and the rest are stablehands—peasants, sir, much like ours. They don't even show Adelinda much respect. They should be easy to subvert, once they're frightened."

"Perhaps, provided that the woman is not among them to bolster their loyalty. H'mm . . . go tell the woman that I have decided to offer her the hospitality of the Bishop's Palace, since she is obviously of high rank in her own land. And don't let her refuse you!"

Li-Mun was shocked. "A woman? Here? If word of it gets to the initiates . . ."

"If word gets to the initiates that we have imported a bunch of unconverted outlanders and set them to work among the peasants where they could do the most damage, we'll be bishop and bishop's secretary of the Seaward Islets and up to our necks in saltwater at every high tide."

Li-Mun gulped. "I'll try to persuade her. She won't want to leave her people."

"Do better than try. Oh, while I'm thinking about it, I've arranged for a raid of slavers to carry away some of the young breeding-age women tomorrow. See to it that the out-landers are well out of it. I've had to let the night stalkers in, too, to thin out the old and infants, but they won't bother young healthy stock. Better have a care for the cripple, though."

Adelinda made less difficulty than Li-Mun had antici-pated. The accommodations offered them in the village, though much better than the conditions the peasants lived under, were crowded, and one less would make a consider-able difference in the comfort of the others. Besides, she judged it as well to find out as much about An-Shai as she could. "That bishop means us no good," she told Karel and Orvet, as she gathered her things. "I knew it the minute I saw him. I'm going to keep an eye on him."

"I think you're right," agreed Karel, easing his aching leg up onto the sleeping bench. Adelinda's leaving meant that he could stretch it out and that Ina could have a little curtained-off corner for privacy. "Just remember that when in enemy territory it's always wisest to speak sparingly and listen well."

Orvet followed her outside. "Take this," he said, handing her a little bag. "Keep it in your possession all the time. It's an herb that tends to discourage attacks by the supernatural. It won't protect you if you're attacked directly, but it might encourage a supernatural predator to look for easier prey."

Adelinda made no objection. She slung the bag around her neck by its long drawstring. "Are there supernaturals here?"

"Several kinds. I haven't identified them all yet. The traces of some of them are completely unfamiliar to me. Be careful."

"I don't think the supernatural is nearly as dangerous to us as the bishop is."

"You deal with the bishop and I'll concern myself with the supernatural. Karel can look to our defense from more mun-dane perils."

"I think you had better get him aside and tell him what you are. He needs to know what resources he has available.

But don't tell the farmer folk; they'd be more frightened of you than of the real dangers."

Orvet sighed. Adelinda assumed that the farmer folk were the mental and moral equivalent of children. The prejudices of her class blinded her still. But this was not the time to argue. "I'll tell Karel," he agreed.

Chapter 4

As she carried her pack into the palace, Adelinda thought about the bishop. "An interesting man," she mused. "Too used to having his own way, but still unsatisfied. There's something uncanny about him. He's cold as ice, but as full of fire as a volcano. Handsome, but not interested in women. People like that are dangerous. They aren't easily distracted from their own ends. I'd like to try sparking some of that fire—but I might regret it if I succeeded."

The Bishop's Palace was not palatial. It was large, with many rooms and chambers. But it was starkly furnished, with few comforts. Sleeping arrangements were stone benches along the walls, which served as seats during the days, just as in the poor huts they had seen. The only decorations were simple watercolor paintings, never more than one to a room. At least she was given a room to herself, for which she was grateful. Privacy was evidently more important to the subjects of the King than to Godsland's simple folk. It did not occur to her that there was safety in numbers nor that she might have been separated from the others in order to render her more vulnerable. She thought she had been invited to the palace so that she could not protect her people.

At dinner, a meal even more ascetic in its simplicity and sparseness than those they had been given, An-Shai and Adelinda took each other's measure. Wills had clashed, and neither had prevailed; now the arena shifted An-Shai found that the woman fascinated him. She was as different from

40

the dutiful women of Godsland as an eagle is different from a barnyard hen.

"Is it the custom in your homeland to send women on long voyages without the protection of their men?" asked An-Shai.

"Not exactly the custom, Your Grace, but among my people women are considered to be fully capable and responsible. Few of our people, men or women, travel. We are a home-loving folk. Is it the custom here to prevent women from traveling?"

"The women of Godsland are conscious of their duties as wives and mothers. The idea of traveling would not occur to them."

"What of those who are not wives or mothers?"

An-Shai glanced into his plate as if seeking a special morsel from among the attractively arranged vegetables. "All adult women are wives and most are mothers. We have a constant shortage of marriageable women in all classes." He did not add that it was machinations such as he was currently engaged in that kept the ratio of women to men artificially low. "If women in the Kingdom are permitted to do as they wish, how are marriages made there?"

"Most women wish to marry and have children. Those who wish to do something else can usually do so."

"In Godsland the women are not asked their opinion of the matter, but are allotted in marriage by the priests."

Adelinda was aghast. "Whether they want to marry or not? What if they don't love the man they are allotted to?"

An-Shai looked at her in his cold way. "It is their duty to love the man they are given to. If people were allowed to marry whomever they chose, hereditary weaknesses would decimate the population, and the stock would deteriorate until the peasants and nobles were useless."

Adelinda shook her head. "It must be very hard for your women, forced to marry without love. I'm surprised they tolerate it."

"Surely even in your undisciplined land people are not allowed to marry indiscriminately. What if they are closely related? What if they are completely unsuited to each other?"

"Close relatives don't marry, of course. And if two people

find they can't get along, they separate and find other mates."

It was An-Shai's turn to be shocked. "Do you mean to tell me that your people are actually permitted to . . . er . . . lie with more than one mate?" He shuddered in disgust. "In Godsland such infidelity is punishable by death."

Adelinda hastily decided not to tell him about her own early escapades. "It doesn't happen often. For one thing, our people don't usually marry until thirty or later, so they have made up their minds whom they want. But I thought Li-Mun mentioned that he had two wives?"

"Li-Mun is a hierarch. He may take as many wives as he wishes, and the two girls were sisters and did not wish to be parted. He is soft-hearted and acquiesced when they begged."

Adelinda thought it well to change the subject. "Your Grace, if we're to spend a year here, we need to know more about Godsland. May I ask you something about the government of this land?"

"Government?"

"Yes, the rulers or administrators of Godsland."

"There are none."

"But who makes the laws?"

"There are no laws."

"Then who protects the people?"

"The Quadrate God grants His initiates the power and the responsibility to guide and protect the people, and the initiates inform the hierarchs of His will. The hierarchs in turn pass this information on to the village priests who guide the people in their everyday lives. We are all the servants of the Quadrate God."

"Then is 'God the Father' one of the Quadrate Gods?"

"There is only one Quadrate God. The Fourfold One is known by many names, but He is only one. But the concept of one God with four aspects is too complicated for the peasants and nobles, so 'God the Father' is the name by which He is known to the nobles and village priests, while the peasants are taught to think of Him as the spirits and gods which animate the trees and fields, the storms and many other things."

"And what do the initiates call him, Your Grace?"

An-Shai shifted uneasily. "As I'm not an initiate, I don't know." It was the hierarch's turn to feel that the conversation would be better channeled in other directions. "Do your questions imply that in the Kingdom, the governing of the people is in the hands other than those of the Church?"

"We have many religions, none of which have anything to do with the government. Some of them would like to, of course, but the King is the head of our government. The day-to-day tasks of governing are carried out by thousands of civil servants, each with his or her own special concerns, so that none becomes too powerful."

"Why do the people obey this government, without God's power to force them to?"

"Well, sometimes they don't obey, but mostly they do because they understand that it's really to everyone's best interests to have a good government. The real lawbreakers are controlled by the King's Constabulary, and wars and insurrections are dealt with by the army."

"Here we have no wars or insurrections, and those who choose to place themselves outside of God's will also place themselves outside of His protection. They are soon destroyed by the many perils from which He protects His own."

Adelinda, of course, regarded this as so much metaphysical nonsense. Had she listened more carefully, she could have understood the Church's whole strategy for controlling the laity of Godsland. It never occurred to her that the perils of which the bishop spoke might be provided by the Church itself. An-Shai, assuming that he was dealing with the sort of utterly ignorant and credulous person that might be, for example, one of the nobility of his own land, felt no hesitation in revealing the secrets of his Church, couched as they were in allegorical language. Too, he still thought of Adelinda as a woman, and to the bishop women were only a shade more perceptive than the beasts of the fields. He failed to connect her penetrating questions and ready understanding with the wary shrewdness and clear intelligence from which they issued.

So, by underestimating each other, both Adelinda and

An-Shai missed their best opportunities to estimate the resources of the enemy against whom they were ranged. Dinner over, they sat for a while in the deepening twilight of the balcony, watching the blue evening shadows fill up the Vale. They talked idly of the Vale and its people, and Adelinda learned a very great deal more than the bishop thought she did. As they parted for the night, An-Shai was startled and perturbed to receive a long, slow, knowing look from beneath Adelinda's half-lowered eyelashes. It was not precisely provocative, but it was measuring. It showed, and was meant to show, that she was aware of his maleness. Had he reacted eagerly, she would have discovered one thing about him. Disgust would have told her something else. That he reacted with astonishment gave her much to think about.

Later, arranging the thick quilted pad and her own blankets on the sleeping bench, Adelinda mulled over the day. "An-Shai means us no good, I'm even more convinced of it. Well, possibly he doesn't mean us harm, exactly, but he certainly means to force us into his own mold—and that comes to the same thing," she mused. "Why does his attitude irk me so much? Ah, I have it. He doesn't expect me to understand anything he says. I'd like to shove his superiority down his throat . . . but it's just as well that he thinks that; as long as he does, he'll keep giving away his plans. Maybe I should play dumb, like Iona does when Felim's around. No, I can't; I'd gag. It's hard enough to keep from telling him what I think as it is. . . ." Her thoughts trailed off into dreams.

Adelinda had settled into that deep slumber from which it is as hard to awaken as to swim to the surface of a pool of quicksand. She heard the first dismal groans of the thing that hung above her sleeping form only as from a great distance. As she struggled back to consciousness, a stench of rottenness assaulted her nostrils. The thing groaned again, and she opened her eyes to find hanging over her a face—a rotten, maggoty face, squirming with obscene life. Nor had it been a human face before it had decomposed, for slimy great fangs protruded over the putrescent lips and the withered eyeballs bore slotted pupils like a goat's.

Adelinda absorbed few of the details. After one appalled glance, she flung herself sideways off the sleeping bench, snatching the short sword which lay beside her right hand— she had not forgotten that she was in enemy territory— slashing at the disgusting thing as she rolled. Had the vision had any corporeal existence, it would have been halved by that blow.

For the space of a dozen breaths, the two regarded each other across the width of the chamber, Adelinda half crouched, short sword raised; the apparition floating just off the floor. With the whole decaying body visible, the thing was even more horrible. The rib cage protruded from the tattered rags of flesh. Moldy rags of ancient finery draped its shrunken limbs. Instead of fingers, claws, incongruously sharp, considering the advanced decomposition of the rest of the thing, were raised to strike. A green and lolling snake twined about the eviscerated basket of the pelvic girdle and coiled about the half-exposed spinal column. The nauseating stench emanating from its rotting flesh filled the room. An entourage of bloated rats and spiders lolloped around its ankles, showered by the dripping brown fluids of decay.

It surged forward again, looming over its victim, stretching as if to strike, spattering her with its noisome fluids. Adelinda swung the short sword at the thing with all her might. It slashed the vision cleanly in two, severing it across the breadth of the chest and upper arms—or would have severed it; the sword met no more resistance than that of the polluted air. Swung around by the force of her blow, Adelinda staggered half across the room.

Catching herself, she whirled to face it. It was upon her once again, the rats and spiders making little darting charges at her feet. But Adelinda had learned that ordinary weapons were ineffectual; lowering her sword, she raised her left hand and experimentally felt at the vision. There was no palpable presence there. Adelinda straightened. "I guess if you can't touch me, you can't hurt me. You certainly are an unpleasant roommate, though. What do you want?"

There were, in fact, many ways that An-Shai, whose consciousness animated the apparition, could have endowed his creation with the ability to do actual physical damage to a

living human being, but he hadn't done so. He didn't want
to hurt the woman, just bring her into submission. He was
completely taken aback. He had expected screams, terror,
panic-stricken flight. He hadn't prepared himself for defiance, and he absolutely had not foreseen the possibility of
being questioned by his construct's victim. Nor was he ready
for Adelinda's next move.

"Someone sent you here to scare me, I suspect. And I'll
bet I know who. Where does the bishop hang out?" Without
waiting for an answer she stalked out the door, her sword
still in her hand. And if led by instinct she turned toward the
bishop's library, where his temporarily abandoned body lay
sprawled helpless in its chair.

An-Shai hastily let go of the substance with which he had
made his specter, allowed it to mix back with the amorphous
stuff of the overmind. Invisible, he abandoned the control
which had resisted the tendency of his selfness to flow back
into its rightful vessel. Frantically he willed himself back to
the library and into his body.

Adelinda was delayed in her search by not knowing exactly where she was going. Not finding the bishop in the hall
where dinner had been served, she was forced to search
through the public part of the palace room by room. So
An-Shai had time to insert himself wrenchingly back into his
corporeal envelope before she found him, and even to overcome some of the attendant giddiness and nausea. When
Adelinda flung open the door of the library, he was standing
beside his desk, pale but composed.

"It is not considered proper for women to enter uninvited
into the quarters of the bishop," he said coldly.

"Then you had better invite me," Adelinda said, closing
the door behind herself. "How does polite Godslandish society feel about unwelcome specters intruding into a guest's
sleeping quarters?"

"Polite Godslandish society is properly submissive to the
will of the Quadrate God. Being under His protection, they
don't suffer from unwelcome visitations."

"Nonsense. Why did you send that . . . whatever it was
. . . to pester me?"

Again An-Shai was astounded. He was a subtle man, not

used to direct frontal attack. Nor was he an accomplished liar, for no one had dared to question his actions for a very long time. But he was skilled at keeping his countenance; by no flicker of expression did he reveal that Adelinda's shrewd guess had struck home. He stared at her coldly. "You're very brave, to question your bishop in this manner, and dare the wrath of the Quadrate God."

"The wrath of the Quadrate God doesn't bother me, but I'm beginning to be a little concerned about the wrath of the Bishop An-Shai. That was quite a production; I hope the smell has cleared out of my room. I notice you don't bother to deny that you sent it." She crossed the room to his desk, let the point of her sword fall onto its top with a little ting. An-Shai looked at the sword. She made no threat, but the possibility of the weapon was implicit. "It seems to me, Your Grace, that we have an agreement, made through your agent Li-Mun, of benefit to us both. We agreed to provide horses and instruction in their care and use; you paid us an agreed-upon sum for the horses and salaries for the time we remain here. Is this the way you understood the business?"

An-Shai regarded the woman coldly. Behind that facade his thoughts were racing. The tiny metallic note the sword had made when it hit his desk had shattered a great many preconceptions in the Bishop's mind. In all of Godsland, there was no one, man or woman, brave or rash enough to even consider bearing a weapon into a bishop's presence uninvited. There was not one who would conceive the idea of implying that rights would be maintained with violence. Quite suddenly, his perception of the woman standing before him altered radically. He might have been looking at a heretofore unknown species—a dangerously unpredictable species. The techniques that worked so well with ordinary human beings, he saw clearly, would not affect this fascinating tawny-maned creature before him at all. He must think, must plan. Already the pause was lengthening uncomfortably. An-Shai seated himself at his desk with grave dignity.

"Let us sit and be comfortable." He waited while Adelinda reluctantly removed her sword from his desk and seated herself in the chair at the end of the desk before he continued, "Yes, that's exactly how I understood the bargain to stand."

"Then why, ever since we started off, have I had a feeling that Li-Mun and now you have something quite different in mind? You're not my bishop, Your Grace, and your gods are of no consequence to me. Your superstitions don't frighten me. But your malice does. If the original bargain isn't satisfactory to you, if you want something different from me and my people, then let's discuss it. If we can come to an agreement, fine, and if not, we'll leave with our own horses. But sending your peculiar, er, servants to frighten people in the night is no way to do business."

An-Shai regarded her steadily. For the first time he was seeing her, not as an aberrant member of the inconsequential class of woman, but as a dangerous adversary in her own right, and measuring and assessing her with that in mind. "Perhaps I do wish something different from you than was included in the original bargain. I am concerned for you and your people. You make light of my religion and of the protection of the Quadrate God, but that's only because you don't realize that He can protect you from some very real perils. Whatever bad dreams you had tonight couldn't harm you, but there are many evil beings abroad in the land that could. I only wish to bring you to the realization that the Quadrate God would gladly take you under His protection, caring for you as He cares for all His children. I hope that you understand that being under the protection of the Quadrate God means, of course, that you are also under the protection and care of the God's Shepherd on earth, his bishop; that is to say, myself."

"Your concern for our welfare is touching, Your Grace, but I can't help feeling that there must be a price for all this solicitous care, and a pretty steep one, at that."

"Why, no," An-Shai said, leaning forward, intense in his will to convince her. "There is no price. The Quadrate God asks nothing of His people except that they submit themselves to His will. Can a parent care for a disobedient child? If the sheep don't obey the shepherd, are they not likely to dash themselves over some cliff or wander into inhospitable wastes where they may perish in misery? The Quadrate God and His representatives on earth only ask that you accept His guidance."

Adelinda heard the meaning behind the fine words. "You mean," she said levelly, "that all we have to do is turn over to you all our freedom and that in exchange, you will be willing to defend us from these dangers you keep talking about! Well, we're neither children nor sheep. We're quite capable of defending ourselves and we give up our freedom to no one, man or god." She sprang from her chair and paced restlessly across the room. "No, Your Grace, the additional bargain is not acceptable. Our freedom is too heavy a price to pay for anything."

"Even for life?" An-Shai said, softly, rising to his feet. He caught her free hand, turned her to face him. "I cannot have you teaching these heretical doctrines to the people of the Vale. They are not capable of defending themselves, nor would they know what to do with this freedom of which you speak, unless it would be to wander off, taking no thought for the needs of the morrow, until they perished like sheep." He paused for breath. Perhaps for the first time in his life, An-Shai was speaking straight from the heart, and the blazing sincerity with which he spoke nearly sent Adelinda reeling, except that the crushing grip on her left hand prevented it. "You scoff at the dangers I've warned you of, but they are very real, and if you persist in this proud defiance of everything right and orderly, I'll have you and your people destroyed as I would a pack of mad dogs."

"I see," said Adelinda quietly. "I think I understand your concerns. I hope you understand that we can and will not surrender our free will to you or anyone. But I think we can fairly promise not to teach our ways to your people. Otherwise, I can't see anything before us but open war."

"It is not enough. By behaving as you do, fearlessly and without the proper respect, you are an evil example to the simple folk of the Vale that they may be tempted to follow."

"Then can we agree to treat you publicly as you wish to be treated, if you will agree to leave our consciences alone?"

It was still not enough. An-Shai, though he hardly realized it himself, would never be satisfied with anything but the complete subjugation of this woman to his will. He didn't know there was a strong sexual motivation behind this unconquerable urge to domination, for he was considerably more innocent in such matters than the virgin Orvet. But he realized that now was not the time to provoke the final confrontation. "I believe it will serve. You must stay by me so that I can teach you how to behave. Your people must begin teaching the farmers how to manage the horses, because time is growing short." He thought to himself with some satisfaction that by keeping her with him, he would soon learn how to overcome her.

Adelinda was doubtful, but she realized very well that there were only six of them among thousands. If this man before her, whose power in this place as absolute, decided to destroy them, he could do it, though the cost might be more than he reckoned on. She, too, dissembled her real intentions. "It seems to me that it might be a workable solution," she said, thinking to herself that she would stay with him about as long as it took to saddle Red Hawk. She had no intention of letting her folk be dispersed among the villages.

An-Shai, pleased with the apparent success of his scheme, smiled at her, something he almost never did. He was unaware that besides triumph, he felt admiration for this worthy opponent, but Adelinda, more experienced and far more sensitive, recognized it, and pulled her hand away from him. He was not a man, she felt, who did things by halves, and his admiration was more dangerous than his hatred.

CHAPTER 5

"No, no! Don't drop the reins! Hold on, he won't hurt you. Here, let me show you." Sweating, Len grabbed the lines leading to the giant gelding's bit and gently guided him back into the furrows. The gelding had shied at an unexpected shout from one of the farmers, and had been further upset by his frightened driver's panicky abandonment of control. He heaved a great sigh when he felt a steady hand on the lines and calmed down. He was basically a docile creature, as all the greathorses were, and asked only to be told what to do in a manner that was comprehensible to his limited intellect.

"Here, take the reins," Len said to the trembling farmer, who had never in all his life seen anything nearly as big as the greathorse, "and start him up. Keep a gentle pressure on the bit so he'll know you're there—don't yank, you'll hurt his mouth—and pull on the right rein to turn him right." Len wiped the sweat off his forehead with his sleeve and reflected that it would be a lot less work to do the plowing himself. As it happened, he liked plowing and had done a lot of it back home. The long days alone in the fields with just a team for company gave him plenty of time to think—a seasoned team knew how to turn a field as well or better than most of their drivers and needed only a minimum of attention. And at the end of the day there were the long, smooth furrows of newly turned earth to look back over, and a pleasant sense of accomplishment.

A sense of accomplishment was all too rare for a young man of the farmer folk, Len reflected sourly, especially one who had dreams and ambitions beyond his station. If, like the rest of his contemporaries, he had been willing to marry early, rent a farm that could barely feed his family, and scrabble all his life for bare subsistence, he could have been content with the few pleasures that went with such a life. But all he could see in following that path was a soul-crushing trap of poverty and ignorance.

The farmer was gaining a little confidence as he found that the huge animal would obey his signals. Len dropped back a little to let him see that he was in command.

Orvet fell quietly into step with him. "How's your boy doing?"

"Pretty well. The horses must look pretty big to him; he's scared to death of them."

"I think donkeys must be the largest animals they've seen before. He's doing all right. Come and sit in the shade; you look as if you could use a break and I've got a bottle of wine cooling in the spring."

"Sounds good! It isn't as hot here as it is at home, but somehow it takes more out of you—you sweat more." Len wondered briefly at Orvet's friendliness; back home he had kept to himself. But as cool drink was a tempting prospect and he followed the little man eagerly.

Fishing the bottle out of the icy water, Orvet poured them each a cup. Len drained his in one thirsty draft, the coolness making his teeth ache and spreading deliciously from his stomach. He made a wry face. "This stuff sure is sour. I guess they don't make beer here."

"I haven't seen any. Hand over your cup." Orvet refilled it and handed it back; Len sipped more cautiously. There was already a little alcoholic buzz behind his eyes. The wine was stronger than the beer brewed back home.

Orvet sat down on a grassy spot in the shade of one of the feathery-leafed trees. Len dropped into the soft turf and stretched out on his back, sighing.

They rested for a while in companionable silence, sipping the cold, sour wine. Presently, Orvet said, as one who is just making conversation, "You don't seem happy here, Len. Is there something back home you're missing—or someone?"

If it were not for the wine, Len probably would have

sneered at Orvet's question, but he was feeling uncommonly friendly toward the man. "I don't have a girl, if that's what you mean. Tobin does, and I expect he'll get married as soon as we get back. But I can't see tying myself to a woman and a farm and a bunch of children I can't give any future to."

"What do you want to do when we get home, then?" Orvet asked idly.

"What I want to do and what I will do are two different things. I want to finish school and go on to a university in one of the river cities. What I will do ... well, keep on working for the horse folk, I guess, if I can get a job, and when I get too old to work, I guess I'll starve, like old Tom that was found dead in his bed last winter and weighed no more than ninety pounds when he died."

Orvet glanced at him, disturbed by the bitterness in the young man's voice. "Surely continuing your education isn't an unreasonable goal."

"Not for horse folks, but it's pretty unreasonable for the farmer folk. I had five years of schooling and I've been out of school for ten years now. It would be hard to find a school that would take me for the other five years."

"Why did you quit?"

"Five years is all that's offered in our schools. The horse folks' kids get ten, and a chance to get into the universities."

"Couldn't you have gone to one of their schools? I've heard them say that they take worthy farmer children."

"The local school wouldn't have me. There was no money for boarding in Black Mountain Town. There were seven children in the family, and my dad's farm is no better than most. The schools in Black Mountain Town wouldn't have had me, either; my grades weren't any better than average except in arithmetic." The truth of the matter was that Len had a very original way of looking at things, and his teachers, themselves graduates of the same substandard schools they taught, had been sure that any answer they didn't understand was certain to be wrong.

"What would you like to have done, if you had been able to go on to a university?"

"Study history." For a brief moment, the sullen expression that Len had worn for years slipped away, animating his face

with enthusiasm, making him not merely good-looking, but
blindingly handsome. "There's nothing more interesting than
knowing what people really did, and how they thought and
acted. I don't mean the pretty little stories they teach you
about the Founders of the City and the heroes of the First
Civilization—no real person acts like the stories say they
did. I mean what they really were like. Do you know where
you can look to find the truth about people?"

"No, where?"

"Not in the history books! You have to read the account
books. You can look in the things people wrote about them
who lived in their own time, but you have to remember that
all those writers see things in their own way, with their own
biases. Take Lord Quarmot, for example. He's the most horrible villain in all history, right?"

"So I was taught," said Orvet, filling Len's cup again.

"Maybe he was and maybe he wasn't. The terrible bur-
dens of taxation he laid on his own people were not for his
personal profit; if you read between the lines you can see
that he used the money to defend his domain and to help the
forest folk, who were starving. But they were counted
scarcely human by the plains folk, and they saw a great
injustice in Quarmot's taking the money they wanted for lux-
uries to buy food for savages. The only accounts we have of
Quarmot's life come from those same nobles of the plains,
who hated his guts. The forest folk might have told a different tale, but they were illiterate at the time."

"I don't think taxation was the only thing Quarmot did
that was considered to be evil. He's said to have debauched
every virgin in his domain, poisoned his enemies, betrayed
his friends for his own profit, sold his folk into slavery—I
don't remember all of it."

"So the stories say. But they were written down by his
enemies, the men that murdered him. They were justifying
what they did. I'm sure he wasn't a model citizen. Possibly
he did have an eye for a young girl. But every virgin in his
domain? Come on, when would he have had time, considering all the other things he's supposed to have done? The
thing is, we'll never know for sure if all we do is read accounts written by his enemies. What we need to do is look

into his account books and study them day by day. If we find in there things like 'debit, ten silver pennies, for cyanide for the soup' and 'received, one thousand gold pennies for slaves sold to the Republics,' then we'd know for sure."

"It sounds to me as if you've got some very worthwhile and original ideas. Have you talked about them with any of the mountain folk?"

Sullenness settled back over Len's face. "No, why should I? Even if they understood, they wouldn't care."

"You don't know that. The universities aren't as hard to get into as you think, not if you have a little support and backing. Adelinda isn't a stupid woman. Talk to her sometimes as you've talked to me."

Len's lips twisted bitterly. "Her." The single word was spoken like a foul expletive, laden with scorn and hatred. And he would say no more. Orvet, sensing that Len had retreated into his usual sullen reserve, pressed his questions no farther.

They were talking back to their respective students when the commotion broke out. They were up the Vale some distance from Bishopstown near the village of Two Falls. Adelinda, having adamantly resisted any suggestion that the outlanders be distributed one to a village, had sent them word to deliver five of the greathorses there and to begin their lessons, though they hadn't seen her. The rest of the folk from the Kingdom were giving lessons in nearby fields. Karel had stayed mounted on his old gray gelding; when the screaming and the clangor of arms broke out, he wheeled the horse into the grove where the rest of mounts were tied and loosed them as their riders came dashing up. Vaulting into their saddles as they had been taught and snatching up their lances, they formed a line abreast and charged down into the village.

Karel's orders were terse. They swept through the turmoil in the village square, splitting it into a dozen eddies of action. Reining in, they wheeled their horses as one, facing back the way they had come. Even Ina's lance point was steady and level as they awaited the order to charge again.

Karel surveyed the plaza. A dozen or so rough-looking men had been searching through the village, seizing the nubile girls. Their screaming captives were herded into a hysterical huddle of other girls, shackled and guarded by more of the strangers. A couple of sprawled bodies bore witness that the villagers had at least tried to defend their daughters. The raiders, though of the same race as the villagers, were obviously of a different type than those gentle and peaceful farmers and weavers. They were dressed in dark, well-worn clothes with leather tabards and caps, armed with curved swords and clubs. At the moment, they were standing thunderstruck. The mounted attack by strange-looking outlanders had taken them completely by surprise. Their slave-raiding activities had always been clandestinely encouraged by the Church, although they themselves didn't realize how important a role they played in the initiates' manipulation of population. They had never been met with any more than the most perfunctory of opposition.

They stared at the wickedly sharp lance-points leveled at them as if they had been wielded by supernatural beings, as they may have thought they were. For an instant the tableau held; then at Karel's muttered command, the outlanders set their heels to their eager horses again and charged. The slavers scattered like chickens before the falcon's stoop; Karel guided his sensitive gray to cut the guards away from the captive girls. Len, a savage grimace on his face, skewered a burly raider who was dragging a struggling girl of thirteen or fourteen by the hair. The man screamed shrilly as the lance pierced him through, driven by the weight of a charging horse and rider. Unready for the shock of the raider's weight and the throbbing that vibrated up the lance's shaft as the man thrashed in agony Len dropped the lance and left it standing in the rapidly expiring body.

Tobin was hacking at a raider with his saber, while the fellow, parrying the blows frantically with his club, backed away. Ina herded the hysterical girls out of harm's way, trying to hush their screaming. Orvet chased one fleeing raider out of the village, pricking him with his lance at every stride (exorcists were forbidden to kill) and wheeled back to chase another. Karel's heavy war crossbow thudded and the most ornately dressed of the raiders flung up his hands and crashed to the earth, dead before he hit the ground.

Red Hawk came sailing over the low wall that divided the village from its fields and Adelinda drew rein in the midst of the battle. As it happened, she was unarmed, An-Shai having convinced her (for his own protection) that weapons were unnecessary in the peaceful Vale. Far behind, the greathorse stallion Blackie lumbered along, swept by the excitement into following the much fleeter Red Hawk at a ponderous gallop, while the Bishop An-Shai himself clung precariously to his back, cursing weakly, reins trailing.

"Slave raiders," explained Karel, succinctly.

"Good job. Don't kill any more of them than you can help; we don't know what the local customs for dealing with such vermin are," answered Adelinda.

"Right." Karel raised his voice to a parade-ground bellow. "Let them go. They're licked. Meet in the plaza. Ina, I expect that dead one there has the keys to the girls' shackles on him."

Blackie came wallowing into the square at that moment and Adelinda absentmindedly caught him, gathered up the reins, and handed them up to the bishop. "Don't let go of the reins, Your Grace. The horse will run away with you."

An-Shai gathered up his tattered dignity. "So I've discovered. Why did your people interfere in this battle?"

"The village was attacked by slave raiders, Your Grace," Karel answered. "We happened to be armed and at hand. I'd say they've been at the villages farther north, from the number of captives they'd taken."

"My people didn't intentionally interfere, Your Grace, but slave raiders are the worst sort of scum. Surely you want to see these poor girls returned to their families." Adelinda was looking a little askance at the bishop. His attitude was not at all what she might have expected.

"Of course. But the Quadrate God would have protected the girls and taken vengeance on the slavers."

"Would He have brought these two men the slavers killed back to life? Would He have restored the girls to their grieving families?"

"No," the bishop admitted. "Sometimes His purposes are a little hard for mortals to understand. Nevertheless, I'm grateful for the assistance your people provided. Doubtless

the God meant for them to prevail." Seeing that the outlanders were gathering around Adelinda, he drew her aside.
"Now we will return to Bishopstown a great deal more
slowly than we came, and you can show me how to stop this
creature. Why does your little horse run so much faster than
this one?"

As the two rode off, Tobin said, staring after them, "It
sure seems like he doesn't want to let Adelinda talk to us.
What's going on?"

"I wish I knew," said Karel. "I don't like it. He's up to
something."

"He's good-looking enough, in an oily sort of way," commented Len contemptuously. "Maybe she's found herself a
new bedmate."

Karel turned his gaze on the younger man, and his eyes
were like ice. "You may think you have a right to your opin-
ions, farmer, but keep them to yourself." Dusty, Karel's
mount, sensing his rider's tension, sidled closer to Len's
gray mare. "Or if you can't, bring them to me and I'll demonstrate to you just how wrong they are."

Karel may have been crippled, but on horseback he was a
formidable warrior, well able to overcome Len, who had
only a few days' training in the arts of war. Len knew it. His
resentful gaze fell.

"Gentlemen," said Orvet softly, including Len under the
term that was usually used only for men of the horse folk,
"we're among strangers here. It isn't well to let them see
dissension among us. Karel, I don't think it's fair for you to
use your superior skill as a fighter to bully the rest of us.
Len, we all know that Adelinda wouldn't involve herself in
an affair with an enemy."

"Not to mention," added Ina unexpectedly, "an iceberg.
There's nothing but coldness in that man. He might look
handsome, but if you look into his eyes, all you see is pride
and ice. I've met fish that were more attractive, no matter
how good-looking he is."

"What difference does that make?" asked Tobin. "Len
here never lacks for girls to set their caps at him, and he
never gives them the time of day. With his looks, what
woman cares what's inside?"

"That's where you're wrong. Len's not a bit like the bishop. He's cold on the outside, but he'd be as warm and loving as any man if he met the right girl. The trouble is, you men judge a woman just by her looks, so you think we judge you the same way. But we don't. Nine tenths of a man's attractiveness is in his personality. You're no beauty, but you've never lacked for girl friends. Any one of you is a hundred times more attractive than the bishop."

This set the men to blushing and clearing their throats, all except for Orvet, who grinned. "Now that we men have been thoroughly routed by Ina, let's get back to work. But keep your eyes and ears open. There's more going on here than we know about, and the more we can find out, the less in the dark we'll be." Silently, he resolved to himself to talk to Adelinda that evening, no matter what obstacles were put in his way.

Adelinda, riding slowly back to the palace with An-Shai, instructing him on the art of horsemanship, formed much the same determination. It had not escaped her notice that she had been neatly maneuvered away from the rest of her party. The bishop had apparently given up all attempts to convert her to the faith of the Quadrate God, though his conversation was still laced with references to his religion. Instead, he was exerting himself unaccustomedly to be genial and friendly. Adelinda found this as unsettling as his former arrogance. Every instinct warned her against this man, and yet she found in him an enemy that she could respect. She could even like him, warily. But she still underestimated both his cunning and his ruthlessness.

An-Shai, behind his genial facade, was ready to grind his teeth in frustration. He had not expected the outlanders to interfere in his plans, and the abortive slave raid left him in a difficult situation on two counts. The people of Two Falls Village had seen the slave raiders, who they had always been told were too powerful and fearsome to be opposed and whose raids must therefore be suffered with whatever equanimity they could summon, put to flight by a much inferior force of numbers. This made the Church's protestations of helplessness look foolish.

The bishop also realized that unwittingly he had imported into his diocese a force of fighters, few in number perhaps, but formidable by the standards of Godsland, especially mounted upon their lightning-quick mountain horses. Worse yet, these fighters were not under his control, and were motivated by other customs than his.

The key to the problem was Adelinda, he thought. If he could bring her under his control, then he would control the outlanders. Failing that, and he was beginning to realize, with a stirring of respect, that controlling Adelinda might well be a more difficult task than he had ever faced, he would have to alienate her people from her, destroy her credibility with them, convert or subvert them to his cause.

He left Adelinda consulting with builders on the design of stables and paddocks for the breeding stock and summoned Li-Mun to his library. "The outlanders put a neat stop to the slave raid. Schedule another one, with a more impressive force this time."

Li-Mun made a note. "Yes, Your Grace."

"Li-Mun, you traveled for a time with the woman Adelinda. What are her weaknesses? How can she be brought under control?"

Li-Mun shrugged helplessly. "She's bold to the point of imprudence. She's sometimes hasty in dealing with her underlings. Propriety has no meaning for her, and I mean not only our notions of propriety, but those of her own people, too. She's not good at getting along with people—they often don't understand her and she's too impatient to explain herself." Li-Mun paused thoughtfully. "I'd guess that she's lonely. She doesn't make friends easily, and her family seemed almost glad to get rid of her. As to weaknesses—she doesn't have many vices, though I hear that she took a number of lovers when she was younger." He glanced warily at his bishop, wondering if he was offended. An-Shai was sitting—gingerly—at his desk, listening intently, but there was no sign of emotion on his face.

"What you say accords with my own observations, but it isn't much help. What is the woman afraid of? What threat will break her will and send her running to me for help?"

"That, I don't know. I've never seen her afraid of anything. I find it hard to image what she would be afraid of that wouldn't kill her. I can't picture her turning to anybody for help with anything. I'll tell you this much, Your Grace. I'd be willing to bet that if you could win her loyalty she'd be the best servant you ever had."

An-Shai sighed. Breaking her spirit is going to be hard enough. How could I ever win her loyalty? She would know if I lied to her. She doesn't trust me now, but at least she doesn't hate me, and she's still willing to carry out her part of the bargain."

"Perhaps we should just let the outlanders do what they came to do and send them home as we agreed."

"No!" The bishop tossed his head as if challenged. "No. If I give up, she's won, she's beaten me. I'll have lost control of the Vale, of the people, of myself. I might as well cut my throat and be done with it, because I'll be as good as dead."

"No one would ever know," said Li-Mun soothingly. "I don't think the woman herself has the slightest idea what's at stake. After all, Your Grace, we have to keep our eyes on what's important here. Your goal is to be summoned for initiation. If no one knows you lost the struggle, where's the harm?"

"I'd know. And if I know I'm beaten, what's the good of being an initiate? Don't suggest such a thing again. Just find me a way to break her."

"Yes, Your Grace," said Li-Mun, wondering how he was going to carry out the order.

"The first thing we need to do is get at her people. There must be ways to convert or buy off or frighten them. They can't all be as tough-minded as she is. Find out what each of them wants or needs or is afraid of. Assign someone to each of them. Separate them, alienate them from each other. Especially, find ways to turn them against her, but be very sure that she doesn't suspect that we're behind it. She won't be quite so bold when she's all alone in a strange land. Maybe when she finds that there's no one else to turn to, she'll turn to me."

"Yes, Your Grace," said Li-Mun, grateful to have something specific to do. "One of the peasants seems to resent her; that'll be a good starting place. Maybe he'd like an opportunity for revenge. And the peasant woman . . . she's plain. Perhaps she'd be vulnerable to affection offered by some sympathetic man. I know just the man. The light-haired peasant isn't too bright, and he's lazy, too. The other two are going to be harder."

An-Shai gestured impatiently. "The cripple is in a lot of pain. Poppy gum is addictive. He's the easiest one of the lot to subvert."

"Very true, Your Grace. I should have thought of that. What about Orvet? He's different from the others; I don't entirely understand him."

"Try buying him. If that doesn't work, threaten him. If that doesn't work, then I'll use one of my supernatural servants to scare him into line."

"Very good, Your Grace." Li-Mun hastily scribbled more notes and scurried out.

An-Shai sat at his desk for a long time, staring at but not seeing his clenched fists. In his daydreams, he pictured dozens of variations on a theme: a broken and repentant Adelinda and his own magnanimity as he graciously received her tearful oaths of undying loyalty and kindly stilled her terrors.

Chapter 6

"Are your people unable to go on without you for even a single day?" An-Shai inquired coolly. One of the palace servants had brought word that Orvet was seeking to speak with Adelinda. The two of them were just finishing a scanty dinner.

"Of course they are, but I want to see him. I need to find out how they did today and what they plan to do tomorrow." Adelinda rose.

"You saw them today. And it is not polite to leave the bishop's presence without permission."

"I didn't have a chance to talk to them."

"I believe we agreed last night that you would observe our courtesies."

Adelinda sighed and sank back into her chair. "So we did. May I be excused?"

"No, but I will have the man brought inside. You can talk to him in more comfort here."

Adelinda would much have preferred to speak privately to Orvet, but it seemed wiser not to make an issue of the matter. When the Exorcist was ushered in and seated at the table with a cup of wine, they stiltedly discussed the delivery of the greathorses to Two Falls Village and the plans for the morrow, which involved a similar visit to Woodsgarth, a village in the south.

"Karel was hurting pretty badly after the workout today," Orvet mentioned. "Li-Mun sent a healer who gave him some kind of chewy medicine that seemed to help a lot. He's asleep."

"I'm glad they had something to help him. That leg gets bad when he does too much. Maybe he'd better rest tomorrow."

Adelinda and Orvet had been speaking the language of Godsland out of courtesy to the bishop. Now Orvet stumbled deliberately over some of the words. "Ah . . . Len, umm . . ." He turned politely to An-Shai. "Will you excuse us, Your Grace, if we speak our own language for a moment? My command of your tongue is still imperfect and we must discuss one of Lady Adelinda's employees, a subject that you will find of little interest."

"By all means," An-Shai said graciously, deciding to have Li-Mun give him secret lessons in the outlanders' language immediately. He would have given a very great deal to have understood the conversation of the next few minutes.

"What does Len have against you?" Orvet asked in the king's language.

"Len?" said Adelinda bewilderedly. "Nothing that I know of. Why?"

"He seems really bitter, but he won't say why."

"Against me personally? I can't imagine. He didn't hesitate to take the job when it was offered."

"Did you have anything to do with keeping him out of the school in your town? He seems to carry a grudge about that."

"Why would I want to keep him out of school? Even if I could, which I couldn't. I would have still been in school myself at the time—what is he, about five years younger than I am?"

"Not that much, I think. Be careful, the bishop isn't your only enemy here—and speaking of him, he's starting to grind his teeth because he can't understand what we're saying. He seems determined to keep us from talking privately."

"That's not all; he's been setting nauseating visions on me. Meet me tomorrow night in the grove of trees at the bottom of the slope and I'll tell you about it." She turned to An-Shai and switched to Godslandish. "I'd like to thank you for sending your healer to help Karel. He's my kinsman, and the pain is pretty bad sometimes."

"I'm happy to help. There's plenty of the medicine available whenever the pain gets too bad. All he has to do is ask the healer."

"Thank you. If you'll excuse me, Your Grace, I'll walk my employee to the door."

"Certainly," An-Shai said, rising smoothly. "Very courteous of you. I'll come too."

Adelinda and Orvet exchanged speaking looks behind the bishop's back, but were effectively prevented from any further private discussion. An-Shai seemed prepared to stay with them all night, if necessary, so they made their farewells and parted.

Adelinda's sleep that night was troubled only by her milling thoughts. She had known that Len was a bitter and sullen young man, but that his smoldering anger was directed at her personally she had had no idea. She had never harmed him or any of the farmer folk. In fact, she thought self-righteously, her attitudes toward them were a lot more liberal than most of the mountain folk. Orvet, she decided, didn't understand them the way those who had lived all their lives around them did. Len carry a grudge because he hadn't been admitted to the mountain folks' school? Nonsense, the farmer folk all hated school and were glad that they only had five years of it to endure. She dismissed the matter from her mind.

Less easy to dismiss was the realization that An-Shai meant to keep her effectively isolated from the rest of her party. That gave her an uneasy feeling. Evidently the agreement they had struck last night was not satisfactory to him, but what did he want? Was he so religious that he couldn't bear to know that there were people who were not followers of his Quadrate God in his Vale? Then why keep her so closely by him? Or did he regret having agreed to spend so much on his foreign employees? But if that were the case, why didn't he just send them home? Adelinda had a lot more questions than answers. She slept lightly and restlessly that night.

An-Shai spent the greater part of the night searching through his scrolls for mention of a supernatural that he could use to master the outlander woman. It would have to be one with the power to inflict real physical punishment on its victim; Adelinda had already proved that she was not easily frightened. On the other hand, it had to be one he could control, and not one that would kill its victim. That would be as bad as having her escape him—no, worse. Death was far too final an escape.

In the small hours, he fell asleep with his head on his desk and dreamed that he pursued Adelinda down an endless hallway, ever and again drawing close enough to seize her, only to have her melt like fog from between his clutching fingers and flee onward with a mocking laugh.

It was morning then and Li-Mun was shaking him. Those who meddle with the supernatural are always at risk, and the secretary had been startled to find his superior sprawled untidily over his scrolls—very unlike him. An-Shai could not very well be described as a man who liked his comforts; the regimen that the Church's rules prescribed for a bishop contained little that could be described as comfortable. But he was a man who didn't go out of his way to be uncomfortable. He blinked blear-eyed at his secretary and rubbed a stiff neck.

"What is it?" he grouched.

"It's morning, Your Grace, and the outlanders have already started out for their day's work. I assigned the woman Ina to teach the noble Cho-Hei how to drive a cart hitched to a team of the greathorse mares." Seeing that An-Shai was staring at him without comprehension, he added, "Cho-Hei's wife died last winter, Your Grace, and he's a man who likes women. More importantly, he knows how to make women like him. His priest would have had him married again, for the safety of the village girls, if you hadn't proscribed marriages this spring."

"I see," said An-Shai, remembering that one part of his scheme to isolate Adelinda from her countrymen was to place a romantic distraction in Ina's way. "Have you talked to him about what he's expected to do?"

"Yes, and I must say he seems enthusiastic about the idea. He said that this was one command from the bishop that was no hardship."

"Harumph! I hope you explained that there was no need for him to actually . . . er . . ."

"Oh, yes, Your Grace, quite clearly. He said he knew there must be a catch in it somewhere, but that the hunt was always more fun than the kill—whatever that means."

"Cho-Hei's a competent man, and if you're sure he understands what he's to do I suppose we can trust him—but keep an eye on the situation just the same. Where's the woman Adelinda?"

"I told her you wanted another riding lesson, so she's waiting for you where the carpenters are building the new stables for the breeding stock. I sent the healer with another dose of poppy gum to the crippled one. The dark-haired one I asked to give me a driving lesson today, and I'll sound him out about his feelings about his employer then. The light-haired one is off to deliver horses to the northern villages, and if I read my man correctly, he'll dawdle along the way enough to make a whole day's journey out of it."

"Very well, I'll get some breakfast—God's knees!" An-Shai had made a feeble attempt to rise. Pain laced him from a dozen—no, a hundred different places on his body. He sank back into his chair weakly. "Did you tell the woman I'd ride today? Man, I don't think I'll be able to walk!"

"Oh, you'll be fine, Your Grace. The same thing happened to me the first time they put me on one of their horses. I thought I'd be crippled for life, but they told me that all I needed was to get back on a horse and ride even farther, and they were right. Up you come!" With the callous lack of sympathy of one who has recently been through the same agony, he hoisted the bishop to his feet and guided his tottering steps into his sleeping quarters.

By the standard of the people of Godsland, Cho-Hei was a handsome man, with the sleekness and grace so much admired there and a perfectly magnificent mustache. Even by the standards of the Kingdom, he was good-looking, taller than the average of his countrymen, with flashing dark eyes and a ready smile. Ina felt his charm as she felt the glowing warmth of the sun. He was a willing pupil as they drove up and down the narrow roads of the Vale, two greathorse mares pulling a hastily converted farm cart, but he seemed more interested in her than in what she had to teach him, and that she found intriguing.

"That's good. Keep a light pressure on the bits. Don't start the turn too soon or the cart will hit the gatepost. The left rein now—very good! Your learn fast, Lord Cho-Hei."

"It's easy when one has such a fascinating teacher." Cho-Hei leaned toward her and smiled down upon her. "Show me again how to arrange these thongs in my hands."

"Reins." There were no words for many of the items of horse tack the horse folk used, so they were teaching their own words to the students. "Like this. This goes to the near side of the near horse, here, and that goes between these two fingers, and when you need to use the whip you switch both of these to this hand and then back again."

"I don't understand why I need to use a whip; the horses seem willing enough to go."

"It isn't a punishment, but a signal. See, your off horse is lagging and not taking a fair share of the load. Touch her with the whip and she knows she's to move into the collar. Good! Oh, dear."

The last was because in switching the reins back, Cho-Hei had gotten them tangled and was fumbling with them. Confused by the random tugs on the reins, the near horse threw up its head and stopped; the off horse tried to turn sharply right. The whole equipage ground to a halt. "Never mind," the noble said gallantly. "You can show me again how to hold the reins and then how to start them up. It's going to take me many days to learn to drive properly." He was clearly pleased by the prospect.

Ina sighed. "It's really very easy. Maybe you'd learn faster from one of the men."

"But I shouldn't enjoy it nearly so much. No, I think I really must insist on your company for as long as it takes to learn . . . and didn't you tell me that sometimes four or six horses are driven at a time?"

"Sometimes, with very heavy loads, even more, but I've never driven more than two myself."

"Well, then I really think that as soon as I have learned to drive I ought to learn to ride. Now where do these reins go?"

* * *

Several miles away, Len was putting Li-Mun through much the same sort of exercises, though his pupil was a good deal more attentive and had no trouble at all figuring out how to hold the reins. After a good spell of trotting and backing, Li-Mun halted his team in the shade of a grove of pale lacy-foliaged trees. "We'd better let the horses breathe a bit," he said, wiping the sweat off his forehead.

"You don't need any more instruction, anyway. All you need now is practice."

"It doesn't seem unduly difficult . . . Tell me, do you think these horses could be used to pull a chariot like the bishop's?"

"Well, it would have to be bigger. The tongue that fits those onagers would be way too small for greathorses, and it rides so low to the ground that I don't think the driver could see over the horses' rumps. But it seems kind of silly to have two horses pulling a man around when he could just as well ride one."

"You don't make allowances for the bishop's dignity. He isn't just concerned with getting from one place to another; he has to do it impressively. It's the same as it is with your employer, Adelinda. She could just as well be friendly to you and treat you like equals. But she has to keep a distance and treat you like you aren't quite responsible adults, so that you'll all remember who the real leader is."

Len gave the hierarch a startled glance. "Adelinda treats us all right. She pays the best wages of anyone in the mountains."

Li-Mun feigned surprise. "You mean that your people like being treated that way? Or does she pay you extra so you'll put up with it?"

"She pays extra because she knows we have a hard time making ends meet. All of us are saving money this trip?"

"Indeed? She's very kind to share her profits with her employees."

"She'll do all right out of it, too."

"Of course. It just doesn't seem right that she should be so proud. After all, where would she be without you?"

Len gave the secretary a suspicious stare. "I don't understand what you're getting at."

Li-Mun sighed. "Why, nothing at all. I had just observed that she was a trifle arrogant toward her employees. In Godsland, no woman is permitted to behave like that toward any man. If she were one of us, she'd be put in her place fast enough, believe me! It rather seemed to me that you resented it, too." He laid his hand on Len's shoulder in a brotherly way. "And I for one certainly wouldn't blame you. Women like that deserve a good sharp setdown. I wouldn't be surprised if you weren't just the man that could do it, too, if you had half a chance."

"Adelinda is my employer. She's always treated me fairly. If there are any hard feelings between us, that's for her and me to work out. I'll tell you this much, too: as long as she pays my wages I'm her man."

Li-Mun nodded approvingly. "Your loyalty does you credit, Len! I wonder if she knows how you feel. Does she feel the same about you? If the chips were down the other way, would she feel quite so obligated to back you?"

Len stared at the hierarch as if stunned. Li-Mun had struck a staggering blow, he could tell, though he had no idea why. Len had no answer for him, and he resolved to let the thought he had planted fester for a while. In a few days the conversation could be resumed, and he could drive home the resentment and turn it to advantage. Len, he considered, was as good as subverted, at least if he could discover what "hard feelings" there were between him and Adelinda and exploit them. He changed to the subject and chatted of inconsequential matters as they drove back to the half-completed stable yard, noting with satisfaction that Len was exceedingly quiet and thoughtful.

Orvet had noted and was disturbed by the deft way all the outlanders were sent off in different directions. With Adelinda kept out of contact with the rest of the group, her actions hampered by the constant presence of the bishop, and Karel dozing in their quarters, mercifully free of pain for the first time in years, Orvet felt responsible for his fellow travelers. He was teaching a novice stable crew how to clean and care for the big horses, and saw Ina and Len depart with their respective students in different directions, and Tobin ride out with a string of three greathorses to deliver to a distant village. He was even more perturbed when Ina returned with a dreamy expression on her face. Len came back later, his face dark with brooding thought. Tobin had not reappeared long after he should have been back. Orvet was deeply concerned.

Adelinda, too, was worried. An-Shai, even though he was obviously in agony, had insisted upon another riding lesson, and then a return to the palace, where he began her lessons in the complex etiquette surrounding a bishop. Her suggestions that her time might better be spent teaching some of those who were actually to use the horses, were brushed aside.

"Since I'm paying for your time," he said haughtily, "you must leave it to me to decide how it can best be used. You must try to understand that I must never be contradicted or even spoken to unless I speak to you first. The right to decide whether or not to open a conversation is mine."

Adelinda sighed. "Then how am I going to teach you anything?"

"When you're giving me a lesson you may consider that you have my permission to speak. Likewise, when only the two of us are present, you may speak to me as you would to your own countrymen, bearing in mind of course that you call me 'Your Grace' and not by my given name as I have heard them speak to you."

"Is that a universal rule, that people can only talk to you when they're alone with you?"

"No, it's a universal rule that no one may speak to me under any circumstances unless I speak first. If I had a wife, she would have to obey the rule, or if my aged parents were here, they would have to obey it. I'm making an exception in your case."

"You certainly seem to be surrounded by rules. Even the clothes you wear and the food you eat are prescribed by rules, aren't they?"

"Of course. I consider myself privileged to wear a bishop's simple robe, restrict myself to a vegetarian diet, sleep on a single blanket spread on a stone sleeping bench, rise at dawn, and live by all the other rules that a member of the Church must obey."

"It hardly seems fair."

"Eh?" An-Shai blinked, astonished by the unexpected response. "Why not?"

"You work hard running the Vale. I've seen you. It seems to me that things would be easier for you if you were allowed a few friends, a good meal, and a more comfortable house than this pile of rock. Back home, the poorest farmer family has more comfort than you do, and I daresay gets more pleasure out of life. Why does anybody want to be a member of the Church?"

"The Church is the only way a boy can use his life to some effect in the world. If you don't choose the Church, you are choosing to spend your life in the same ignorant rut as all your ancestors. It is a man's duty to do what he can best do to serve the Quadrate God, and the brighter and more ambitious can best serve Him through his Church."

"I see," said Adelinda, noncommittally.

The discussion of etiquette went on for some time, but only half of An-Shai's attention was on his lecture; he was grappling with extraordinary experience of having been treated like a person. It hadn't happened to him since he joined the religious life.

In the afternoon they walked down to the new breeding farm, which had been placed at the foot of the slope below the palace, where An-Shai could keep an eye on things from his shady balcony. So it happened that they as well as the rest of the travelers were present when Tobin came lashing his foaming chestnut mare down the valley at a dead run. It was so unusual for Tobin to put himself to any exertion that they all stopped whatever they were doing and stared—and when he pulled the mare to a sliding stop, peeled off, and came running up to them they were even more dumbfounded. His face was a mask of horror, pale, eyes starting from his head. He was breathing in such gasping gulps that for a few moments he could not speak. Orvet led him aside and seated him on a pile of timbers intended for the stable.

"What is it? What's the matter?" Adelinda asked him kindly, almost soothingly, sitting beside him.

"There's some kind of monster in this valley. I was riding back from delivering the horses when I saw a nice little stream. It looked cool and I was hot so I decided to stop and take a swim... and let my horse rest," he added hastily, a little shamefaced. "I rode downstream, looking for a deep hole. I came to this pretty little clearing on the bank of the creek where there had been a farm. It all looked neat as a pin, fences mended, sheds painted, a real picture of a small farm, and I couldn't understand why such good farmers would leave old rags all heaped in piles around their front yard. Something was spooking my horse, too, so I got off and went over to investigate." He stopped, swallowed hard.

"I found all the people, the farmer and his wife, the old folks... and... and the babies... killed and partly eaten." He stopped again, mouth working. "The tracks were almost human, but whatever it was had teeth and claws. Only the insides were gone on the adults, but the babies were mostly gone. I hurried back here—I thought the bishop ought to know. If we get saddled up and get going, maybe we can catch the... whatever they were... before dark. They left a plain trail."

An-Shai swore internally, though he arranged his face into an expression of deep concern. The outlander had found the work of night stalkers. It was not often that they wiped out a whole family like that, but occasionally, if there was a large enough pack of them and if they found an isolated homestead, they might do so. An-Shai resolved to have a word with the village priest who was responsible for the family; they shouldn't have been permitted to move out of their native village.

He was more than a little startled by the explosion of activity that followed Tobin's story. Almost before he could draw breath to forbid it, horses were being saddled, arms fetched, and the outlanders were mounting up to ride out. He shouted futilely after them, but if they heard him over the clatter of galloping hooves, they failed to respond. Even the crippled Karel rode with the outlanders, and Adelinda was gone quite beyond his careful control. He shouted for his greathorse to be saddled, but since the newly chosen stable-hands were far from expert, by the time Blackie was saddled and he had scrambled awkwardly onto his back, the out-landers were long gone.

Chapter 7

The six travelers took little time to inspect the grim remains at the clearing. Only Orvet dismounted and looked around; the rest preferred to keep a bit of distance between themselves and the grisly heaps in the well-kept farmyard.

"Night stalkers would be my guess," he reported grimly, as he swung back onto his nervous mount. "They will have bedded up somewhere when the sun rose. We're lucky; they're not hard to kill for a healthy, active person. If it had been a werewolf we'd have had a job on our hands, and likely lost some of our people."

The three farmer folk were listening with amazement. "Who's the best tracker?" Adelinda asked.

There was a short silence. "I've been on a few hunts in the mountains," Len offered diffidently. "My folks needed the meat."

Adelinda forebore to comment on his poaching. "Can you follow the trail?"

"I think so."

"All right then, let's go. Are the creatures truly nocturnal, like vampires?"

"No," Orvet answered. "They're just rather cowardly and prefer the dark. Watch yourselves, though. They're true predators, and if anyone goes down, they'll tear him to pieces in an instant."

The riders followed Len at an easy lope, for the tracks were clear and easy to follow. They led away from the stream, and before long the riders found themselves on a steep trail carved into the low cliffs that marked the western boundary of the Vale. Here they were forced to slow down; the trail was narrow and rocky and the tracks were harder to see. For horses accustomed to the vast ranges and perilous trails of the Black Mountains, though, the climb was not a difficult one. Soon they were topping out, to see before them a very different landscape.

It was a broken land, hilly, cut with gullies and washes. The terrain was made more difficult by the tangled, thorny scrub that clustered in the bottom of every declivity. The summits of the hills were grassy and windswept. The trail of the night stalkers followed a broad and obviously well-traveled path. The riders turned their horses into it. They soon discovered, however, that the path had been made by creatures considerably shorter than a horse and rider, for wherever the path passed through the thornbushes they were forced to dismount and lead their horses through. The spiny branches arched over the trail at a level of about five feet. Len, in the lead, found it an uncomfortable experience; visibility when down in the thornbushes was limited to a few feet in front and a few inches on the sides, and he could easily imagine the vicious creatures which had mangled those poor peasants leaping out at him from the dimness.

An-Shai lashed his lumbering mount along in the wake of the outlanders. He was angry and upset, and he knew that Blackie was nowhere near fast enough to catch up before they found the night stalker nest. He failed to even consider that the stallion was too big and clumsy to tackle the trail up the cliff, but put him at it determinedly, and the animal tried gallantly. An-Shai realized his error when he found that his leg was nearly scraped off against the cliff, and when he remembered that he really didn't ride very well, but he shut his eyes and made it to the top.

The bishop knew that he had to regain control of the situation. Events had moved so rapidly, and he had been so unprepared for the vengeful departure of the outlanders, that all the initiative had passed to them. Not that he was exactly unsympathetic with their anger and determination to wipe out the evil little supernaturals; he had long thought that Godsland would be better off without them. But if anyone was going to wipe them out, it ought to be he, or at least by his direction. It was simply intolerable that they hadn't even asked him if they could chase the night stalkers.

An-Shai was so wrathful that it never occurred to him to get off and lead his horse through the thorn thickets. Blackie was so big and powerful that he plowed right through the tangled branches, but even so his rider was scratched and bleeding.

The horses first warned Karel that they were approaching the nest of the night stalkers. He had learned long ago that a horse's senses are far more acute than a human's, and that a wise soldier in enemy territory pays close attention to his mount's actions. When Len's gray mare lifted her head and whuffled disgustedly as the stench of the night stalkers reached her nostrils, Karel quietly called a halt. Within an instant, all the horses were snuffing the tainted air and staring up the trail with huge eyes and working ears.

Orvet squeezed past the horses on the narrow trail and slipped on ahead to survey the situation. It was not long before he was back. "They're bedded up, all right. They've made a sort of village of stick and bark huts."

Karel rubbed his chin. "Can we use the horses in there?"

"We'll have to," said Orvet evenly. "They're small but they've got incredibly sharp teeth and claws. If they get one of us down, I doubt that we'd be able to pull the pack off in time to save the victim."

"All right," said Karel, "let's split up. Three of us work around to the other side with crossbows. The other three charge from here with lances. Crossbows take the outliers and those that try to bolt. Lancers take the center and the fighters. Len, Adelinda, with me to the far side. Orvet, Ina, Tobin, give us fifteen minutes to get into position, then charge. If anyone's unhorsed, everybody drop everything and get to him immediately. Questions?"

There were none. Quietly, grimly, each prepared him- or herself for the task ahead. Karel, with Len and Adelinda close behind him, swung wide around the night stalker nest, approaching it again from the west. Easing their horses into position where their bolts could command the boundaries of the camp, they even had a few moments to observe the vicious supernaturals.

They were like hideous little caricatures of human beings. About five feet tall, weighing perhaps a hundred pounds, they were covered with sparse, wiry hair, mostly brindle in color. Their forelimbs, or arms, were disproportionately long, and the stubby fingers were armed with such large curved claws that they could have been of very little use as manipulating organs. Their bellies were swollen, and the jaws and chest of many of them were dabbled with dark dried blood. Their faces were the least human. Massive brow ridges, like those on apes, shaded bloodshot little eyes. The nostrils were mere slits. The jaws were entirely unapelike, being as wide and massive as a bulldog's, and filled with too many teeth. Long canines projected over the opposing lips, and were backed by smaller canines, while the enormous muscles of the jowls gave promise of an incredible shearing force. In the heat of the late afternoon, the nasty creatures were mostly somnolent, lying about in the patches of shade cast by their crude huts. Many sprawled unconcerned in the dung that lay carelessly about. There were no artifacts other than the huts in evidence, no signs of fire or other elements of culture.

From across the clearing, the three riders burst out of the scrub, grimly silent except for the thud of hooves and the creak of accouterments. Adelinda sighted on a large specimen on the south flank, and in spite of Red Hawk's mincing —he wanted to join the battle below—skewered it neatly on her bolt. It flopped and convulsed, but she was cocking and loading her bow and paid its death agonies no attention. Another of the creatures bolted out of the melee in the center; she shot it, crippling it, and Ina swung her horse out of the melee long enough to administer the coup de grace with her lance. For a few moments, no more of the creatures attempted to escape on her side, and she saw Tobin hacking at them with his saber and doing a bloody slaughter; Orvet's proscription against killing did not apply to supernaturals, and having trapped a clot of the night stalkers in a circle of greenish powder, he was finishing them off at his leisure. She could hear the thudding of Karel's crossbow on the left, and then Len broke out of the scrub, impatient with the slow slaughter possible with crossbows, and charged into the thick of the fight.

The night stalkers, confused and dazed, were easy prey for the first seconds of the fight, but they soon turned on their tormentors and fought desperately. One leaped onto the crupper of Tobin's chestnut, claws extended, while another sank its fangs into the horse's flank. Squealing, the chestnut wheeled, but the rest of the night stalkers, sensing a wounded victim, mobbed Tobin and his horse. The rider was fully occupied with trying to keep the razor-sharp, filthy claws of the night stalker out of his flesh. Adelinda set her heels into Red Hawk's sides and charged down into the battle. As she came, she drew her saber, but Red Hawk was a herd stallion and one of his mares was threatened; he plucked the creature off the chestnut's rump in his teeth, and, flinging it to the ground, trampled it into the earth as he would have a wolf. Adelinda's sweeping saber accounted for two more.

The riders pulled up their sweating horses and looked about. There were no living night stalkers visible. The crushed and bloody remains of the pack lay about them, stinking even more in death than they had in life. They had wiped out the nest.

That was the scene that An-Shai came upon when he finally caught up with the outlanders. He rode into the clearing at a lumbering gallop, holding for dear life to Blackie's mane, his bishop's robes hiked up over his thighs, scratched, ragged, bloody, and breathless. The outlanders sat their horses in the midst of an abattoir of night stalker carcasses. Tobin had dismounted and was anxiously inspecting the damage to his chestnut mare's flank, but she was the only casualty, and thanks to Red Hawk she was not seriously hurt. An-Shai pulled his mount to a stop and stared about him, torn between chagrin and pleasure. He hated the night stalkers venomously; he was far more aware than the outlanders of the death and terror they had spread. He could not be sorry that they had been so completely destroyed. Then he saw Adelinda, and was surprised to find that he felt relieved.

"Your Grace!" said Adelinda, shocked. They had had no

idea that they had been followed. They were no less surprised than the Bishop when Li-Mun and a contingent of hastily recruited peasants armed with hoes and scythes came laboring into the clearing on foot, to halt and stare about wide-eyed.

An-Shai hurriedly gathered his thoughts. He couldn't very well castigate the outlanders for killing the night stalkers without arousing their suspicions, and certainly not in front of the awe-stricken peasants. "Good work!" he said heartily, letting the very real pleasure he felt at the destruction of the vicious little beasts show in his voice. "I'm more sure than ever that it was a wise move to bring the horses here, and you, too, of course. My own servants have never been able to catch them in daylight."

"Yes, indeed," seconded Li-Mun, who had been staring with nearly as much amazement as the peasants. "We're well rid of the creatures. We owe you considerable thanks."

"You're welcome, I'm sure," said Adelinda. "I'm surprised to find that you know about these creatures and haven't done something about them."

"If we're going to get back to the palace by dark, we'd better get going," An-Shai said. "Doing something about them is easier said than done. Our farmers are not as warlike as yours appear to be, and can't be relied upon in this kind of situation. We have made appeals to the army of the Church, but there are many demands upon them which they consider to be more important than this little Vale." As he spoke, the bishop moved his horse away, drawing Adelinda with him.

"Just a minute, Your Grace, I really must talk to my people." She swung her horse away before he could object, leaving him grinding his teeth at her disregard for his consequence.

In the clearing, Li-Mun was directing the peasants in the unpleasant task of cutting wood and piling the carcasses for burning. Adelinda gathered her friends around herself. "I just wanted to say," she said diffidently, almost shyly, "what a magnificent job you all did. Tobin, you did exactly the right thing to bring the news to us, and that was quite a fight you put up. Len, your tracking is what made it possible for us to find the night stalkers. Ina, you were really brave and I want you to know that I'm proud of you. You all showed courage and initiative. Karel, Orvet, all of you, I can't tell you how glad I am that it was you who chose to come with me." She choked a little with emotion.

Ina blushed with pleasure at the praise. Tobin glowed. Len looked down at his horse's mane and mumbled inaudibly. Karel leaned over from Dusty's back and gave her a quick one-armed hug around the shoulders. Even Orvet smiled as if pleased.

An-Shai watched the exchange. How on earth could the woman expect to keep her inferiors under control if she treated them like that? he thought impatiently. Why, she's acting as if they were . . . well, people, people she cared about. He silently vowed to keep her away from the rest of her party and to speak to Li-Mun about hurrying along the process of subverting them. It shouldn't be hard, he thought contemptuously; they weren't the least bit afraid of her.

On the ride back, he kept her close by him with various subterfuges, and she had little opportunity to speak again to the rest of her party. They trailed far enough behind that An-Shai and Adelinda couldn't hear their discussion of the events of the day. They didn't talk about the slaughter of the night stalkers. It had not really been a battle, only butchery, the advantage given them by their horses rendering the vicious little supernaturals almost helpless. They considered that they had done a good job of extermination, no more.

They did talk about the other events of the afternoon, however. "How is it that you know so much about supernaturals, Orvet?" asked Tobin.

Orvet and Karel exchanged a glance. Adelinda had told them not tell the farmer folk about Orvet's position, but they judged that the three would not be content to be foisted off with lame explanations. "Better tell them," advised Karel.

Orvet related a condensed version of the story he had told Adelinda. THe farmers were surprised, but not frightened; they knew Orvet too well to hold him in superstitious awe. "That's lucky," commented Len. "From what people tell me, there are lots of supernatural creatures around here."

"I've heard so, too," contributed Tobin. "I guess they don't have anybody like our exorcists to combat them."

"There's some human agency involved," said Orvet. "At the head of the trail up the cliff there was a guardian stone that should have kept the night stalkers out, but a releasing symbol had been drawn over the barrier symbol. Somebody let the creatures into the Vale."

"Bandits, maybe, or those slave raiders," speculated Karel, "hoping to profit by the confusion and disorganization."

"Why would slave raiders want their merchandise eaten?" asked Len.

"We should tell the bishop what you discovered," said Ina, indignantly. "He should be glad of your help."

"I'd just as soon he didn't know too much about me just yet. Right now he thinks that Adelinda does all our thinking, just as he does for his people," said Orvet. "As long as he thinks that, the rest of us are a secret weapon."

"Do you think we need a secret weapon?" she asked, wide-eyed.

"I don't know. Maybe. I don't like the way he keeps Adelinda away from the rest of us, or the way they try to send us all in different directions."

"That's right," said Karel, softly. "Divide and conquer. It's one of the oldest rules of warfare. Everybody be on your toes."

"I don't believe it!" cried Ina. "Nobody's trying to conquer me. Cho-Hei has been as kind as he could be . . ." Her voice trailed off. Her expression was stricken. Experience told her that no man was so attentive to her unless he had a reason, but she desperately wanted to believe that Cho-Hei was the exception.

The rest of the travelers rode along in silence for a while, respecting her painful struggle between truth and inclination. Karel shifted uneasily in his saddle, trying to find a comfortable position for his aching leg. "When we get back," said Orvet kindly, "you'd better ask the healer for another dose of that medicine."

Karel shook his head emphatically. "That stuff knocks me out too much. It helps the pain, but I feel like I'm floating in

a warm bath where nothing matters. I can't afford to be
drugged out of my mind. I'll make some willow bark tea. It
helps some."

Len had been riding along, preoccupied in his own
thoughts. "Do you really think they're trying to split us?" he
said, almost shyly.

Orvet looked keenly at him. "I don't know, but I think
they might be. Why, have they been at you?"

"Li-Mun was being very sympathetic this morning about
how badly Adelinda treats us."

"I don't think Adelinda treats us badly," said Ina, indig-
nantly. "She's just sort of insensitive, like all the horse folk.
Oh, I'm sorry, Karel, I didn't mean . . . well, you know what
I meant." She colored in embarrassment.

Karel smiled kindly. "I know what you meant. You're
right. She treats us that way too, sometimes. She's impetu-
ous, and she doesn't realize that other people are a little
overwhelmed by her . . ." he floundered for an accurate
word.

"Determined character," offered Orvet, helpfully.

"Yes. But she can be as warm and sensitive as any woman
at times. Of all my friends and relations, she's the only one
who didn't avoid me as if I had some infectious disease
when I came home crippled. Without her, I think I'd have
died when I finally realized that I wasn't ever going to be
any better."

"The problem with her," said Len bitterly, "is that she
thinks everyone else is as tough as she is."

"In a way, that's a compliment. She thinks of other people
as being adult, responsible for their own lives. She doesn't
nurse along any emotional cripples, but she's never asked to
be nursed."

"That's easy enough for her. She's never had an emotional
problem in her life."

"Do you think not?" interposed Orvet. "Then you're not
very observant. I've never met anyone whose conditions of
life were so completely suited to make her miserably unhappy, and who was so little willing to submit and take what
crumbs she could find in an impossible situation."

Len was silenced, but Orvet resolved to talk to him again

at the first opportunity to be private. At the head of the trail, he dismounted and restored the barrier symbol on the guardian stone. They were forced to abandon the conversation when they started down the trail. At the bottom, Karel called them into a huddle.

"I've been thinking about the bishop. If he is really trying to divide us, we need to know why. I'd suggest that we all play along and try to find out. Try not to fall for their game," he said with a warning look at the downcast Ina, "but try to find out what they want."

"Nobody's offered me anything," said Tobin.

"I expect I'm their main target. Li-Mun thinks I resent Adelinda and would be happy of an opportunity to do her a bad turn," said Len.

"Do you resent her? Why?" asked Tobin interestedly, if not very tactfully.

"If I do, it's between her and me, and no business of any foreign preacher. It doesn't mean I'd throw her to that bishop to do what he likes with."

"As long as they think you would, though, they might let slip what they've got in mind," said Karel.

"What we need to do is get a look at their account books and letter files," said Len, ignoring the startled glances. "Words can say anything the speaker wants them to, but facts and figures speak for themselves."

"None of us can read their language," said Orvet.

"Adelinda can," said Tobin. "She learned while we were on the ship. I was too sick to pay much attention, but I heard her reading the labels on everything."

"She's the one with the best chance to get a look at them, too, living in the palace," said Orvet. "I'm going to meet her after dark; I'll suggest it to her. That's a really good idea, Len."

"I'll jolly Li-Mun along, too, and see what I can find out."

"Don't be too eager. Let him persuade you."

Len snorted. "Trust me! I haven't lived in a cave all my life."

* * *

An-Shai had never been so glad to see anything in his life as he was to see the palace. Comfortless and cheerless as it was, it was still not the back of a horse. He felt as if he had been split from his crotch to his chin; his scratches stung; his second best bishop's robe was no better than tatters; his careful plans for the reduction of his excess population were in ruins; and by tomorrow the outlanders would be heroes from one end of the Vale to the other, where he had ruled so long in undisputed control. He debated whether or not to give the hapless Li-Mun a truly epic scoring for bringing peasants onto the scene, thus insuring that the news would get out; but his sense of fairness niggled at him until he had to admit that Li-Mun, knowing no more than he knew, had done exactly the right thing. Who could have foreseen that the outlanders would have killed all the nasty little brutes? He himself had been convinced that he was rushing to their rescue.

He would have said that at the end of a day when almost everything had gone awry, nothing else could go wrong, but he would have been mistaken. When he wearily climbed off Blackie's back and dragged his aching body into the palace, leaving Adelinda to take care of both horses, and sought the sweet privacy of his library, there was a surprise awaiting him. The initiate Tsu-Linn was comfortably seated at his desk, in his chair, reading his papers. An-Shai stared at him aghast. He was not ready to explain himself to the initiate. He had not yet reduced his population, put the imported horses to impressive use, brought the outlanders under control, increased his food production—he wasn't ready!

"You don't seem very pleased to see me, Bishop An-Shai."

An-Shai recovered himself. "Certainly I am, sir. This is a very pleasant surprise. I had not expected you back so soon!"

"I hadn't expected to return so soon, but I can see that it was a good thing that my duties brought me back this way. What on earth have you been doing to yourself? You look like the loser in a cat fight."

"I was riding through the thornbushes up on the mesa."

"Why were you up on the mesa?"

An-Shai groped for a reasonable explanation that the initiate would accept. There was none. In desperation, he offered the truth. "Well, some of my . . . er, employees were hunting night stalkers, and I went to save them."

"Hunt night stalkers? You have rash employees! Were you able to save them?"

"No, sir. . . . That is, they didn't need to be saved. They wiped out the nest."

"Wiped out the nest! Why did you permit that? How do you think you're going to control your population without night stalkers? And furthermore, I find that the slave raiders you ordered were attacked and driven out of the Vale without taking a single slave. Employees? Since when do bishops hire employees? All the labor you need is available for the ordering. And as if that weren't enough, those new buildings and paddocks are full of some sort of monstrously huge animal I never saw the likes of before. I'm waiting for your explanation with bated breath, Bishop An-Shai. I'm sure it's going to be a good one."

An-Shai's hopes of ever attaining initiation were fading rapidly. The chubby little initiate was looking at him with an expression that showed the steel beneath the jolly exterior. He took a deep breath. He might as well face up to it and tell the whole truth, and if the initiate didn't like it he could do what he liked about it. It was what Adelinda would have done in his shoes.

"The huge creatures are horses. The farmers in the Vale were hampered by the lack of good draft animals, so I sent to the Eastern Continent and purchased fifty horses. Since no one here knew how to care for the animals, I also hired six of the natives of that continent to teach my peasants how to use and care for them."

The initiate swelled up like a bullfrog. An-Shai pulled himself straight and waited for the blow to fall. It was upon this scene that Li-Mun and Adelinda walked in. Li-Mun was in the lead, and had taken three steps into the room before he recognized the initiate. He promptly wheeled, grabbed Adelinda's wrist, and tried to yank her back out the door. Her natural reaction to being manhandled was to jerk away, and Karel had taught her some of the techniques of self-defense; she broke Li-Mun's hold and sent him reeling across the room, to bring up with a crash against a stack of book-shelves.

She saw An-Shai standing before a stranger seated at his desk, for all the world like a schoolboy about to receive a scolding from the master. The funny little man at the desk was staring at her in open amazement; the expression on the bishop's face was icily grim. She realized belatedly that the dazed Li-Mun might have had a very good reason for not wanting her in the room. "Excuse me!" she said, hastening across the room to offer the staggering Li-Mun her support. "I didn't realize you had company, Your Grace. I'm sorry, Li-Mun; I didn't mean to hurt you but you startled me. Are you all right?" She steered him toward the door.

"No, don't leave, Adelinda," said the bishop. "I would like to make you acquainted with the initiate Tsu-Linn. Sir, this is the leader of those outlanders I told you of, the Lady Adelinda." He hesitated for an instant, decided that things had gone too far for tactful reticence. "She's living here at the palace."

"How do you do, Your . . . er . . ." said Adelinda, cheerily, unaware that the only really proper reaction for a layperson in the extremely unlikely event of meeting one of the awe-some, powerful initiates was abject terror.

Tsu-Linn's reaction was as unexpected to An-Shai and Li-Mun as hers had been to the initiate. He crossed his arms and surveyed her coolly. "I'm fine, thank you. The proper form of address, which I perceive that the Bishop An-Shai has failed to explain to you, is simply 'sir.' We initiates have little need of titles."

"I see, sir. Well, nice as it is to have made your acquaintance, I have things to do, so I'll run along now." Then seeing by Li-Mun's horrified expression that she had once again violated the elaborate rules of etiquette, she added, "That is, if I have your permission?"

"Please stay for a moment, Lady Adelinda. Perhaps you can be of assistance in clearing up this situation. An-Shai," and his voice cracked like a whip, "do you actually have the gall to stand there and tell me that this woman and five others have destroyed a whole nest of night stalkers, that you are permitting them to teach our peasants, and that you have let this outlander female move in with you? What are you thinking of, man?"

The last feeble hope of advancement flickered and died. In its place came a wash of rage. How dare the little toad speak to him so in front of the woman? An-Shai drew himself to his full height. "That is exactly what I have told you, sir. Furthermore, I'll tell you now that I heartily endorse and support their attacks on the night stalkers and the slave raiders, and that the woman stays here in my palace because I want her to." The tall bishop fairly bristled with fiery defiance.

Tsu-Linn smiled coldly. "Do you realize what you're saying? Keeping a concubine is punishable by death even for a hierarch."

"Just hold it a minute!" exclaimed Adelinda, striding forward. "I sleep in the palace, not with the bishop. Not that I consider it to be any of your business. But I am not anyone's concubine . . . sir!"

An-Shai's indignant response followed hard upon Adelinda's. "Certainly not, sir. Lady Adelinda is the leader of the outlanders, and I need her by me to help plan the usage of the horses."

"H'mm," said the initiate, glancing at the open-mouthed Li-Mun. "Very well, then if there has been no impropriety, you may go about your business, Lady Adelinda, with my apologies."

"Your apologies are accepted, sir." Adelinda stalked out of the room, followed by a shocked and confused Li-Mun.

"Sit down, Bishop An-Shai," said the initiate, when they were alone. "I see we have some things to talk about. Why have you let the woman run out of control like that?"

An-Shai sank wearily into a chair. "Bringing her under control is easier said than done. But I'm confident of success in the near future, sir."

"Tell me what you intend to do."

"I have Li-Mun working on ways to alienate her countrymen from her, leaving her alone and dependent upon me.

I'm searching for an appropriate supernatural to use to frighten her into turning to me for help."

"Do you intend to make her your concubine?"

"Certainly not, sir! I've always obeyed the rules of the Church."

"So you have, but even I can see that this woman is a totally different type from our sweet and submissive females. It would be quite possible for an unusual man such as yourself to fall under her spell."

An-Shai flushed. "Hardly, sir. It will give me the greatest pleasure to bring the insolent creature to heel. I anticipate with great joy the moment when she comes crawling to me to beg brokenly for my help and protection, but to actually wish to . . . er, lie with her . . ." He shuddered. "I don't find the rules of the Church unduly harsh, as I am told some of my colleagues do."

"Hmmph!" The initiate eyed him for a moment, dubiously. The Church's most useful servants sometimes understood their own motivations the least. The initiate was a cynical man, and had seen a lot of human nature in his day. "In any case, I didn't come here to discuss your outlanders. What do you hope to accomplish with these giant horses?"

An-Shai wearily explained his plans for improving agriculture and transport. "I had hoped with these more efficient methods and by limiting marriages to be able to support the whole population of the Vale without recourse to harsher measures," he said.

"Don't you approve of the use of supernaturals to control the people?"

"No, sir," said An-Shai, bluntly. "Oh, a few ghosts and goblins to scare would-be evildoers into righteous behavior are a good idea. But night stalkers and their ilk—no. We're supposed to protect and care for the people, not set such cruel and evil creatures on them. I'm glad the outlanders killed them, and I'll tell you what: if you send Fire Priests here to corrupt my people I'll have the outlanders destroy them, too."

"I'm a little surprised to hear you claim to have such complete control of them."

"They're quite willing to fight, sir."

"No doubt." The initiate's face took on a grave expression. "However, I feel obligated to warn you that if you persist in this extraordinary aberration, that the full power of the curses of the Quadrate God will be called down upon your head." He spoke these phrases with a rolling solemnity that sent a shiver of apprehension down the bishop's spine.

An-Shai took a deep breath and cast his hopeless ambitions away forever. For an instant, a mental picture of Adelinda laughing in this very room flashed across his inner vision. "Nonsense," he snapped. "Save the stories for the credulous. We both know that the Quadrate God is as much a construct as God the Father and the spirits of the fields. If the curses of the Quadrate God are all I have to worry about, I'm a safe man."

Brave words notwithstanding, for an apprehensive instant An-Shai expected to be struck down where he sat, until amazingly, the initiate chuckled. "Bravo! Of course we know that, though it isn't considered polite to shout it out." Tsu-Linn leaned back in his chair. "We know the Quadrate God's a fraud, just like every other religion that was ever invented to keep the laity under the ecclesiastical thumb is a fraud." He leaned forward again, suddenly intense. "But what about me? Am I such a fraud that you feel able to stand against me in a supernatural duel? Are your powers well enough developed? Do you have such a good command of the supernatural and of yourself that you don't fear to challenge my powers?"

"If I must, I will."

"You would die, terribly."

"Perhaps."

Tsu-Linn tented his fingers on the desk. "You haven't asked me why I came, but I'm going to tell you anyway. I've heard rumors of these goings-on and came to check them out. You've been walking a very thin line, Bishop An-Shai, and I came to see how tottery you are on it."

"Now that you know, sir, what are you going to do?"

"Submit your name for initiation."

An-Shai stared at the initiate, speechless.

"You can expect to hear in a few weeks if my recommendation has been accepted—it always is. Quit goggling.

Granted that the religion of the Quadrate God is an utter fraud, the last thing we need in the governing body of the Church is a true believer. Theocracy is the most absolute form of government, but it can only work if the theocrats themselves know better than to fall for the superstitious pap they feed the populace—or the middle-level Church administrators. The penalty for revealing this to anyone—anyone! —is instant death, and don't think for an instant you won't be watched every moment. Anyway, you wouldn't be believed." Tsu-Linn paused thoughtfully. "Your outlander woman might believe you. Something is going to have to be done about her."

An-Shai recovered his breath. "I won't have her killed."

"Did I suggest such a thing? No, I think you should take her for your first wife, once you've got her under control, of course."

An-Shai lost his breath for the second time. "Never!" He shuddered eloquently. But it was not entirely a shudder of distaste.

Tsu-Linn laughed. "Better think about it. Before you can receive the final initiation you have to be married, and an initiate's wife can be no common little drudge. It's a constant struggle for power and supremacy, and having the right wives can make all the difference. The most intelligent, ruthless, ambitious women in Godsland are taken for initiates' wives. It keeps them out of trouble and it helps their husbands. Mine are right little cutthroats, the darlings."

"I told you already that the mere thought of . . . lying with the woman is distasteful to me."

"Oh, you wouldn't have to make love to her unless you wanted to, and if I were you I certainly wouldn't try it without her permission; I have a feeling she'd take strong exception." He chuckled again. "I made that mistake with my third, and I carry the scars to this day—I won't show you where. But I brought her around, and it was certainly worth the trouble. You have to consider your breeding potential." An-Shai gasped indignantly. "One way in which religions with a celibate priesthood have insured their own destruction is by excluding the best and brightest from the breeding pool. That's why our religious men are required to marry, and encouraged to marry as many and as bright and ambitious women as they can handle. Think of the children she could give you! We weed out the children of the dull, the unambitious, and the commonplace, and replace them with the children of the bright, the ambitious, and the uncommon."

"Changelings!" breathed An-Shai, interested in spite of himself.

"Exactly. The peasants wake up one morning and find their baby replaced with an exceptionally large, alert, active baby. Their village priest warns them that they must love and care for it as if it were their own, because otherwise the spirits who have taken their own to nurture will fail to care for it properly."

"Do the real parents never see their children again?"

"Of course they do. I know where all of mine are and what exactly is happening to them."

"What happens to the peasant babies?"

"They are raised to be servants and farmers at the Initiates' Hall, and are probably the most pampered peasants in Godsland. Of course they are never told their origins."

An-Shai rubbed a hand wearily over his brow. "I still find it hard to believe that I'm to be offered initiation, sir. Things are disorderly here."

"I certainly can't argue with that. You'll want to get things straightened out here before you report to the Hall for instruction, both for your own sake and so the new bishop won't find the Vale in turmoil."

"I'll push along the plans to subvert the outlanders."

"Yes, do, and I have some suggestions for getting the woman under control, too. You aren't supposed to learn about this technique until after you've been initiated, but I'll make an exception in your case."

"Thank you, sir. The supernatural vision I tried to scare her with didn't work at all."

"We run across people like that occasionally. Hierarchs, for example, who get the idea that they know everything they need to know about the supernatural and decide, from greed or for whatever reason, to break away from the Church. Your Adelinda might well be that willful. If anything supports the contention that women ought not to be allowed to learn anything, she certainly does. Educated women are dangerous!"

"God's knees, sir, you don't think all women would be like that if they were allowed to get an education, do you?" An-Shai was startled and upset by the idea.

"Who's to know? Certainly some of them would be. There are certain of the liberal initiates—a group to which I do not belong, I might add—who think that exceptional girls ought to be educated just as exceptional boys are and inducted into a sort of sisterhood. They maintain that these women could then help with the studies of the four attributes—but you don't know about that yet, and I've said more than is tactful already. Showing them this woman Adelinda ought to convince them that theirs is a risky proposal indeed."

"Oh, I don't know," said An-Shai, intrigued in spite of himself. "If the girls were as carefully indoctrinated as boys destined for the priesthood are, I don't think it would be risky. Women have a lot more potential than any of us ever suspected."

"Which is not the least of the dangers of the plan," pointed out Tsu-Linn. "Who knows what they would be getting up to if they were given a chance? Imagine, if you can, a female hierarch." There was a short silence while the two men contemplated the unthinkable. "I see I've recruited an initiate who will find himself in sympathy with the opposing party. They also feel, as you do, that the more malevolent kinds of supernaturals ought not to be employed against our own peasants. I think myself that constant thinning is good for them. Weeds out the unfit and keeps the survivors grateful to us."

An-Shai, feeling that he had tempted fate quite far enough by arguing with the initiate as much as he had, forebore to contest this statement, but he kept some very severe reservations to himself. Instead, he turned the conversation to the technique Tsu-Linn had mentioned for bringing Adelinda under control.

"It isn't easy to learn, and it isn't exactly safe for the operator, either, but it will work if you've read your victim right. You'd better get a healer to deal with those scratches of yours and get a bath and a change before supper. Then I'll teach it to you this evening. Does the woman Adelinda eat with us? Good. It'll give me a chance to estimate her potential to resist."

Chapter 8

Adelinda slipped down the hall in the darkness. There was a murmur of voices and a light under the door of An-Shai's library. She moved as silently as a ghost past the hall that led to it, carrying her boots in her hand. The guest rooms were in the same wing as the dining room, and the Bishop's quarters were off a hall that led directly past the dining room and out the main entrance, so there was no way that Adelinda knew to get out except past her enemy's rooms. The halls that led to the other wings all radiated out of the dining room, and though Adelinda was sure that there were other ways to get out of the building, given the labyrinthine design of the place and the near surety of meeting someone, she preferred the main entrance.

An-Shai's balcony opened into the dining room, too, and she stepped out on it and peered out over the darkened grounds. There was no movement. Still in stocking feet, she hastened down the vast entrance hall. The main door, though wide enough for several men to walk through abreast, was so cleverly hung and carefully maintained that Adelinda pushed it open as easily as any cottage door. Leaving it a little ajar—she had no desire to have to climb back in through a window—she took a deep breath of the sweet-scented heavy air and sat on the bottom step to pull on her boots.

She was bone-tired, and the moist, syrupy air seemed to clog her nose and throat and make drawing each breath an effort. Still moving quietly and keeping to the shadows as much as possible, she made for the grove of featherleaf trees at the bottom of the slope. Orvet was not there yet, and she settled herself on a low limb, bracing her back against the trunk of the tree.

The night was warm and moist, like a soothing bath. Adelinda fell into a half-dozing state, listening to the shrill insect cries and the ever-present murmur of the waters, her mind drifting as aimlessly as a leaf caught in the current of the placid little stream that ran nearby. Orvet could have told her that it was a dangerous state of mind, here where the supernatural lay so very near to the surface of reality, and so could the spirit of the tree in which she rested. But the dryads were little concerned with human folk, unless the safety of their beloved tree homes was concerned, and this one shrugged unfeelingly as it directed the roots of the tree far down to the mineral-rich water.

Adelinda felt the presence first. It didn't seem strange to her that Dep had followed her to this far land. She was tranquilly happy to see him again; the only contentment she had ever known had been in the little times she had spent with him, and peace filled her unquiet soul to know that he stood behind her, leaning over the branch to kiss her on the cheek as he had often done when she waited for him.

How different Dep had been from the supercilious and austere young men of her own class! He had been warm and loving, often hugging, patting, or snuggling, as her equals would have thought it beneath their dignity to do. Being with him had satisfied a deep hunger for affection that she had not even known she had, a hunger that none of her other lovers had even touched.

She turned without rising to find him standing in a dappled spot of moonlight, the familiar warm smile lighting his brown eyes. "Dep!" she said. "It's so nice to see you." How much handsomer he had grown since she had seen him last, and taller, too, and how she yearned to have him take her in his arms and just hold her close as he had always done whenever they met after some little separation. He had never kissed her or caressed her upon these occasions; that was for later and the passion that followed, but only held her as if he could never get enough of nearness, and Adelinda treasured those moments of closeness as if they had been precious jewels. She drew her legs over the branch and rose, holding her arms out to him, bemused by the moonlight and the nearness of her lover.

"Get out of here! Begone, incubus!" There was a crash as Orvet leaped between them, and Dep shrank back.

"Orvet . . ." protested Adelinda. Dep held his hand out to her, pleadingly, as he had done when she sent him away, and she tried to crowd past Orvet to reach him. The exorcist thrust her back and flung a pinch of some white dust at him; Adelinda gasped as he turned, and changed, and shadowlike withered and fled.

With the departure of the incubus and the fading of its spell, Adelinda sank back down on the limb, cold with horror and yet bereft again. All the pain and loneliness of the original loss flooded back over her, as it had not done for years, and she found that she was having to bite her lip hard to force back the stringing tears. Orvet glanced at her and then turned away and subjected the peaceful grove to an intense scrutiny.

At length Adelinda regained her composure. "Thanks, Orvet. Would it have killed me?"

The exorcist turned back. "I don't think so, although I don't know much about them. I think it would have just drained some of your vitality, your life force, and compelled you to keep on meeting it until you cared about nothing but it."

"It looked like . . . like someone I used to know. How did it do that?"

Orvet glanced at the naked pain in her face and then away, hastily. "It must pick the picture out of your mind, or perhaps it lets you shape it to match your own heart's desire."

"Did you see who it looked like?" she asked, averting her face.

"No," lied Orvet. "I was digging for the antidote powder. I'll give you some in case it comes back when I'm not around. Do you think you can withstand it now that you know what it is?"

"I don't know. It casts a sort of spell. If I had been able to think, I would have realized that—that he—the person it was supposed to be couldn't be here, thousands of miles and an ocean away from home."

"Then you mustn't let yourself be caught out at night and alone."

"Do you think An-Shai could have sent it?"

Orvet considered. "I've never heard of them being controlled by any human agency. They have only one interest in humankind, and that's as prey; they aren't, strictly speaking, material creatures at all. They can't be bribed or forced to do anything. When you were under the spell, was there a feeling of An-Shai's presence? A sort of flavor you can't taste, but that still gives a sense of his personality?"

"No, there wasn't. I knew right away that he had something to do with the other one."

"That's one of the things you wanted to tell me about."

Adelinda quickly told the exorcist of the disgusting specter she had seen, and what happened when she faced An-Shai with her accusation. He laughed. "I would have liked to have seen his face. It sounds to me as if he was just trying to scare you. But why? Do you have any ideas?"

"I was hoping you would. And also some idea of what I can do about it if he tries it again. It could get to be a nuisance."

Orvet sobered. "It could get to be a lot worse than a nuisance. There are supernatural manifestations that are considerably more dangerous than a spook. He doesn't seem to want to hurt you, though I don't understand how it could be to his advantage to frighten you."

"Maybe it's foreigners in general. Have any of you been bothered by such things?"

"No, but we are being paid a little special attention by Li-Mun and some of his friends. He's been trying to alienate Len, and Ina has found herself the object of attention of a very handsome and very sophisticated gentleman. The medicine they've given Karel puts him out of action, besides helping the pain. I wish I knew more about medicines; I know that some painkillers are dangerous to give because the patient can become addicted to them, but I don't know what they are or how they work."

"What about you and Tobin?"

"So far they aren't bothering us. I think Len and Ina can hold out; neither one of them is as stupid as An-Shai and Li-Mun seem to assume they are."

"I hate to ask Karel to quit taking the medicine. You don't know how much pain he's in sometimes."

"He's quit of his own accord."

Adelinda mused for a moment. "An-Shai's trying to lure Len and Ina away from the rest of us; he's seen to it that Karel is given a medicine that may be dangerous; and he's trying to scare me. We know what he's up to, but not why."

"What do you think he's up to?"

"He's trying to split us up so we can be handled more easily. For some reason, we scare him, or bother him, and he wants to get control of us just like he has control of every soul in his Vale. But why? None of us has ever done him any harm."

"He must have his reasons. We really don't need to know them, though. As long as we know that he really is deliberately trying to manipulate us, we can guard against him."

"Know what? If it weren't for the horses, I'd say let's saddle up and get out of here tonight."

"What do the horses have to do with it?"

"These people don't know how to take care of them. They'd suffer, certainly, and they might die. I agreed to teach the peasants how to take care of them and I intend to do it. But I sure do wish the bishop weren't sneaking around behind my back; it's going to be a very long year."

"Maybe our best bet is to pull in our horns and act more like the local peasants. None of them would say boo to a mouse. I used to think of myself as a peaceful man, but I'm positively adventurous compared to them. Whatever it is that An-Shai doesn't like about us, it no doubt has something to do with that."

"I'll treat him with more deference. He likes that. But I can't grovel."

"No, I don't suppose you can. Tobin tells me you learned how to read the local script."

"Yes, on the ship. I didn't know he'd noticed."

"He says you went around reading all the labels out loud.

Try to get at the account books and daily journals, if the bishop keeps them."

"Whatever for?"

"Len says that the best way to find out what's really going on is to look at accounts and business letters. What people say is likely to be lies. If you went to the bishop and demanded to know why he was trying to split up our group, he'd just fob you off with some story. But if you find written in the accounts, 'Five gold pennies to bribe Orvet,' you'd know something was going on."

"Len says that?"

"You keep on underestimating that young man. I wish you'd talk to him."

"Maybe you're right. I will talk to him. I'll try to get a look at the bishop's papers, but I'm not sure I would know what to look for."

"We could smuggle Len in and he could help you."

"Or I could demand to have him with me. No, I'm going to be more deferential. All right; if he's willing, we'll try it tomorrow, very late. An-Shai works until all hours. We'll meet here."

They went their ways, and Adelinda got back into the palace and to her room without incident. The light in the library was still shining and the voices were still murmuring. She paused at the junction of the corridor, but couldn't make out any words.

By that time even the hard, narrow stone bench seemed attractive. Adelinda went straight to bed, but tired as she was, she didn't sleep immediately. The incubus was to blame. It had brought back with painful poignancy the sadness and loneliness she had felt when she had had to send Dep away from her. It was the only thing she could have done, for Dep's sake as well as her own. There had been no possibility of a future for them, as she had known from the very beginning. They had had nothing in common, neither interests nor social class nor intellectual equality. For a short time they had needed each other, and then they had passed out of each other's lives to pursue their very separate destinies. She couldn't even have guessed where Dep was or what he was doing, though she would have speculated that he had married and was the father of a large family by now. He would be, she knew, a good father, warm and caring, if not the disciplinarian he ought to be. She hoped he had found a wife that deserved and appreciated him, and that his farm was flourishing so that poverty and care was not spoiling his sweet and merry nature. She hoped he thought of her fondly once in a while.

In the close, dark privacy of her narrow bed, a lonely tear welled out of the corner of her eye and trickled down her temple into her hair.

An-Shai was fascinated by the insights he was gaining into the lives of the initiates. "It's a constant struggle for supremacy," Tsu-Linn told him. "There's never any truce. You'll be the last and youngest of the initiates, the thirty-eighth in rank out of thirty-eight, and before you've wiped the wine of consecration off your hands, number thirty-seven will be eyeing you with fear and loathing, wondering when you're going to challenge him for his position. And you'll have to soon, too, or number thirty-nine will be snapping at your heels, wanting your position. You'll have to keep moving up, because there are only two ways to go: up the scale or down it, and the higher you go the harder you'll be pressed. When you're not worrying about challenging the next higher initiate or when the next lower one is going to challenge you, you'll be scrabbling to learn as much as you can to get ready for the next challenge. Besides all this, you'll be fighting to get your views and aims recognized and put into action by the Convocation, the meeting of all the initiates. Do you see why your choice of wives is so important? At the Initiates' Hall, they're the only ones who're on your side, the only ones you know you can trust."

"Yes, I see. Of what do these challenges consist?"

"Anything the man who's challenged wishes. The junior initiate makes the challenge, the ranking initiate chooses the nature of the contest. Usually they choose duels of magic or will, but I've known there to be trials of strength and courage, and occasionally even a gambling game. By the time a man has worked his way into the highest ranks, he's been severely tested for every quality a man might have."

An-Shai tented his fingers, elbows supported on the arms of his chair. "I assume that this information isn't usually given to hierarchs."

"No. I wanted you to understand the uses of the technique I'm teaching you. You'll be going into the brotherhood with a tremendous advantage over other new initiates. You'll know about this technique and you will have had a chance to practice it on a person of formidable strength of will, but still with very little risk, since she won't know what's happening. I shall look to see you rise fast, An-Shai."

"I'll try not to disappoint you, sir."

"I'm afraid you won't—I'll be facing you myself someday, if you don't. This is how you use the overmind in a battle of wills. As you know, the stuff of the overmind can be shaped by a strong mind, but what you probably don't know is that you can draw another into the overmind with you and confront him there. If you are the aggressor, the shaping of the battlefield is yours, and the victim can only try to master the scenario you have designed. It's difficult even if you know that it can be done, but I should say that to someone who doesn't even know of the existence of the overmind it would require an enormous strength of character to withstand the aggressor's will for even a moment. You'll have to be careful not to kill your victim outright or drive her mad. You'll have to design your scenario so that there are some familiar elements in it, to give her some traces of reality to hold on to. You can be sure that the first time you face an initiate, he'll not be so solicitous of your mental health!"

"How should I design the scenario?"

"Ah, well, that's where your experience and judgment of the woman come in. I don't know her well enough to know what experience will crush her spirit without destroying her mind."

"I'm not sure I do, either, but I would guess that having to turn to me for help would do it."

"Then design your scenario so that she must beg you for help. The nice thing about this technique is that if you find that one thing doesn't work, you can always switch strategies—sometimes just the inconsistency will have the desired effect."

The two men worked far into the night, practicing and polishing the technique. To the unaided eye, there were only two clerics, resting peacefully upon the benches of the library, but there were mighty stirring in the ether that night, and supernaturals for many miles around, sensitive to the tremendous forces that the men handled, slunk cowed to their lairs or haunts or dens.

In the morning, Orvet continued his lessons for the budding stablehands. He was giving a demonstration of grooming techniques to an attentive audience when Li-Mun came strolling up. The hierarch watched quietly as Orvet finished his explanations and put his pupils to practicing on patient greathorses. Then he joined the teacher.

"When will you teach them how to breed the horses?"

"In the spring, during the breeding season."

"They don't breed the year around, then?"

"Some mares may come into heat all year, but most don't, and it's better if the foals are dropped just when the new green grass is coming. The mares can make plenty of milk on the lush feed."

"Very interesting. Come, walk with me a little. Have you seen the count's mansion?"

"I've noticed it. Very impressive. Your noblemen don't seem to have much to do, though."

"The officers of the army are recruited from their ranks, and most of the noblemen have extensive business interests. The noble Tai-Din, whose mansion that is, for example, is one of the foremost cloth merchants of Godsland. He has two sons in the army, and his third son helps in the business. The noblemen lead a very comfortable and satisfying life. You don't have different ranks in your Kingdom, do you?"

"There are a few hereditary offices, but no real class of hereditary noblemen."

"Yet you do have social classes."

"As most societies do. They aren't determined by birth, though, more by occupation."

"I was under the impression that Adelinda and Karel were of a superior social class, and that Len, Tobin, and Ina were inferior."

"In a way. Adelinda and Karel are horse-breeding and landowning folk who belong to the Guild of Beast Merchants. The others are from farming families who rent their land and belong to no guilds."

"I see. How do you fit into this?"

"I'm neither one nor the other. I'm from King's City, and I suppose you might say that I belong to an educated subclass that draws its members from all the other classes according to ability and desire."

"Could you join the upper class if you so desired?"

"If I wanted to work that hard at it."

"The way things are, though, you're just another employee, like the farmer folk."

"That's true."

"How would you like to be a nobleman and live in a mansion like that one, with servants to wait upon you and an important role in the affairs of the Vale?"

Orvet surveyed the hierarch. This was a bribe indeed! "I think," he said carefully, "that I could get used to it."

Li-Mun laughed. "I thought you could. If I were you, I'd think about my loyalties and what each employer has to offer very carefully over the next few days." He slapped Orvet on the shoulder and went off in a high good humor to find Len and see how he was fermenting. His program was succeeding very well. He could see Ina giving Cho-Hei another driving lesson, and the nobleman was leaning very close to his instructor, who was not at all withdrawing from the contact.

Len was giving another set of plowing lessons. The sullen expression on his face was even more marked this morning, and Li-Mun nodded encouragingly to him before moving on about his business. Let the boy stew a bit longer and he'd be a weapon ready to the hand to turn against his employer, the hierarch thought.

That left only Tobin to be dealt with. Li-Mun sought him out. He was showing a group of awed farmers how a team of the powerful greathorses could snatch a recalcitrant stump out of the ground. Li-Mun watched, amazed himself at the power of the harnessed giants as they flung themselves into their collars, squatting behind as their enormously muscular haunches bunched and knotted with the gargantuan effort. Their harness creaked and jingled; their huge heads were lowered almost to the ground. They drove their brute power against the groaning roots. Hitched to these behemoths, the stump shuddered; a great root broke free of the ground; the trunk heaved complainingly over as the taproot broke, and the stump was dragged, defeated, to the side of the field. The peasants broke into delighted applause, and the great animals stood, blowing and nodding their heads with placid dignity as they accepted the applause as their due.

Li-Mun congratulated the grinning Tobin. "You've been working awfully hard," he added. "Come and take a break in the shade."

Tobin acquiesced readily. "The horses could use a drink of water," he said. "They've pulled about a hundred of those stumps today." He hooked the dragging trace chains into the harness and led the team to a nearby stream, where they drank thirstily. He tied them in a shady spot and joined the hierarch with the air of one who intends a good long rest.

"Adelinda certainly does work you hard," Li-Mun observed sympathetically.

"We all work hard," said Tobin, uneasily.

"Yes, but you more than the others, I think."

Tobin knew very well that wasn't so. He was a lazy man and he knew it. Much of his time and energy was spent devising ways of doing things that would cause him the least amount of effort. He saw no reason to do anything extra; he was not one, for example, to polish the harness just so his team would look smart. On the other hand, he was conscientious enough about things that really mattered. He wouldn't let his horses go thirsty just to save a little work, for example. He also knew that he probably put in the least amount of work of any of the travelers, and if they were more liberally rewarded than he, he was willing to admit that that was fair.

Tobin thought. Li-Mun was probably testing him to see if he could be subverted, as Len had said he was tested yesterday. If that were so, he should play along and see what came of it.

Li-Mun had sat quietly while Tobin mulled these thoughts

over (he was not a particularly quick thinker). "You seem to have a lot to do," the hierarch prompted.

Tobin sighed theatrically. "I do get tired of doing all the work," he admittted.

Li-Mun glanced at him suspiciously, but there was such an open, candid expression on the young man's good-natured face that he dismissed the thought that he was being gulled. "Our farmers only work as much as they need to. The rest of the time they're free to relax and take life easy," he lied. "The easiest kind of work is herding goats. All the herders have to do is take the goats out to pasture and then sit in the shade and watch them all day."

"That sounds like a good job."

"It would be even easier for you. You could ride your horse to the pasture and back."

"She isn't my horse. She belongs to Adelinda," said Tobin.

"She could belong to you. If you were working as a herder we'd have to see that you had a horse. You'd need a nice cottage in one of the villages, too, and a biddable little wife to wash your clothes and cook your meals and wait on you when you rested in the evenings."

"You make it all sound heavenly."

"Well, think about it for a few days." Li-Mun went happily off to report to An-Shai that his program to subvert all of Adelinda's employees was proceeding very well. He frowned a little when he saw Karel riding on the old gray as he checked on the progress of the various groups, but then he shrugged. A few more doses of the poppy gum and Karel was theirs to do with as they pleased; let him ride around a little today if he wished.

Li-Mun found that An-Shai was napping in the cool of the morning after having spent most of the night closeted with the visiting initiate. Adelinda, freed of his constant supervision, had ridden off on Red Hawk to explore the valley and check on the welfare of the horses that had been dispersed to the villages.

She enjoyed the day. She rode north in the morning, taking it easy, stopping at fountain or grove as the whim took her. She visited with the peasants she met and enjoyed the dreamlike beauty of the Vale. She and Red Hawk tasted the mineral-laden waters of the artesian springs. These fountains almost sparkled as they rose up from far below, so cold they made the teeth ache, incredibly refreshing. They splashed through a dozen creeks and brooks, startling the lazy little trout and perch out of their midday somnolence. They galloped over pastures so lush that they could all but hear the grass grow, and when she paused and looked back, the traces of their passage had been obliterated by the resilience of the vegetation.

At noon she returned to Bishopstown and ate lunch with the rest of the travelers, and they were pleased to see her laughing and bright-eyed from the morning's exertions. They had white crumbly goat cheese to eat with their vegetables and grain, and it almost reminded them of home, for they raised goats and made cheese of the milk there, too. They were starting to miss bread, which the people of Godsland did not bake, and meat, which was served only on festival occasions, but they were getting used to the thin sour wine that was served at every meal, even breakfast. Tobin said wryly that he could understand why there were no alcoholics in Godsland; the wine would curdle in the stomach before one could get drunk on it.

Lunch finished, the travelers stretched out on the springy grass for a few minutes' rest. Adelinda stretched luxuriously. "Len," she said, "I'm going to ride south this afternoon. Would you like to come with me?"

"If you like." His tone was almost surly.

"I'm not ordering you to. I'd like to talk to you, but if you'd rather not come, you don't have to."

Orvet shot a sharp look at Len. "I'd like to go," the young man said hastily, with a little better grace.

"All right, then, saddle up and we'll move along." Adelinda went to saddle Red Hawk, who had been freed to graze nearby.

The two rode in silence for a while. The land to the south was more sparsely settled, more broken and wooded, with frequent rocky outcroppings and not quite so lush a ground cover. They came to one of the artesian fountains, a huge one that sent its twin streams of sparkling water higher than their heads as they sat their horses. At the highest point of each jet, someone had placed a clear hollow glass ball, blue and green, that danced there upheld by the force of the water. The water cascaded back into a rock basin, escaping through a break to flow away in a frothing brook.

"Come and taste the water," said Adelinda, smiling at her young companion. "It's different from any you've tasted before."

They dismounted and sampled the water in the basin, finding it tangy, ice-cold, and subtly flavored, different from the ones Adelinda had tasted that morning, but invigorating. The chill of the water radiated out to drive back the sultry warmth of the afternoon sun; they were sprayed with an impalpable chill mist that soon drove them back from the basin's brim.

"You're right, I've never tasted anything like that. Why do you suppose it's so cold?" said Len, swabbing the beads of mist from his face with his sleeve.

"It must come up from really deep in the earth under tremendous pressure," speculated Adelinda, shuddering. "It's a scary idea, isn't it? Hundreds of feet down into the rock, darkness and the terrible weight of the rocks above are forcing this water up into the light of the sun, still carrying with it the cold."

"I've read that in very deep mines the temperature goes higher and higher the deeper they go, until it becomes too hot for human life."

"Really? Then this water must come from somewhere else."

"Perhaps not such deep layers. I've been in caves myself, and it gets cool under the surface of the earth as far as I've gone."

Adelinda shuddered again. "Weren't you afraid of being trapped?"

Len regarded her with a trace of surprise. "No, I was careful not to go into dangerous caves. There are lots in the cliffs to the west of the valley back home. Didn't you ever explore them?"

"Once, when I was little, I went with my brother. He and his friends thought it was a wonderful joke to sneak off and leave me in the dark. I was too petrified to scream. If Karel hadn't come hunting me with a candle, I probably would still be there." She laughed. "Poor Karel was always rescuing me from some scrape or other. I nearly choked him that time. I wouldn't let go of his neck and he had to carry me all the way home."

As they spoke, they drew aside to some convenient boulders, shaded by fragrant spicewoods and offering a view of the crystalline spring. "I think we need to talk, Len," began Adelinda, waving him to the boulder next to hers.

Len sat down. The rock was closer to Adelinda's than he would have liked; their knees almost touched, but it was the only one nearby. Apparently Adelinda noticed his discomfort. She hitched herself a few inches away under guise of stretching her legs. "Len, Orvet tells me you have a theory about finding out what An-Shai's up to by looking into his papers and records."

Len shrugged, his face averted. "Since I can't read their script there isn't much I can do about it."

"Ah, but I can read their script, and I don't suppose anybody but Li-Mun has the slightest idea about it. With me to do the reading, do you think you could find out what the bishop has in mind?"

"Maybe. But what would you need me for if you can read the papers yourself?"

"I don't have any idea what to look for or what it would mean if I found it. Will you sneak in and take a look?"

"If you like."

"If you're afraid, forget it. I won't blame you."

Len flared angrily, "I'm not afraid. I'll do it." He hesitated. "If you're sure you want to be associated with someone like me." This time the contemptuous sneer was blatantly obvious.

Adelinda was taken aback and beginning to be a little angry. "What does that mean?"

"Just that I'm farmer folk and you're horse folk. I thought maybe you'd rather not be around such trash." The sullenness of his demeanor was being replaced with such a bitter rage as Adelinda had never seen. She realized that if she

returned his rage with anger or reproaches he might be lost
to them for good.

"It's you who called the farmer folk trash, not I," she said
gently. "I can tell that something happened to make you hate
us, and I'm sorry for it. When we get home, if you'll tell me
what it was that happened to you I'll try to do what I can to
right it, although you must know that I don't have much
influence among my own folk. For now, I'd be proud to help
you figure out why the bishop is persecuting us."

For the first time, Len looked at her. At last he muttered,
"I don't hate the horse folk, and it's way too late for you to
do anything about it. But I'll look at the bishop's papers. I
said I would."

Adelinda took a deep breath. "Good. Then come to the
front door of the palace about two o'clock and I'll let you
in."

CHAPTER 9

As Adelinda stole down the corridor from the guest room to the entrance hall of the palace, she paused at the junction of corridors that led to An-Shai's quarters. All was quiet; no crack of light showed under the door of his library. The bishop had apparently gone to bed at long last. He had been working hard at something, cloistered in his library with a servant posted at the door to keep intruders out. Even Li-Mun had been denied admittance.

Adelinda retraced her route of the night before, yawning mightily. This necessity for sneaking around after dark was wearing her down. Nervously clutching the packet of white powder that Orvet had given her to ward off the incubus, she opened the door and peered out. There was no sign of life. She edged out onto the head of the stairs.

Len materialized out of the shadow beside the door, startling her and very nearly getting the powder in his face. "Oh, it's you," she hissed.

"Who else were you expecting?"

"Keep your voice down. You never know around here. I haven't gone through a single night yet without being set upon by some kind of supernatural being. Come on—no, take your boots off."

They slipped through the entrance hall and paused at the junction of the corridors, where Adelinda had left an unlighted candle. "The library's down this way," she was whispering when the door to the room farther down the corridor from the library was flung open and Tsu-Linn came out, followed by An-Shai. Adelinda and Len, who had been about to light the candle with his flint striker, shrank back into the shadows.

". . . ought to be asleep by now," An-Shai was saying.

"I'll check. You take the drug and get ready. Where's her room?"

"It's the first guest room on the right. I'll get you a candle." They went into the library.

Adelinda gasped. "That's my room! Come on!" she whispered.

"I can't go into your room with you."

"Don't be an idiot! I'm not going to attack you."

"I didn't think you were going to," said Len with dignity. "But these people take a very serious view of—er, sneaking around at night. If I were found there it could mean trouble."

"You can't get out; the only way is past the bishop's quarters. I don't know where else to hide you. Come on!"

They hurried back to Adelinda's room. She had pushed her packs under the sleeping bench on the opposite wall from her usual bed place. Pulling them out, she motioned Len under the bench and pushed the packs back in front of him. It was fortunate that he was rather slight of build, for Adelinda believed in traveling light, and there was only a scanty cover even when he drew his knees up. Then she leaped into her bed and pulled up her blanket.

She was barely in time. The door opened and Tsu-Linn came in, a candle in one hand and a pear-shaped black object in the other. This was a magical apparatus called a suffumigator, and Adelinda found out almost immediately what it was used for. As the initiate entered, she raised herself and said sharply, "Who's there?" She deemed it wise not to try to feign sleep or to give the nocturnal visitor a chance to hear that there were two breaths being drawn in that room.

"You sleep very lightly," said Tsu-Linn calmly. "Don't be afraid." He stepped closer to the bed, pointed the small end of the pear into her face, and squeezed sharply. Naturally enough, Adelinda gasped, and as she did so, her lungs filled with an acrid smoke. She made a strangled noise and sank back onto her pillow. Tsu-Linn stood for a moment, watching her struggle for breath. When she sagged loosely, he smiled with satisfaction and left.

Len had watched through a tiny opening, paralyzed with astonishment and horror. As soon as the door closed on the initiate's heels, he shoved aside the packs and crawled out. Quickly, he went to Adelinda's bed and bent over her. Her eyes were open, but stared unseeing past him, nor did she respond when he called her name. Frantically, he shook her, without result.

Clearly, Adelinda had either been poisoned or had a spell placed on her. In either case, Len was unable to help her. But perhaps Orvet could. Quick as thought, he dashed to the door, intending to fetch the exorcist. When he reached the main hall, though, he stopped abruptly. Tsu-Linn stood at the junction of corridor that led to An-Shai's quarters, and past them to the entrance hall and the door. Len couldn't hear what he was saying to one of two palace servants, but shortly he left the man there and led the other one back down the hall toward the corner that Len peered around. Len nipped back into Adelinda's room and applied his eye and ear to the tiny opening he left in the door.

"Don't let anyone come down this hall," he was telling the bewildered servant. "No one is to disturb the foreign woman. You may hear her call out or scream. Ignore it. On no account go to investigate, no matter what happens."

The servant took up his post, and Tsu-Linn turned back toward the bishop's quarters. Len clenched his fists. What was he to do? Adelinda needed Orvet's help, but there seemed to be no way to fetch him. For a moment he considered just walking past the guard or possibly overpowering him, but an alarm was sure to be raised by the other guard. He went over to Adelinda's bed and peered down at her. The darkness was too impenetrable for him to see much; he risked lighting a candle. By that flickering light he could see that she lay as before.

Suddenly, for no reason that he could see, an expression of astonishment crossed her face, quickly followed by alarm, and then terror. She began to breathe in short gasps, as if running hard, and her limbs twitched. Len looked around wildly, feeling more helpless and bewildered than ever before in his life. He hated Adelinda, with what he considered to be good reason, but as he had told Orvet, that

was between him and her, and if he wished her to be made
sorry for what she had done, he would not have wished this
weird supernatural affliction on her. She cried out, a sound
laden with hopeless terror, and he winced.

To Adelinda, it was like wakening. When Tsu-Linn
puffed the smoke in her face, she was immediately seized
with a dizzy, wrenching sensation and a feeling of nausea
and disorientation. When her senses cleared, she found herself lying in the dust of a gray and lifeless plain. The powdery soil was strewn with pebbles and rocks of various sizes
from gravel to small boulders, but there was no life, neither
plant nor animal. The air was heavy with the same acrid
scent the smoke had had, and it burned her nose and throat
as she inhaled it. Her lips were as dry as if she had been on
this waterless plain for days; she wavered weakly as she
drew herself to her feet and looked around for a landmark.

There were no shadows. The sky was lit with a sourceless
luminescence that cast the same gray light from all directions—if there could be said to be directions. There was
only one feature visible, a small structure of some sort, possibly two or three miles away. Otherwise the lifeless plain
stretched to the horizon unbroken, behind her and to either
side. For the lack of a better goal, she began to trudge toward the building. The dust dragged at her feet, making
every step an effort, and the bitter air burned her lungs.

She had gone only a few yards when a fellow traveler
hove into her ken, seemingly from nowhere. He staggered
into her peripheral vision, staring with the glare of madness.
He had obviously been here a lot longer than she; his lips
were cracked, and he licked incessantly at the blood that ran
from them with a tongue too dry to absorb the fluid. He
croaked something that could not be distinguished as words,
and whether he lunged at her or merely staggered in her
direction could not be told.

From behind her came a yammering cry. The man cast a
glance over his shoulder. With a hoarse scream of purest
terror he shoved her in the direction of the cry and turned to
flee. But his strength was spent. He fell, scrabbling to gain

his hands and knees even as he hit the ground, raising a choking cloud of dust.

Past her came a flood of creatures, somewhat manlike, yet also, from their narrow, chinless faces and elongated hand-paws, owing some of their descent to the rat. They were dressed in filthy leather and tattered rags, and each wore a necklace of withered human hands strung by thongs laced through the dry skin of the severed wrists.

They swarmed over the prostrate man, and Adelinda watched, paralyzed with horror, as they tore the living flesh from the man's bones and crammed it still quivering into their bloody mouths. In seconds the flesh was gone from his limbs and they were tearing at the internal organs. A stench as of the gutting of an animal rose into the tainted air; the screaming stopped. One and then another rose triumphant above the moil, brandishing a hand. Adelinda began to withdraw backward, step by silent step.

The creatures knew she was there. There was nowhere near enough flesh on the emaciated corpse to satisfy them. Nothing was left now but stained dust and pink bones. One by one the bloody-mouthed creatures left the gruesome pile and began to slither toward her, their beady eyes fixed on the warm, sleek flesh of her body. Her nerve broke; she turned and fled toward the house she had seen, the only possible place of refuge on these barren plains.

The creatures were not fast. That was all that saved Adelinda. The dust slipped treacherously beneath her feet; her lungs labored agonizingly in the poisoned air; her head swam with the terrible effort of running; but though they snapped at her heels, they could not come quite close enough to bring her down. Several times she looked up from her dogged stride to find that she had veered from the direct route to the building; she moaned in terror to see how much distance she had added to that she must still cover.

At last the building loomed darkly in her blurring vision. She staggered the last few steps and sagged against it, turning to look back. The creatures had fallen behind in the last few hundred yards, but they were coming, they were coming! Slowly but inexorably they drew nearer, yammering with insatiable hunger. Adelinda turned back to the building, searching for an entrance. There was none on the near side, but when she turned the corner, holding to the rough stone wall of the building for support, she found a grillwork window and a door.

Gasping with relief, she made for the door. But there was no handle on the outside, only a thin crack that even her fingernails would not fit in. She hammered on the door, without result. The window—perhaps she could get in that! But the iron bars were fixed.

Peering through, she saw a patio with a chiming fountain. A current of sweet air wafted through the window. Seated with his back to her on a cushion-strewn bench, surrounded by delicate flowering plants, shaded by a featherleaf tree, was a man.

"Hey," Adelinda shouted. The yammering was coming very close. "Let me in!"

The man stood and turned. It was, as she had almost known it would be, An-Shai. When he saw her at the window, an expression of concern shaded his handsome face. "Adelinda, my child, what are you doing out there? It isn't safe." He crossed to the barred window.

Adelinda gulped. She could almost smell the fetid breath of the creatures. She could hear the whisper of the dust beneath their foot-paws. "You're telling *me* it isn't safe out here. Can I come in, please, Your Grace?"

An-Shai looked distressed. "No, I'm afraid you can't come in here, my child. This place is only for those who acknowledge me their master. It's the law. You can't come in."

Adelinda whirled, bracing her back against the wall beside the window, breathing in great ragged gasps. She could hear the creatures' nails scrabbling on the wall around the corner. Their yammering had sunk to a low gobbling mutter.

"This is a nightmare," she said to the blank sky. But she could not believe it.

"Adelinda!" came An-Shai's kindly, anxious voice. "If you would only take me for your master, I could help you. If you will submit yourself to my protection, you can come in here where it's safe."

Take him for her master? Submit to his protection? Outrage flooded Adelinda's soul. "An-Shai!" she called.

"Yes, my child?"

"Stuff it in your ear!" She launched herself away from the building, rounding the far corner, and running away from it on the opposite side from the pack, lashing her failing body on by a terrible effort of will. Outrage burned away in terror when she heard the triumphal yammering of the pack as they sighted her and took up their pursuit. She struck out across the featureless plain, running away from the only safety she knew of.

In the fitfully lit bedroom, Len leaned over her as she moaned and thrashed. He wrung his hands helplessly. What could he do? She was utterly unresponsive to any efforts to wake her. She had broken out in a cold sweat, was gasping for breath as if running for her life. She muttered; he leaned closer. "An-Shai!" he heard. The rest was lost in incoherence.

Adelinda's run had degenerated to a shambling trot. The creatures were in little better condition, however; they could not quite reach her. A break in the horizon caught her eye. Was that a line of hills far away, or boulders close at hand? If they were hills, they were unlikely to be of any help; she was almost spent. No, they were boulders. Thankfully she plunged in among them. The creatures raised a yammering yell as she disappeared from their sight.

Within the boulders, the land began to rise steeply, further sapping her waning strength. The boulders, higher than her head, seemed to crowd her upslope and to the left. Without warning, one of the creatures leaped out at her, slashing at her face with a filthy flint knife. She threw up her arm and deflected the blow. Seizing a rock, screaming with rage and the burning pain of the ragged gash that spouted blood the length of her forearm, she smashed the creature's head and left it twitching as the rest poured out of a slot between two boulders and fell upon their fallen packmate. Adelinda took advantage of their cannibalistic preoccupation to renew her flight, but she knew the scrawny carcass would not hold their interest long. Indeed, they raised their yammering pursuit cry before she had gone more than a few hundred feet, and now she was leaving a reeking crimson trail of bloody drops to lure them after her!

In the bedroom, Len recoiled when a bloody gash suddenly opened in Adelinda's right forearm. She screamed and convulsed. His breath hissing between clenched teeth, he snatched a piece of cloth from her pack and pressed it tightly against the wound in spite of her thrashing. The bleeding slowed, but it was becoming clear to the young farmer that Adelinda was in deadly peril. Whatever happened to her in her unconsciousness could appear on her body here, evidently, as the gash had done. If she died there, would her body die here? She moaned again and he bent to examine the wound. The flesh around it was already hot and swollen, inflamed as if with several days of virulent infection. He felt her forehead. The cold sweat was gone; her skin was dry and hot as if with fever. And these changes had taken place in minutes! Len went to Adelinda's pack and rummaged for a weapon. If she died, someone was going to pay, and the same if her sufferings went on much longer.

Cradling her wounded arm with the other, Adelinda struggled up the steepening slope. Gravel rolled under her feet and she floundered awkwardly. At least she seemed to have distanced the pack, or at least she could no longer hear them. But her gashed arm burned and throbbed. The site of the wound was swollen, oozing a stinking greenish pus, and she could feel her skin parching with fever. Thirst consumed her, though she felt weak and queasy. Only a dogged determination to keep going kept her from sinking to the earth to die. Irrationally, she felt that if she surrendered to pain and fear, An-Shai would have won.

Two boulders loomed up before her, leaving a narrow passage. Too weak to contemplate walking around, she squeezed through, to find her passage blocked by an ornate wrought-iron gate. She fumbled with the latch; it was locked. She sagged against it, too exhausted to turn and seek the way out.

"Adelinda, my child!" It was An-Shai, shock and concern in his resonant voice. "Let me help you!"

She raised her weary gaze. The gate closed off a beautiful little dell, with a crystal spring gushing from a crack in a great boulder that made Adelinda's mouth feel even dryer. A couch strewn with cushions and cool silken sheets sat near the spring, and beside it was a table laden with medicines, bandages, and pitchers of fruit juices beaded with condensation. An-Shai stood just inside the gate, watching her with a compassionate gaze.

Adelinda tried to form words, but her mouth was too dry, and all that came out was a formless croak. She licked her lips with a tongue almost as moistureless as they were. "Could I have a drink of water, please?" she managed to whisper.

Great sorrow shadowed the bishop's face. "I'm so sorry, Adelinda. I wish I could help you. The water, and the medicines, and this refuge are only for those who have accepted my protection."

Adelinda sighed. "I thought that might be the case," she whispered, and turning away, supporting herself against the boulders with her unwounded arm, she trudged back out into the sloping boulder field.

Surprisingly, as she walked, she began to feel a little better. The pain in the wounded arm eased, and her fever subsided. But now the yammering of the pack began to draw closer again, and there was no strength in her to run. She looked about for a refuge. The boulders crested in a ridge not many feet in front of her. She drove her exhausted body to climb that. At the very top were two great flat sheets of rock, and she scrambled onto the right-hand one just as the pack made its appearance from the boulder field. They made as if to climb onto the rock; Adelinda withdrew to the far edge of it. The rock teetered and groaned. The creatures drew back, evidently unwilling to trust to the unsteady surface.

Adelinda glanced over her shoulder and froze in horror. The huge boulder was teetering on the very brink of a drop of thousands of feet, grinding over the underlying bedrock as it inched inexorably toward the cliff. Far, far below, roads traced across an indistinct farming country, divided into fields, laced with streams, blotched with darker patches that must have been mighty forests. Between her and this distant land was nothing but hazy blue air and a wobbling rock.

She shifted her weight, intending to draw away from the brink, and the boulder rocked alarmingly. The creatures, with a yell of rage, began to push on the edge of the boulder, urging it over the edge of the cliff. Adelinda looked about desperately for some means of escape.

"Take my hand, quickly! Let me help you!" An-Shai, secure on the other sheet of rock, which was part of the bedrock of the cliff, reached out toward her. Adelinda started to take the offered hand, then drew back suspiciously.

"I suppose your hand is only for people who have submitted to your protection."

An-Shai sighed. "Adelinda, you've shown more courage and determination than anyone I ever met, man or woman. You've overcome deadly dangers and terrible hardship. I only want to help you. Why won't you accept my protection before it's too late?" As if to underscore his words, the boulder heaved suddenly another foot toward the brink.

Adelinda crouched and clutched dizzily at the boulder's slick surface. It was tilting so steeply that she was in danger of sliding off it. "The price of your help is too high."

"How high a price are you willing to pay for not accepting it?"

"I don't believe this is real," she said desperately. "This is just another one of your creations."

"Make no mistake, this is real enough to kill you or cripple you. Your body is back in your bedroom, but if your soul dies here, how long can your body survive mindless?" The boulder heeled over even farther, gratingly. "Take my hand. Let me help you. Everybody needs someone to help them sometimes. You need me now. There's no shame in needing other people. I'm strong enough to pull you off that rock before you fall off it or it carries you over the edge, and I'm strong enough to take care of you for the rest of your life, too."

"You're crazy!" Adelinda cried. "You want to make a slave of everybody. Leave me alone! I won't take your help!" With a despairing yell and a terrible convulsive effort, she flung herself off the rock and into the milling pack, striking at the slinking little monsters with her good arm. Thrown into confusion by the sudden attack from their formerly fleeing prey, they scattered momentarily, and Adelinda dashed through the opening and ran headlong down the slope.

In the bedroom, Len started up from the floor by the bedshelf as Adelinda thrashed convulsively. ". . . help!" he heard her mumble as she tossed. He looked at the wound. It was nearly healed and the fever was gone! The short hairs on the back of his neck bristled.

Adelinda plunged down the slope, falling as much as running, held up only by momentum and luck. The pack was in full cry after her, and she was horrified to discover, glancing back over her shoulder, that the man-rats had been joined by slinking, mangy canines, huge brindled beasts that slavered as they loped along. If they catch me, she thought, there won't be more than a bite apiece for them.

The glance back over her shoulder had been a deadly mistake. Without warning, the gray light was blocked off, and she found herself pitched down an ever-increasing slope into the dark maw of a tunnel. She tried desperately to stop, but the steepness of the powdery, sliding soil and her momentum carried her into the cave's mouth and down, out of control. She scrabbled at the moving surface and tried to dig in her boots, but it was too late; she was carried beyond the reach of the light, and her last sight of the day was of the man-rats and their hounds, balked at the entrance to the cave, yelling in baffled rage.

The last spark of light vanished; she was hurtling downward, banging into rocks and the wall of the tunnel as it twisted and turned. She grabbed at anything she could, but could not break the long slide. Her speed was too great. Her hands were battered and bleeding and there seemed to be no part of her body that had not crashed into something with bruising force. But worse than the physical pain was the terrible fear that the slope would steepen even more or drop off into a sudden pit and that she would fall to dash herself to death on unyielding bedrock. Her broken body would lie forever in the dark depths, and somehow that thought was as unnerving as the fear of falling.

At last, after what seemed like hours of helpless sliding, the slope began to level out, and she came gently to rest at the bottom of the immensely long chute. She lay for a long while, drawing ragged, sobbing breaths, while the pain of all her myriad bruises and scrapes soaked into her consciousness. She had received the equivalent of a severe beating as she hurtled down the chute, and it felt as though she could never move again.

She opened her eyes to look about her. There was nothing to be seen. She was in blackness so utter that red sparks swam before her eyes as they strained to make out even the slightest image. The air lay heavily on her chest, stale and lifeless. The thin, dry whisper of a tiny fall of sand from somewhere was the only sound, save for the labored pounded of her own heart and rasping breaths. Above her, the weight of millions of tons of rock and earth bore down upon her with a palpable pressure, crushing her spirit as the rocks themselves threatened to crush her body. She could not scream, as some might have done. The dark was a living thing that pressed hungrily at her from all sides, drinking in her terror. She could only whimper and cower on the sandy floor, babbling to drown out the fearsome silence.

Len was not surprised when great livid bruises began to appear on his employer's body. Grimly, he laid aside Adelinda's sword and dabbed away the blood that welled from the scrapes. But when she huddled herself into a ball and began to whimper as one in the utter extremity of hopeless terror, the hatred that had festered for so long in his heart melted away at last, to be replaced by pity and a great fear for her sanity. Moved by an unreasoning desire to comfort her, he sat down beside her on the narrow bed-shelf and gathered her into his arms, holding and rocking her as he would have a frightened child. "Adelinda, Adelinda," he whispered into her ear. "You're safe. Nothing can hurt you here. You're going to be all right. Please, Adelinda, try to wake up. I'm here with you, and I'll keep you safe until you can wake up. Try to come to me, Adelinda," He kept repeating the same phrases, over and over, holding her trembling body tightly, projecting comfort and safety to the utmost of his ability.

Adelinda cowered on the floor of the cavern for a long

while, her nerve utterly gone. Her half-healed arm burned like fire; every bruise and scrape ached clear to the bone; thirst tormented her. But none of those would have broken her will. The darkness and the depths did that.

An-Shai, watching her with a light that shone in the over-mind only for his eyes, tasted triumph as a rich wine, knowing that he had only to speak and she would take his offered protection gratefully, eager to accept him as master if only he would take her from this place. He paused to savor the picture of her, humbly grateful to him, worshipping him as he showered her with kindness, coming at last to be glad he had broken her spirit and her proud heart.

Through the extremity of her terror, Adelinda knew he was there. She knew, too, that as soon as he had enjoyed her fear long enough he would speak, and the depths of her self-loathing were abysmal, for she knew that when he did, this time she would yield. She would have called out to him, had she not been stunned with fear, her tongue swollen in her mouth until it threatened to choke her.

But then, just as An-Shai was preparing to speak with infinite sorrow and pity, a third presence entered into that hellish place. A powerful personality with a keen intelligence, freed at last of the fetters of self-pity and hatred that had crippled its development for so long, Len's spirit was a bolt of lightning illuminating the pit. He poured his strength and courage into Adelinda's flagging soul lavishly, and she rose from the floor of the cave with a glad cry. Irresistibly, he summoned her out of her trap and back to him, and, newly invigorated, she fled to him, obeying his call freely as she would never have done An-Shai's.

An-Shai was livid with rage and disappointment. He had had her in his hand; she had been on the very verge of capitulation and some insolent outlander had intervened. He would pay, whoever he was. The bishop wrenched himself out of the overmind, letting his savage little universe dissolve back to its constituent nothingness, plains, buildings, man-rats, and all. He started up from his bed-shelf, his face contorted, considerably startling Tsu-Linn, who was standing by to offer assistance if needed.

Adelinda returned to the real world to find herself cradled tenderly in Len's arms, as he rocked her soothingly, murmuring comforting words in her ear. Convulsively, she clung to him, racked by a storm of weeping. The remnants of terror, bitter humiliation, and incredible relief rendered her speechless for minutes.

When at last she was able to catch her breath, she said, quietly but with great intensity, "Len, I don't know why you hate me, but whatever I did to you I'll make it up, if it takes every penny I have and every drop of my blood. You saved me from—well, from something more horrible than you can even imagine, and I owe you a debt that nothing could ever repay."

Holding her gently, he answered, "Hush, hush. You're upset. I don't hate you. When you feel better, let's get out of here."

"Oh, yes, let's. An-Shai must be insane, and he's a more powerful sorcerer than we ever imagined. Let's get the horses and make a run for the ocean."

"Without his help, how will we get ships?"

Adelinda was silenced. "I don't know," she said at last. "Maybe we can run for the northeast, where the continents are supposed to come together so closely that you can see across on a clear day. We'll talk it over with the others."

Adelinda's trembling had almost quelled itself when the door burst open and An-Shai charged into the room, followed by Tsu-Linn, Li-Mun, and a contingent of the palace servants. The bishop took in the scene before him. Adelinda was half lying in the embrace of one of her young employees, the dark-haired one, holding on to him as if he were her lifeline, as indeed he had been. An-Shai drew himself up, his face glacially cold, bolts of invisible power playing about him as lightning plays about some high and rocky peak.

"So!" he said, controlling his rage. "You've dared to bring your lover into my very palace. Are they all your bedslaves?" A bitter burning feeling welled up in the bishop's breast and added itself to his anger at being balked in his plans; he failed to recognize the sensation as jealousy.

Len released Adelinda and scooped up the short sword he had laid aside. Adelinda came to her feet, fighting to subdue the trembling that An-Shai's entrance had caused to break out anew. If An-Shai had taught her nothing else, he had taught her fear. Shoulder to shoulder, the two outlanders faced the crowd defiantly. "Len is not my lover. He's much more than that; he's my friend. If it weren't for him, you'd have succeeded in destroying me. You're a treacherous, vicious madman, and our contract is ended. We're leaving Godsland."

"Do you think so?" snarled An-Shai, nearly beside himself beneath his icy demeanor. "You aren't leaving. You and this peasant are going to stay here and pay for your crimes." He raised his hands suddenly, clutching as he gathered his invisible power into them. He flung it at the defiant pair. It was like being struck by lightning. The sword was dashed out of Len's grasp and flung across the room to clatter against the wall. Len convulsed as he was flung the other way, to skid across the floor and land crumpled in a corner. Adelinda dropped as if shot, unconscious before she hit the floor. The air sizzled and stank of ozone. The palace servants cowered in awe, and even Tsu-Linn's jaw dropped. He had had no idea his protégé could command such powers in the real world.

All his forces spent by the efforts of the past few hours, An-Shai sagged and would have fallen himself if Li-Mun hadn't caught him and supported his body. "Lock them up," the bishop gasped weakly. "Tell them what the penalties are for what they've done. I want them to suffer."

"Yes, Your Grace," said Li-Mun, soothingly. "I will. Er —what are the penalties?"

"Use your imagination!" snapped An-Shai, pettishly as an old man. "And tell the woman she'll have to watch the peasant suffer them first."

Li-Mun gulped. He had never imagined that his bishop was capable of such malice. "Yes, Your Grace. Where shall we lock them up?"

"Do I have to do all the thinking? There must be a storeroom with a lock on it, or you can have some bars installed on the outside of one of the guest rooms, or something. Just make sure it's uncomfortable." Sagging weakly against Li-Mun, An-Shai looked down at his unconscious prisoners. "She's going to be very, very sorry she didn't accept my protection."

CHAPTER 10

"For God's sake, man, forget it," expostulated Tsu-Linn. An-Shai's cold rage had survived the night. He stood at the window of his library, his inner turmoil expressing itself in the vibrating tension of his tall, slender frame as he stared out over the northern Vale. "If this try at mastering the woman failed, you have all the chances in the world to try again. If the peasant is her lover, you have an excellent leverage against her. She must care what happens to him, but you don't, if you take my meaning."

"I understand you. You think that if he's threatened, she'll do anything to save him. I don't think so. I'm not sure I can do anything to him in the overmind, anyway. You didn't feel the power he poured into her, nor the strength with which he called her out of the overmind."

"Far be it from me to suggest crude methods, but I'd like to point out that you don't have to deal with him in the overmind. She's seen what night stalkers can do. If he were staked out near a nest of them, what would she do to have him freed?"

An-Shai turned and looked at the initiate, revulsion plain for an instant on his face. "What if I didn't get back to him in time? He'd really be killed. No, it isn't worth it. Besides, if he were eaten by night stalkers she'd hate me forever."

"She's not fond of you now."

An-Shai shook his head. "If I could master her, I could win her over with kindness. If I actually harm her or her friend, the psychic power her hatred would generate would probably burn out both our minds. She's very strong, if only she knew it. If she knew as much as I do about the overmind, I wouldn't have any chance of mastering her."

"I'd bet that she's learning rapidly. She isn't stupid, either."

"Li-Mun says that the peasant resents her. There must be some way we can use that."

"He was quick enough to help her last night."

"Not really. It was hours of subjective time before he intervened. If he cared about her he'd have been into it at the first episode."

"Then you don't think he's her lover?"

"No, I suppose not, not unless she's forcing him and that's what he resents. But I doubt that she'd do that. She's as honest and straightforward as a punch in the mouth; she says what she means and she means what she says. Think of the trouble she could have saved herself by pretending to give in last night." An-Shai paused reflectively. "Can he help her if they're separated and he can't see her?"

"Not if he doesn't know she needs help. Unfortunately, you'll find that being in contact in the overmind as they have been establishes a bond between people. You'd feel it yourself if she was threatened by someone else in the overmind. You might even be drawn in to help her. Whether these outlanders will be sensitive to such a bond, who can say?"

"Well, then, what can I do?"

Tsu-Linn shrugged. "Kill them both and come with me to the Hall for your initiation. They aren't worth all this agony."

"No! If I did that, she'd have me beat. She'll be worth it all, once I've broken her in. You said yourself that she would make a good wife for an initiate."

"Then bring her to the Hall of the Initiates. There are facilities there that you don't have, techniques that in time will break any will. We've been underestimating these outlanders all along; that's been our trouble. I suggest that you use their names when you think of them, just as you would another initiate. If you go on thinking of them as 'the woman' and 'the peasant,' you can't help thinking of them as stereotypes."

* * *

Adelinda returned to consciousness to find herself lying in a bare room on an uncovered stone sleeping bench. Morning light streamed through the window. Len lay across the room from her, sprawled as if he had been dumped carelessly down. Aside from their two bodies and the clothing they wore, the room was completely empty. She swung her legs down and staggered stiffly to her feet. A quick check showed that Len was unconscious, breathing with some difficulty because of his awkward position. She straightened him out and began to examine the room. One door opened to show the same sanitary facilities that she had had in her room. She used these with considerable relief. The other door was shut and barred, and with no leverage she couldn't hope to force it. An examination of the window showed that it was closed with a hastily installed grillwork. There was a sheer drop of twenty feet or so to the floor of the Vale, certainly far enough to break bones if they tried to jump.

Adelinda returned to the place she had been left and sat down. Running a sticky tongue over paper-dry lips, she set herself to think her way out of imprisonment. Neither doors nor window offered any avenue of escape. She was considering all the various stratagems she had ever heard or read about when Len groaned and began to stir. He levered himself to a sitting position and stared blankly about, his handsome young face marred with a livid bruise across the left cheekbone.

"Are you all right?" Adelinda asked inadequeately.

"I guess so. I feel like I took a nap in the path of a stampede. Is there anything to drink?"

"No, but there's a facility through that door, if you need it."

Without answering, Len struggled to his feet and limped through the door. When he returned, he made the same round that Adelinda had done and made the same discoveries. Then he, too, returned to the sleeping bench and sank down upon it.

They had sat thus for a while when the bars were removed from the door—three of them, from the amount of racket they made. The door was opened, and Li-Mun entered. His quick glance showed him both the prisoners, seated on opposite sides of the room—not hopeful for the bishop's schemes, he thought. "Would you move over beside Adelinda, please, Len? I want to talk to both of you." Sullenly —the old cast of countenance had settled back onto his face—Len complied. "You two have displeased the bishop very much. He's asked me to explain the nature of your crimes and the penalties."

Adelinda's expression was one of courteous disinterest; Len scowled into space as though Li-Mun were invisible and inaudible. "The rules governing marriage here in Godsland are very strict, and the penalty for taking a lover outside of wedlock is death," the secretary said as impressively as he could manage.

"Then it is very fortunate that Len and I aren't lovers," said Adelinda, calmly.

"You must agree that it looks very suspicious for him to have been found in your room, the two of you clasped in a close embrace."

"Oh, quit it, Li-Mun. You know that isn't why An-Shai is angry with us. He's mad at me because I wouldn't play his little power games with him, and he's mad at Len because he helped me out. What is he going to do about it?"

"I believe he intends to invoke the full weight of the custom. He means to have you both put to death. And I'm afraid that he intends for you to watch while Len is subjected to indescribable tortures and then executed yourself after he expires."

Suddenly Adelinda laughed. "Did you say 'indescribable tortures'? An-Shai must have told you to say that."

Li-Mun, who had made up the phrase himself and was rather proud of it, blushed. He had thought that mysterious terrors would be more effective than specific threats, at which his imagination failed him. "I should prefer not to tell you what will be done to him. It doesn't make pleasant hearing," he added darkly.

"Go back to the bishop and tell him that if he'll let us go we and all the outlanders will be out of the Vale by noon and out of Godsland by tomorrow nightfall, if he will arrange for the ships."

"I don't think he'll agree to that. There's only one way to save yourself and Len."

"As if I didn't know. Go ahead."

"If you will go to him and plead for mercy, he might be willing to take you under his protection and spare Len."

There was a stubborn set to Adelinda's jaw that made it unnecessary for her to reject the proposition.

Abruptly Li-Mun abandoned his prepared script. He came and sat down beside Adelinda and took her hand. "Adelinda, he doesn't really want to hurt you or Len, no matter what he says, just like he didn't really hurt you last night." He turned her arm; the scar that only a few hours ago had been a bloody gash was fading away, and the bruises were already gone. "I don't know why, but it has really become important to him that you look to him for protection. What would it hurt? I can promise you that he'd be a kind master. All it would take to satisfy him would be a chance to be magnanimous to you. Can't you give him that chance?" He leaned forward, willing her to believe him. "How could it hurt your pride to let another human being have his pride, too?"

Adelinda sighed and glanced at Len, who was listening with a strange intensity. "It isn't a matter of pride, Li-Mun. Or not any more, anyway. I tried to offer him what deference I could. But he wants too much. He wants to make me a slave. Can you honestly say that he would let us go home if I did—well, surrender to him?"

Li-Mun's gaze fell. "No, I can't. If you really accepted his protection, you wouldn't want to leave him, and he'd know in a minute if you were faking. Would it be so bad to be cared for and protected by a strong man you could trust?"

"I can't do it. I hope he doesn't hurt Len or any of the rest of my friends, but I can't submit my will to him the way he wants me to. I don't trust him. No normal person wants another person to give up all of themselves to him."

"Some do," said Len unexpectedly. "Some men want that from their women. Is An-Shai in love with Adelinda?"

"No-o," said Li-Mun doubtfully. "I don't think so. Not sexually, anyway. He's always obeyed the rules about celibacy, and never seemed to think they were too harsh. But this is important to him. He means to win you over with kindness after you've submitted, I'm sure of that. He'd protect your friends, too, for your sake. I overheard him just now refusing to have Len killed."

"He can't win this fight, Li-Mun," said Adelinda. "This obsession of his is going to get us all killed. Help us escape. Once we're away he can settle down to ruling his Vale or getting to be an initiate or whatever he wants to do."

"You'll never escape him, Adelinda," said Li-Mun sadly. "No matter where you were, even back in your own mountains, he could reach you through the overmind." The hierarch rose and walked to the door. "Think about it. Talk it over with Len and see if he's willing to be sacrificed to your pride. At this time, An-Shai won't hurt you or your friends, but you can push him so far he'd be forced to."

"Wait," said Adelinda. "Could we have a drink of water and something to eat?"

"Of course you can, anytime you're willing to ask An-Shai for them." Li-Mun left the room and the bars crashed back into place.

Len swallowed convulsively. Adelinda tried again to moisten her lips. "He's got us where he wants us, doesn't he?" she said at last. "We've got to have water, and food too. Len, we've got to escape. Watch for any chance, and if you see one, you give the orders and I'll take them, and the other way around if I see one you don't. All right?"

Len nodded. "We won't get far if we're weak, though," he said, hoping she would get the point.

At that moment, the bars began to crash back again. The door opened, and An-Shai appeared, carrying a heavy pitcher. Without giving him a chance to speak, Adelinda rose. "Your Grace, may we have a drink of water, please?" she asked. Her tone, though it could not be said to be humble, was at least polite.

"Of course," the bishop said. "I consider it an obligation to take care of those for whom I have accepted the responsibility." Adelinda's teeth grated, but she held her tongue. Taking large cups from one of the several servants who had followed him into the makeshift prison, An-Shai poured each of them one. It was the sparkling water of the deep artesian wells, cool and refreshing, the faint mineral flavor biting the tongue with a pleasant tang, and they both drained their cups in one draft.

"May we have some more, please?" asked Adelinda, holding out her cup.

"Certainly," responded the bishop, and filled the cups again. "I'll leave the pitcher for you." He gestured, and two palace servants brought in a small table. The bishop set the pitcher down upon it. "Before I go, is there anything else you need?"

"Could we have something to eat, please?"

"Oh, yes." He beckoned again, and two small plates with attractively arranged crisp raw vegetables on them were brought in. There was neither the grain they had come to expect with meals nor the customary sour wine.

"Is this all we get?" asked Adelinda, looking at a lovely fresh salad that was about enough to keep a small rabbit happy.

"Since your activity will be greatly reduced, you'll need a lighter diet—for your health's sake." Without waiting for an answer, the bishop left the room. If he expected Adelinda to call after him and beg for more food, he was disappointed; she was unable to bring herself to do so before the door closed and the bars were replaced.

Adelinda stared moodily at her plate. "I suppose this is better than starvation," she said.

"Lots better. At least we aren't thirsty any more," said Len. "I'll admit that for a while there I was afraid you wouldn't ask for anything."

Adelinda sighed. "I don't have much choice, do I? Promise me you'll tell me if I show signs of groveling."

Len, his mouth full of radishes, grinned. "I can't imagine it."

Orvet and Karel stood before the bishop, their aspects courteous. "Your Grace," said Orvet politely, "we're concerned for our friend and employer Adelinda. She hasn't been seen this morning, even though her horse is still in his pen. Do you know where she is?"

An-Shai leaned back in his chair and tented his fingers. "Yes, and I know where your young friend Len is, too. They were caught breaking some very important rules and are being held until I decide what the penalties are to be."

Orvet and Karel exchanged concerned glances. "May we know what rule they broke?"

"The rule against taking lovers outside the bond of marriage."

"Oh, no, they can't have done that," exclaimed Karel, positively.

"Can't they?" asked An-Shai icily. "Then what was the young man doing in her room in the small hours of the morning?"

"I don't know, but certainly not making love. They don't even like each other."

"If you will permit us to talk to them," interposed Orvet smoothly, "we'll find out."

"No. You're dismissed." The bishop turned to a stack of bark paper he was sorting. Perforce, Orvet and Karel left.

"What do you suppose is going on?" Karel asked, dismayed, when they rejoined Tobin and Ina, waiting outside with the horses.

"I expect he caught them snooping in his papers, or about to, and is using this rule of his as an excuse to hold them. He won't let us talk to them so they can't tell us what they found out."

"Where's the prison?" asked Tobin. "Maybe we can get them out and make a run for it."

"I don't know where the prison is. I haven't seen anything that looks like a jail. Everybody look around and ask a few tactful questions today. We'll see what we can do tonight," said Karel.

Ina was the first to find an opportunity to discover any information. She had been giving Cho-Hei a riding lesson and he had suggested that they rest for a while in a fragrant grove of spicewoods with a peaty amber spring welling out of the ground in the middle, forming a deep, bubbling pool perhaps ten feet in diameter. Someone had walled the pool about with a low circle of stones all golden-stained by the water.

The noble's mind did not prove to be exclusively on improving his equitation, Ina found. He seated her on a mossy bank and sat down so close to her that their thighs rubbed together. When he leaned toward her, which he immediately did, she could feel his soft breath stirring the hair on her temple. She shifted uneasily, all too aware of his proximity. "Tell me about the laws of your country," she gulped.

If Cho-Hei was startled by this sudden introduction of the subject, he was too urbane to show it. "We don't really have laws, Ina," he said, drawing her name out breathily.

"Well," she stuttered, "I had in mind your rules about marriage." Then she blushed as she realized that the noble must think that she meant to apply his answer to them.

"Ah, I see." He smiled his dazzling smile. "Our bishop decides when we may marry and the village priest usually decides whom. Mates are chosen for suitability and for the greater glory of God the Father—also to breed out any defective genes. However," here he leaned even closer, "we may suggest to the priest that we would be unusually pleased if he would choose a certain mate for us, and if the match fulfills all the other necessary criteria, and if the bishop approves, he may sanction it."

"No, I meant, well, sometimes people must, er . . . I mean, what if two people who aren't married, er, misbehave?"

Cho-Hei withdrew a few inches and gave her a shocked look. "I don't mean me!" she exclaimed. "He's holding our employer on some such charge and I wanted to know what the rules were."

"Oh. Well, I certainly can't say that such things don't happen, boys and girls being what they are. If the priest and the bishop want to invoke the full weight of custom, the culprits could be put to death, but usually they're just forced to marry. If the match isn't a desirable one, they're not allowed to have any children."

"I don't believe that Adelinda and Len were doing any such thing."

"Don't men and women do such things in your homeland?"

"Of course. We see nothing wrong in a little affection exchanged between boys and girls, as long as no one's hurt by it. The horse folk, who marry late, may have several affairs before they settle on a permanent mate. We farmer folk usually marry at fifteen or sixteen, so we have little opportunity for experimentation. But Adelinda and Len— well, you'd have to know them to realize how impossible such an idea is."

Cho-Hei shook his head. "An-Shai's a deep one. All the clergy are. He wouldn't hesitate to hold them for reasons of his own. You have to admit that if Len was really found in Adelinda's room, it doesn't look good for them."

"Where would criminals of that sort be held? I'd like to visit them and see if they need anything."

Cho-Hei looked genuinely puzzled. "I don't know. Usually such criminals are dealt with immediately. We don't have any facilities for locking people up."

"What do you do with ordinary criminals?"

"There aren't any." Cho-Hei grinned infectiously. "The bishop has God and all the spirits to back up his commands. He doesn't need to lock people up. Who would dare disobey him?"

"Then where could they be?"

"They must be locked up in the palace somewhere. Come to think of it, I saw a metal worker installing a grillwork over one of the guest room windows around on the south side earlier this morning. I'll bet that's where they are. I'd forget it, if I were you. You'll never get to see them unless the bishop decides to let you."

"I suppose you're right," said Ina, and she threw herself enthusiastically into the spirit of the flirtation that Cho-Hei was trying to carry on, to distract him from her questions. The noble was surprised but pleased, and set himself to charming her.

Later, when she reported the results of this conversation to the other three, Karel shook his head gloomily. "It doesn't sound good. I hope Cho-Hei doesn't report that you've been snooping."

"I don't think he will," Ina answered, patting her disorderly hair into place. "I'll tell you something: I don't think the ordinary people care any more for the clergy than we do. They're afraid of them, and with good reason, but if they could find a way to get rid of them they would. I think

Cho-Hei will follow orders, but I don't think he'll volunteer anything he isn't asked about."

"If they've got Adelinda and Len locked up in one of the guest rooms on the south side, we can at least talk to them and find out what's going on," said Tobin.

"How?" chorused the others.

"If we throw a rope up to them and they tie it on the bars, I can shinny up it and talk to them."

"Really? I couldn't do it," said Orvet.

"I could have when I was Tobin's age, before I got hurt," said Karel. "I believe him."

"I was rope-climbing champion for the last three years in a row at the Midsummer Games," said Tobin, eyes cast down modestly.

"You certainly don't brag about your feats," observed Orvet.

Tobin looked a bit uncomfortable. "Well, if people know you can, they expect you to. But this is an emergency," he added magnanimously.

"One thing is sure," said Karel, thoughtfully. "We've got to be ready to get out of here at a moment's notice. Keep your personal gear packed and ready to go. Light packs, please; your riding horses are going to have to carry them. We won't have any pack stock. I hope nobody brought anything they have any objection to abandoning."

While the rest of the party discussed their fate, Adelinda and Len were facing the bishop in his study. There were no guards; none were needed. An-Shai fairly vibrated with a power kept precariously in leash.

"Let me make myself very clear to you," he said, as cold and distant as winter stars. "Whether you are guilty or not makes absolutely no difference to me at all. You will bow to my will here in Godsland. Late or soon, you will acknowledge me your master. Do you understand what I intend?"

"I understand that you never intended to let us leave when you sent for us, and I call that damned treacherous, dishonorable dealing," said Adelinda. "My folk and I have dealt fairly with you, and would have continued to until our agreement was fulfilled. In return, we find that we are to be kept here for the rest of our lives as slaves."

An-Shai brushed this aside. "Nonsense. Any peasant is better for having a priest and a bishop to care for him and guide his life. Our peasants are happy and content. Can you say the same for yours?" He gestured at Len, standing a little in the rear, the sullen expression of his face even more pronounced. "That one particularly would obviously be better off to have concerned and responsible superiors."

"Len has the freedom to make whatever he wants of his life. He can live where he likes, marry whom he chooses, take whatever job he prefers, and spend the money he earns as seems best to him. Or if he chooses not to do any of those things, he can do that, too."

The bishop's lip curled in contempt. "And all the use he has made of all this freedom is to be miserable."

"Ask Len which he prefers: free misery or serfdom. You might ask your own people the same question, except that they'd be too afraid of you to give you an honest answer."

"Nine tenths of all people are born too cowardly or too lazy to make their own decisions—and to take the responsibility for the consequences."

"I doubt that. Even if it were true, I'm certainly not one of the nine tenths, nor any of my folk. Your best choice is to let us go before you force us all into a situation where no one can survive, much less win."

"You're an arrogant woman, Adelinda. Not only you, but the world will be better off when you have been brought to realize your proper place. And you can ask Len or any of your men if that's not so."

Adelinda was trembling with rage now, too. "The men of the Kingdom are willing to let any woman do whatever she can. You waste half your people keeping your women uneducated and poor-spirited."

"But our women are happy, filling the role for which they were designed. I see no sign that either you or your countrywoman Ina is happy. Both of you need a husband to serve and to take care of you. And how can your men feel that they are men when their women neglect all consideration or respect? It seems to me that everyone, man or woman, needs to have a place in the world and people about him or her whose roles are understood. Your precious 'freedom' is won at great cost. The people who should be able to rely on you can't because you'd rather be free than responsible." As Adelinda grew angrier, An-Shai had been growing cooler; for the first time now, he sat down. "Do you dare to put your concept of 'freedom' to the test against my concept of 'protection'?"

"What do you mean?"

"A test in the overmind, you and Len against Tsu-Linn and myself. Each of us can devise a scenario to demonstrate the point of our philosophies. The more powerful scenario wins."

"I'm not sure I understand what the 'overmind' is."

"The overmind is the stuff of the collective unconscious of the human race. For those who know how to gain access to it in the conscious state, and who have the resolution and the self-command to do it, it is a source of great power. Since a determined will can shape the stuff of the overmind, whole little universes can be created there, designed to suit the creator."

"That little drama last night was your invention." An-Shai inclined his head, gravely. "You've got a gruesome mind, Bishop. I'm not sure I understand the stakes in this little contest you're suggesting."

"Then let me explain. If I win, you will have to concede that my view of the universe is the correct one, and in that eventuality you will be happy to accept my protection. If, on the other hand, your scenario is the more convincing, I would have to admit that there is merit in 'freedom' and to permit you and your folk to keep yours."

Adelinda was tempted to fall in with the bishop's plan. There was no question in her mind but that her view of the universe was the right one. It seemed a way out of a situation that was rapidly degenerating into unguessable catastrophes. Len saw the indecision in her face. "No!" he said, startling both of the others. "Don't agree to anything, Adelinda. The only thing that sort of contest would prove would be that An-Shai and Tsu-Linn know more about this 'overmind' and how to handle it than we do, and we already know that."

Adelinda gave him a look of surprise that quickly changed to gratitude as she assimilated the pitfall Len had pointed out. "You're right," she conceded. She turned back to the bishop. "No. My friend sees things more clearly than I do. No contests. I'll tell you again that the best thing you can do for yourself, for your people, and for us is to let us go. We can guarantee to be out of Godsland tomorrow."

"I'm not sure I shall permit you to refuse my offer. I'll even warn you so that you can prepare. In fact, I'm even willing to concede that your peasants are certainly smarter than ours, and that even if one of ours had observed what Len did he wouldn't have dared to speak up. But I still maintain that he's no happier for it." The bishop rose from his desk, seeming taller and more dreadful than ever, as if some great wrathful force was gathering itself into him, imbuing him with a latent power that threatened terrible destruction.

"You're to remain here. I'll speak to Tsu-Linn now and discover his convenience." He strode out the door, shutting it firmly behind him.

His footsteps had not ceased to echo when Len was at the door, opening it to discover a contingent of palace servants. He shut it again quickly. Adelinda was already at the bishop's desk, riffling through the piles of bark paper that lay there. Len joined her. "What do they say?" he asked.

"Just a minute. Thank goodness An-Shai writes a good clear hand—I don't read these syllabics very fast, you know. H'mm, these are business letters. I can't find the account books."

"Business letters are just as good. Just skim them to find out what they're about—he's likely to be back shortly."

"This one's about cloth to be sent. . . . I don't recognize the name. Here's one about ships, and this one's about a quota—" Adelinda paused, horrified.

"What is it?" demanded Len.

"A quota of slave girls to be taken—or maybe it's stolen —by the bandits. He apologizes for the last raid having been stopped and promises it won't happen again."

"Then he knows about the slavers!"

"If I'm reading this right, he not only knows about the slavers, he sent for them. He says here that only nubile girls are to be taken, to reduce the population of breeders."

"My God."

"Is this his idea of protection? Oh, Len, you were right to stop me from accepting his challenge."

"Look at the rest of the letters."

"Right. This one's about cloth again, and fruit trees to be brought from—somewhere. This is a population report. Here's a letter canceling an order for a team of onagers. . . ."

"Wait a minute. Take another look at that population report. If he's reducing his population of breeders—well, take a look at it."

"All right. It's divided by groups according to occupation. Farmers are in this column, weavers here. Over here the nonproductive parts of the population are listed. Old people, babies, and young children—what's this notation? Thinned, I think. This is a list of deaths. Natural causes, three, night stalkers, nine. This is another list of deaths—no, this verb is in the future tense, I think. That would make it 'to be thinned.' That doesn't make sense. Unless . . ."

Adelinda stopped almost in midword and they stared at each other, aghast. "Unless," said Len carefully, "the bishop not only knew about the night stalker attacks but encouraged them, in order to cull out useless babies and old folks. Orvet said that the protective symbols on the guardian stone had been overwritten. Who all knows how to write in the Vale?"

"Just the clergy. Li-Mun told me that no one else was allowed to learn to write when I talked him into teaching me."

"That means that An-Shai is a cold-blooded monster. All this talk about protecting people is a lie. The lives of his people mean no more to him than flies do to us."

"We've got to get away!" said Adelinda through pale lips.

"If he meant to kill us he could have done it long since. For some reason he has to make us—no, you—admit that he's the boss before he has us killed."

"Because it's all right to have his own people killed, but

not others. Once we let him get the upper hand, all he has to
do is decide that we're excess population."

At that moment the door opened and An-Shai walked in.
He halted in amazement when he saw them at his desk, the
papers in Adelinda's hand, both of them pale and shocked.
"What're you doing? Give me that," he snapped.

"You've been having your own people killed and kid-
napped by slavers!" blurted Adelinda. To her surprise, the
bishop blanched. She had never seen him show any emotion
but anger and disdain before.

"You read this! Where did you learn to read?"

"On the ship. How dare you claim to protect and care for
your people when you treat them like this?"

Slowly An-Shai went to his desk and sat down. "Sometimes a bishop has to consider the good of his whole diocese. It's better that a few should be taken away than that
everybody should starve." There was an expression on his
face that might almost have been shame. "It's unfortunate, I
agree. A really good bishop should be able to manipulate the
population of his diocese by limiting marriages and not have
to use such drastic means."

"Do you have the nerve to claim that you wouldn't have
us killed the same way as soon as you had us under your
thumb?" challenged Adelinda.

"I would not," said An-Shai, steadily. "I have never
meant to have any of you killed. On that I give you my
word. I will prevail in this struggle between us, Adelinda,
and I will care for you and your people for the rest of your
lives. Nor will your lives be cut short by any action or negli-
gence of mine." There was no mistaking his sincerity, but
Adelinda refused to accept it.

"Did you give any of those poor peasants the same guarantee," she sneered, "or did they just assume that they had
as much right to live as anybody?"

"They do have as much—or as little—right to live as
anybody. An accident or illness may end their lives as much
as any plan of mine. The Quadrate God gathers their souls
into Himself and cherishes them until it's time to send them
to earth again. And perhaps their next lives will be more
fortunate."

"Is that what you tell them? That they're lucky to be killed and eaten? You know you're lying. Dead is dead, with no second chances."

"You're wrong, Adelinda. I believe there are second chances."

"I think so, too," said Len. "It's unthinkable that all a person's soul just evaporates when his body dies. I'm not sure what happens to it, but it has to survive somehow."

The two men looked at each other and the tiniest flash of masculine unity traveled between them. "Return to your quarters and prepare your scenario," said An-Shai dismissively.

"I don't agree to the contest and I won't abide by the terms," warned Adelinda.

Chapter 11

"Hsst! Len!" Tobin chunked a rock at the moonlit window above his head. There was no response. "Len! Are you up there?" called Tobin as loudly as he dared. Len's thin dark face appeared at the grillwork. "Catch!" On the third try, Len managed to snag the weighted rope Tobin tossed up to him. The end securely fastened to the bars, Tobin swarmed up it with an agility surprising in one usually so slow of movement.

"What's going on? Why are you two locked up?" Tobin panted, seeing Adelinda's face beside Len's in the moonlight.

"The bishop, up to his tricks," answered Adelinda hastily. "Now listen, Tobin, I want you to take this message to Orvet and Karel. The bishop arranges the slave raids and the attacks by night stalkers and other supernaturals. He means to keep us all here for the rest of our lives—which might not be very long. I want the four of you to get out fast, tonight." Both Len and Tobin made inarticulate sounds of protest. "I mean it. We can't get out. We've tried everything, and if you try to help us you'll just wind up locked up, too. But leave Red Hawk and Len's mare. If we can we'll come after you."

"I can't hold on much longer," gasped Tobin.

"Just deliver the message—and do what I say."

Tobin slid down the rope out of sight. Len untied it and dropped it after him. The prisoners withdrew into their room.

"Why did you tell them to run without us?" asked Len, sullenly.

Adelinda sighed. "It's the only chance they have. And if An-Shai thinks of it, they are four more levers he can use against me. I'm sorry you're caught with me, Len. If I knew any way to get you out of this mess I'd do it, and tell An-Shai to do his worst. It worries me that he may decide to quit messing around with contests and tricks and just hold a knife to your throat. What shall I do, then? I can't give in to him and I can't let him hurt you."

"What happened to one of the farmer folk never worried you before." Len's tone was bitter.

"Don't be silly. I've never been in this kind of situation before. I didn't even know you before I hired you to herd on the mountain pastures. What we'd better do, instead of trading reminiscences, is put our heads together and decide what we're going to do about this contest."

"I'm not sure I know what we can do," said Len, losing his sullen expression.

"Evidently you can shape this overmind into anything you want, if you know how. It must be sort of like a play except that the spectator is the main actor. When he had me trapped in his little drama last night, it wasn't like a dream. The wounds really hurt."

"They appeared on your body here, too, but the bruises formed and the cut healed a lot faster than you'd expect."

"The time seems different, too. It seemed to me that I was gone for hours, but you say it was only a half hour or so to you."

"That's right. Can the actor in the play change the script?"

"I don't know. I didn't try. On the other hand, we know that someone outside the play can reach in and change it, like you did when you called me out. Now what kind of a play would convince the main actor that it's better to be free and miserable than slave and happy?"

"We aren't going to be able to change his mind. It's already made up. The best we can do is demonstrate our point. Maybe if we . . ." Len's voice trailed off and he got a far-away look in his eye.

"What? What? Have you got an idea?"

"Well, a simple example—and one we know a lot more about than he does, so it would be easy to make our point—

is the difference between a well-cared-for games horse like Dusty and a wild horse."

"That's a brilliant idea, Len. It might just work." They set themselves to work out the details, both contributing their share, forgetting the differences between them as they planned.

Tobin's message was not well received by the rest of the group. "We're not leaving without them!" was Karel's immediate reaction.

"No, obviously not," said Orvet. "Anyway, where would we go? The bishop is not likely to provide us ships if we run."

"If Adelinda's right, the bishop has no intention of providing us ships anyway. We'll have to find some other way to get home," retorted Karel.

"The first thing is to get Adelinda and Len out of the palace and all of us out of the Vale," said Tobin.

"No, the first thing is to give the bishop something to think about besides us. From what Adelinda told you, he has been using the supernatural for his own ends. Let's see how he likes it when the shoe is on the other foot."

"Orvet! You wouldn't set night stalkers on these poor people," protested Ina.

"Certainly not!" retorted Orvet with some asperity. "But there are plenty of less harmful supernaturals. And I know some methods of controlling them that His Grace might not know. Ina, come on; I'll need you. Karel, if you and Tobin could make yourselves responsible for figuring out how to get our friends out of the palace, I'll take care of distracting the bishop and his people."

By the time Karel and Tobin had worked out and discarded several impractical schemes for attacking the palace, Orvet was back, bringing with him the most stunningly lovely young woman either of them had ever seen. Lustrous dark hair framed a delicate oval face with huge violet eyes and full, kissable lips. Her form was as lissome as a panther's, yet ripe and curved. She moved with a liquid grace that hardly seemed to touch the earth. Karel and Tobin goggled.

"Hey," said Ina's voice (yet huskier and more inviting than any they had ever heard), "it's only me. Close your mouths before the flies get in."

It was Ina. Every detail, each feature was the same as it had been, yet a glamour had been cast over their plain and simple friend that made her a ravishingly attractive woman, the very embodiment of the allure that had entrapped their forefathers into Serinmathusa's War a thousand years before, when a great civilization had fallen for a sake of a woman's beauty. Len could have told them the story, but as he wasn't there, they could only stare.

Ina, obviously startled and somewhat discomfitted by their open admiration, went to her corner and dug out her little mirror, bringing it back into the light of the candle, where she examined her face anxiously. "I don't look any different," she said questioningly to Orvet.

"No. The kind of attractiveness you have now is found in the way men perceive you, not what you look like. Oh, you can heighten the effect even further with cosmetics and the right clothes; Adelinda can teach you when we get her out." He paused and surveyed her; he too was immune to the spell, being a virgin. There was almost pity in his face, and certainly sorrow. "I've put a very powerful weapon into your hands, Ina, and one that will make it almost impossible for you to live the normal life that a woman of the farmer folk expects. You can use your allure to destroy men if you wish, or to entrap almost any of them. Often you'll involuntarily bewitch those you have no desire to attract, and there'll be no way to avoid hurting them, because there just won't be enough of you to go around."

"How on earth did you do this?" asked Karel, finally able to articulate again. Tobin was still staring at her wistfully.

"There was an incubus hanging around. Adelinda was attacked by it last night. I trapped it and killed it, but before I did that I extracted its glamour and invested it into Ina. An-Shai has been using Cho-Hei to try to win Ina away from us; I thought turnabout would be fair play and Ina agreed."

"Can you undo the spell?"

"No," said Ina. "I don't want him to. All my life men's

eyes have slid over me as if I weren't there. I intend to enjoy being noticed for a change."

"But, Ina," said Tobin. "Who will you marry? Any man would be driven mad with jealousy to have a wife that every other man wanted."

"I don't suppose I will marry, but that's no different than it ever was. Before, no man wanted me because I wasn't pretty; now every man will want me. It's a definite improvement."

Tobin failed to look convinced, but Orvet had more progress to report. "Besides letting Ina loose on the male population of the Vale, I've freed a swarm of imps that were trapped in a cave, and put a command on them to bother and pester every clergyman in the Vale to distraction. They were quite willing, since it was some bishop of two or three hundred years ago that put them in the cave and they've been amusing themselves ever since thinking up things to do to him. They were quite upset to find that he was long dead."

"What do imps do?" asked Karel, fascinated.

"Well, you know that little things always go wrong at the worst possible time? And that sometimes inanimate objects seem to have a perverse will of their own? That if you ever get an itch in a spot you can't possibly scratch in public, it's at the very minute you're standing in front of a huge audience? Those are imps, playing their little jokes. I think they get their sustenance from the aggravation of human beings."

"That sounds annoying but harmless. Do you think they'll distract An-Shai enough?"

"Possibly not by themselves, but I have several other distractions developing. I've put out a summoning call for several other kinds of supernaturals that should keep His Grace busy for quite a while once they arrive. Tobin, how would you like to be a very persuasive speaker?"

"No, thank you! Keep your incubi away from me!"

"Not that kind of persuasion, the political kind. What we need to do is stir up the populace and get them demanding more wages and better working conditions. I have a feeling that the bishop has had his own way for so long that he's forgotten how much power the common people really have,

if they can be persuaded to act together. What this Vale
needs is a really effective labor organizer. How about it?"

"That doesn't sound too bad. What do I have to do?"

"There's not much magic in it. You just have to learn how
to appeal to people. I'll give you some quick lessons and
you can go out and start agitating."

"What about me?" asked Karel, feeling a little left out.

"Your role is the keystone of the whole structure, Karel.
You have to figure out three things: how to get Adelinda and
Len out, how to get all of us out of the Vale, and where we
go then. You'll have to find maps or at least talk to people
who have traveled where we're going to have to go. Plan!
Prepare! When the rest of us have done our jobs, then we'll
turn to you and expect you to have all the answers. You'll be
in charge then. Don't let us down!"

To say that Cho-Hei was stunned by the overnight change
in Ina would be an understatement. He liked Ina and had not
found his assigned chore an onerous one, but he had certainly not expected to find himself falling into an infatuation
with her. He looked into those startling violet eyes—how
could he have thought they were an ordinary muddy blue?—
and discretion vanished.

Tobin was also enjoying some success. He casually asked
some of his pupils in the art of horsemanship why they permitted the bishop to recompense them so poorly for the work
they did. "After all," he said with a fine show of indiffer-
ence, "if it weren't for you there wouldn't be any crops, and
the bishop and the priests would all starve. It is you who
prepare the ground and plant the seed and tend the crop and
harvest it. You're entitled to a fair share of the rewards."

"Is that how it is in your homeland?" asked one of his
awed hearers. "The farmers get a fair share?"

"It certainly is," Tobin lied unblushingly. "Our farmers are
able to sell their crops to whomever they want for the highest price they can get, and to spend the money however they
like. Many of our farmers are able to support families of ten
or twelve children."

This news impressed the farm workers more than the part
about the money, which they understood only imperfectly

anyway. "We aren't allowed to have children unless the priests say we may," said one of them, wistfully.

"Is that fair? Why, I hear the hierarchs are allowed to have as many children as they want, and several wives that they choose themselves. Not to mention the best of the food and clothing. And all of this luxury is earned by your sweat and toil. Rightfully, it should belong to you."

"The clergy know how to read and write. They can keep track of things. We can't."

"In my country everybody learns to read and write. The schools are open to all, and if the parents of a child can't afford the fees, the public treasury pays them."

The peasants were disbelieving. "You mean everybody learns to read and write? But most of us aren't smart enough."

"Nonsense! I learned it, and if I can do it, anyone can. You all know me; I'm friendly but I'm not too bright!" This drew a laugh, as Tobin had intended, and he left them thinking over what he had told them and moved on to the next group. By nightfall, he had successfully spread discontent the width of the Vale and a good third of its length.

Adelinda and Len were unaware of the stirrings and happenings in the Vale. They spent the day discussing and polishing their play. They were hardly able to do more; their "healthy" diet of raw greens and water was already beginning to have its effect, especially on Len, who had been too thin to begin with. They felt lethargic and headachy. But when An-Shai came in the evening to ask if they were ready, they nearly were.

"I think it would be fair for you to show us how to get into this 'overmind' and let us practice manipulating it a bit before you join us. After all, we are two beginners going up against two experienced experts," said Adelinda.

An-Shai looked at her suspiciously, but he could not deny that it was a fair request. "Very well," he said reluctantly. "Don't get lost in there or drive yourselves mad." He went out and came back in a few minutes with a small flask and two tiny cups.

"Take just this much, no more, of this liquor. It will wear off in about fifteen minutes—real time; the subjective time can be as long as you want. You can get out just by willing yourself out."

"Does that apply when we're in your scenario?" asked Len shrewdly.

"Not if I choose that it should not. I am the stronger will and I can keep you within the overmind if I choose, or drive you so deep into it that you will never find your way out." He went haughtily away.

"I wonder if he's as strong as he'd like us to think," mused Adelinda. "Or is all that just a bluff?"

"I guess we'll find out. Here's your cup."

"Better lie down. It hits you hard." They chose to lie side by side on the floor, holding hands, in hope that the physical contact in the real world would facilitate contact in the overmind. Swallowing the bitter fluid, they felt the same wrenching and nausea that Adelinda had felt when she inhaled the smoke.

The overmind, unformed by any will, was a gray, nebulous place, with neither direction nor gravity. There were no features for the eye to light upon, so that they could not tell if their vision extended inches or into infinity. The warm contact of their hands was the only identifiable sensation; they could not even see their own physical forms. Len felt a force of will stirring in the substance with which they were surrounded, and saw a flower forming in the mist before him, a yellow evening primrose, blooming in the midst of nothingness. The bush upon which the flower grew formed. Len, interested, exerted his will; the mountain meadow in which the flower grew began to sketch itself in. Adelinda added a babbling mountain stream. Len put in some stately pines and a breeze to stir them, filling the air with their resinous scent and the soughing of their needles. A herd of deer walked across the meadow, unafraid.

Adelinda laughed in delight. "This is easy!" she said. Apparently it took little effort to keep an illusion going once it was started; they found that they could turn their attention to other creations and the older ones simply stayed where they were put. Details did not fill themselves in without one of them thinking of them, though; beyond the ragged wall of

pines was the undifferentiated gray of the overmind, and
there was no sun, just the shadowless gray light Adelinda
had noticed before.

Leaving their meadow to take care of itself, the two
turned their attention to providing themselves with bodies. If
Len's was taller and sturdier than his real one, Adelinda's
was younger and more delicate, and neither of them commented on the little improvements each had made in his or
her own appearance, nor on the splendid clothing in which
they dressed themselves.

"Let's try a game of wills," suggested Adelinda. "I'll
build something and you try to tear it down."

"All right."

Adelinda built a lovely little cabin nestled under one of
the huge pines, with flowers and an arbor shading the wide
front porch, a friendly little house where one might be glad
to go visiting. "All right. I'm ready," she said, concentrating
fiercely.

"It's so pretty, it seems a shame," said Len. But he ruth-
lessly blasted the arbor out of existence with a bolt of lightning. It flickered for a moment, then re-formed itself.
Muttering, Len summoned forth a voracious herd of cattle
that surged over the garden, devouring flowers and vines,
and whimsically munching on the porch railing and the
cabin itself. Adelinda tried to banish the cattle into nonexis-
tence, but found that she could not. Frowning, she created a
pack of fierce dogs that snapped at the heels of the de-
stroyers and drove them away, leaving a sad shambles. She
hastily re-created the garden, mending the bites in the railing
and walls, and added an orchard of fruit trees and berry
brambles.

Len countered with a horde of birds. Linnets and sparrows
stripped the fruit from the trees and the berries from the
brambles. Woodpeckers drilled holes in every exposed bit of
wood. Towhees flicked in and out of the broken windowpanes. Swallows built muddy nests under the rafters. Jays
dropped trash down the chimney and through the holes in the
roof. Quail ran twittering back and forth across the porch,
leaving their droppings scattered.

An enormous flock of hawks and owls descended upon

the marauding birds, bearing many off in their claws and scattering the rest, while an army of cats pounced upon the unfortunate birds that thought to take cover on the ground from the aerial attack. The birds routed, a corps of brisk and busy housemaids appeared from within, sweeping and cleaning, while carpenters mended the holes in the roof and glaziers replaced the broken windowpanes. These were Len's contribution; he had tired of being the aggressor.

Adelinda fell in with the exchanged roles willingly enough and began to search for ways to pull down the cheerful little cabin, by now furbished up and painted and with a flourishing vegetable garden at one side. While she was thinking, a great horse-drawn van pulled up at the door and began to unload shiny new furniture, an oak dining table and chairs, sofas, comfortable easy chairs, big four-poster beds, bright curtains that the housemaids put up at the windows as fast as they could be carried in, colorful wool rugs, chinaware, boxes and boxes of books—a myriad of things, all shiny new and all designed for comfort and convenience.

Adelinda was completely enchanted and forgot that she was supposed to be destroying the charming little home, as Len had intended she should. She added a roomy stable, its loft full to bursting of the very best hay, and a rustic rail fence around most of the meadow, in which grazed two magnificent riding horses, a driving team of pretty bays, and—significantly—an assortment of gentle ponies. In the carriage house she put a simple surrey, new and shiny, well-sprung and comfortable, with two padded seats and a crimson dash panel. As an afterthought, she lengthened the carriage house and put in a silver-painted sleigh with thick, warm lap robes folded on the seat.

The two of them went on adding comforts and refinements to their creation, now wandering through the cozy rooms, now the spacious yards, calling each other to come and look at some especially delightful little addition.

It was with reluctance that Adelinda and Len abandoned their creation and willed themselves back into the real world. "It seems to be easier to create new things to counteract the old ones than to just destroy what someone else has

created," said Adelinda. "Last night, I should have created
an army of man-rat killers or a nice cool fountain when An-
Shai made me think I was thirsty."

"Would he have let you? I found it pretty easy to keep you
from destroying the cabin after I took over creating it."

Their discussion was interrupted by An-Shai's entrance.
"Well, are you ready now?" he asked coldly.

"I think so, Your Grace. We'll have to ask you to play
along with us until we have made our point, though. If you
intend to make a battle of skill in controlling the overmind,
we concede that you know how to do that better than we
do."

An-Shai looked as if he had bitten into a lemon, but
agreed. For them to concede would destroy any chance of a
victory in this contest.

The bitter taste of the liquor was still in his mouth when
he found himself being kicked in the rump. "Come on, old
fellow, time to get up," someone said. "Here's your breakfast." There was a rustle and a rattle.

An-Shai scrambled to his hooves and looked around. He
was in a stall deeply bedded in straw. Clean grain of a type
that the bishop in him did not recognize and a generous
bundle of sweet-smelling hay was in a manger before him. If
the bishop didn't know what to do with the fodder, the horse
in him certainly did. He found himself devouring the stuff
avidly.

He had hardly rooted out the last grain from the corner of
the box when the man who had kicked him returned, clipped
a rope onto the halter he wore, and cross-tied him in the
aisle of the barn. An-Shai the horse accepted this calmly, as
something to which he was accustomed; An-Shai the bishop
was indignant to find his gray coat being groomed from nose
to tail, brushed, wiped, his hooves cleaned out, and his
mane and tail combed. Blankets and a saddle were slapped
onto his back, the girth yanked so tight around his middle
that he could hardly breathe; he gave an angry squeal of
protest and the man attending him laughed and slapped him
on the rump. Before he had quite gotten his breath back, a
thumb was jammed into the corner of his mouth. Involuntar-

ily, he opened it; a cold, hard iron bit was thrust in and the bridle deftly fastened to hold it there. Then he was left standing in the aisle of the barn for what seemed to be hours. Cross-tied as he was, he could see very little, even though the vision of this strange new body covered a much wider arc than his human vision. If he swiveled his ears back, he could hear other horses being groomed, too, but all of them were returned to their stalls and the generous portions of hay that awaited them.

At long last something happened. A different man, a tall blond who looked a lot like Adelinda, came and slapped him familiarly on the neck. An-Shai the horse accepted this as a gesture of affection. This new man unsnapped him from the cross-ties and led him out of the barn into dazzling sunshine. "Give him a good workout, Felim," said a familiar voice, and Adelinda appeared to walk with them to a fenced-in arena. "He looks antsy to me."

"With all the good feed he can stuff in his face and a workout every day, he ought to be feeling good," Felim answered. He put the reins over An-Shai's head and stepped onto him. The next few minutes were the most exhausting the bishop had ever spent. He was forced to run at full speed, then slide to an abrupt stop for no reason he could see, made to spin to the right and to the left until he was dizzy, hauled around in intricate patterns by the bit in his mouth until his gums were sore. Just when he thought he had figured out the patterns the man wanted, and to try to do them without the punishing pressure on the bit, the patterns were changed. "He's anticipating on you again," called Adelinda from her perch on the fence. "Put him on the bit more."

An-Shai found himself squeezed uncomfortably around the ribs. Since An-Shai the horse took this as a signal to leap forward, he did so. But this time the reins were not slackened. He found himself crashing into the bit with bruising force on his already tender gums as he tried to extend his head. There was nowhere to go but up; he found himself prancing along with great effort, neck bent until all he could see was the ground in front of him, legs pumping ridiculously high. His weight was thrown uncomfortably back onto his hind legs, which were obviously designed more for propulsion than weight carrying. "Very nice collection!" called Adelinda.

An-Shai had had about enough of this. When the pressure let up and the reins were slackened, he stopped, intending to go to the gate and demand to be let out. To his surprise, the light switch his rider was carrying descended on his unprotected flank with stinging force, and again. He wheeled about, only to have his mouth painfully jabbed again, straightening him out. He lost his temper utterly. Squealing in rage, he reared into the air, spun around, and bucked with all his might. Whipping about again, he prepared to bite the recumbent form of his erstwhile rider, but there was no recumbent form to be seen, and the whip slashed his flank again as one of the reins was suddenly yanked tight. His limber long neck was wrenched around, and he staggered dizzily in a circle while the whip fell again and again. When the pull on the rein was slackened, he found that he was glad enough to do just as his rider wished. When he was lathered with sweat and his legs were trembling with fatigue, he was ridden through the gate and up to the barn.

Felim stepped off. "I don't know," he said. "Maybe he hasn't got the temperament to be a games horse. He was really resisting me today. Maybe I ought to sell him and use the chestnut mare."

"The best ones always show a little spirit, Felim. Give him a chance. You've still got two weeks before the games."

"That's true." He tossed the reins to the waiting groom. "Walk him good. He's in a sweat." The brother and sister walked off together.

The next few days were a combination of deadly boredom for twenty-three hours a day and horribly hard work for the other hour. An-Shai was given the very best of feed, which his equine palate relished, bedded knee-deep in straw, groomed to an inch, and generally pampered. The other horses in the stable seemed complacent enough, but horses have very little conversation and for a creature of An-Shai's active temperament, the confinement was excruciating.

When a diversion occurred, he was more than ready to enjoy it. A new horse was brought into the stable, a ragged

black with a tangled mane and tail. He was brought into the
stable by Felim and the head groom, and a struggle it was
even for two; the beast kicked and bucked and squealed and
reared, lashing out with his forehooves until it seemed he
must trample the men. But they always seemed to know
where he intended to strike and be somewhere else, even if
only by inches. At last, with much sweat and swearing they
managed to maneuver the wild creature into a stall and slam
the door behind him. A tattoo of thuds followed as the animal tried to kick the walls down, but though the whole
building shuddered, the stalls were soundly built and with-
stood the assault.

Adelinda had been an interested spectator, from a safe
distance. With the horse safely secured, she came forward.
"Boy, he's a wild one," she commented admiringly. "But
he's a beauty. Do you think you can break him?"

"Seven years old and never had a rope on him," said
Felim proudly. "The really wild ones make the best racers.
They've got the will to dominance we've mostly bred out of
our horses. He can be broke. I'll use the lake. He can buck
and kick all he wants to and all he'll do is wear himself out.
Then it'll be just time and patience and he'll be eating out of
my hand."

"He's certainly worth the effort. But don't neglect old
An-Shai here," his sister said, scratching the horse deliciously behind the right ear. "The games are coming up."

"Oh, he's conditioned. Ride him for me tomorrow, will
you, sis? I want to work this black fellow."

An-Shai huffed indignantly. Was he going to have to put
up with the indignity of being ridden by a woman? And
Adelinda, of all women?

"I think he's jealous," Adelinda laughed. "You'd better
ride him yourself. No point messing him up this close to the
games."

"Oh, all right," grouched Felim.

An-Shai was in fact exercised diligently if absentmindedly
by Felim for the next few days. Then he was given a day of
rest. Realizing that something was in the wind from the
change in routine and the general excitement, he was nearly
beside himself the following day when he was taken out and

saddled with a brightly polished saddle and a colorful saddle blanket.

He found that he enjoyed the games. It was quite the most exciting thing that had ever happened to either An-Shai the bishop or An-Shai the horse, and he strained every nerve and muscle to win every event. Felim was the cool head of the two, and his skilled riding gave the horse the steadiness he needed. An-Shai saw the buntings, the brightly decorated booths, the yelling crowds, and the hundreds of other horses only peripherally. Every ounce of his concentration was needed within the arena, and though they didn't win every event, they came away that evening with a respectable number of shell-shaped winner's tokens clipped on An-Shai's bridle.

He had never been so exhausted in his life, but still he managed a little caper of pride as he was led back to his stall. An-Shai the boy had always been bookish rather than athletic, and he was surprised to find how satisfying a mere physical accomplishment could be. "Look at that!" said Felim fondly. "He's still full of ginger. You were right about him, Adelinda. He is a good games horse."

That night An-Shai was aroused from a contented doze to find that the stable was afire at the far end. Felim and Adelinda and all the stablehands were dashing about excitedly, and it seemed for a moment that the whole structure might go up in flames. The head groom ran down the aisle, opening the doors of the stalls and shooing the horses out into the arena, safely away from the fire. The gate was closed behind them so that the excited animals wouldn't dash back into the burning building or scatter to the four winds, but it was a useless precaution.

The new black racer, only half broken as yet, with the smell of the wild winds still in his nostrils, sensed freedom. Either not seeing the railings on the far side of the arena or just not caring, he threw up his head with a shrill neigh and thundered across the enclosure. He hit the railing going full speed, smashing into it and going down, floundering. The rest of the horses, spooked by all the excitement, followed him without knowing why, pouring through the gap in a rush and galloping off into the darkness. The black regained his feet and was soon in the lead. He really would have made a great racer; he went past An-Shai as though he were still standing. On and on through the night they dashed. One by one the other horses lagged and then dropped out of that mad, glorious flight, but An-Shai was in superb condition. In a straightaway race of under two miles, the black could have left him eating his dust, but over the long haul, An-Shai could run the fleet black into the ground, and so it proved.

By the morning, the black was reduced to an exhausted shuffle and An-Shai was leading the way. They had dropped out of the mountains into the desert wastes where the feral horses roamed, and looking about him, An-Shai could see only themselves of all the stampeding herd. The black came to a weary halt, and taking advantage of his opportunity, An-Shai scraped himself a dust bath with a forehoof and rolled and rolled. It felt so good! He had never been allowed to roll; the groom, understandably perhaps, preferred not to have his charge's laboriously polished coat begrimed. An-Shai felt as if he were rolling away the itches of years. When he finally rose to his hooves and shook off the excess dust, the black was grazing among the sparse vegetation, picking wiry gray grasses almost blade by blade from among less appetizing plants. An-Shai thought for a moment of the grain and sweet hay in his manger, and almost regretted it, but the grass was sustaining, and it felt good to be able to eat when he chose and move as he liked.

Over the next few days, An-Shai learned to search out pockets of the grass, or browse on the tough brush when there was no grass to be found. He drank gratefully and deeply from bitter alkaline pools, once a day at best, for the black preferred to go to water at sundown, grazing the night away at a great distance from the rare water holes, where predators often lurked. During the day, they shaded up under some scant-leaved acacia, drowsing the hot hours away tail to head, whisking the flies off each other's faces with lazily swinging tails.

An-Shai nearly became a desert lion's dinner one evening as they went down to water. He was in the lead, and only the chance-glimpsed flicker of movement out of the corner of his eye gave him warning enough to spring aside, receiving a neat quadruple furrow of claw marks in his flank as he did so. The two horses drifted on out of the old haunts that night, and took up a new territory farther north. The grass was not so good but there were fewer predators.

An-Shai grew as ragged and tangled as the black. His shoes worked off one by one, and he walked sore-footed for a few days until his hooves toughened. His halter he left snagged in a tree limb against which he had been absent-mindedly scratching, and hardly noticed its loss. His well-grained plumpness fined down to a greyhound thinness, all wiry sinew and muscle.

The black had been nervous all day, peering about suspiciously, blowing rollers in his nose. An-Shai, who had learned to respect the wild one's instinct, and who had almost forgotten that he had ever been anything but a horse, was uneasy too. There was something amiss in the desolate land where the two feral horses had their territory. The desert birds were flighty, and once a herd of little gray deer came bounding past, eyes starting in terror, drawing the two horses with them into a panicky flight. They ran several miles, but saw no pursuers and circled away from the deer to examine the back trail anxiously. They saw nothing, but something was wrong.

Something certainly was. They had shaded up in the heat of the day when suddenly a rider burst out of the brush. Both horses jumped from sound asleep to a dead run in one stride, but the black's forefeet were yanked from under him before he could take a second. A thrown noose had looped neatly about them, and the unfortunate animal somersaulted, landing on his side with a thud that jarred the earth. An-Shai ran on, almost unaware of what had happened. Within a few hundred feet, though, he realized that his companion was no longer running by his side. Halting, he looked back.

The black was lying on the ground, his legs tied together, a stout halter already in place on his head. He was again a captive of the humans. There were two of them and their saddle horses. Even as he turned, one stood up and walked a few paces toward him. "An-Shai! An-Shai!" he called.

The voice was familiar. It was Felim. It brought back

memories of a warm, well-bedded stall, a manger filled to overflowing, careful grooming—and the bit and the whip. An-Shai turned again to face the empty desert. He could flee now and they would never catch him. But if he did so, he would go alone. He would be cold in winter and hot in summer, always a little thirsty and always on the verge of starvation, every meat eater's prey. But he would be subject to no whim but his own.

And then An-Shai understood the point of the whole drama. He was being offered a choice. Which was better, perilous freedom or well-cared-for captivity? He looked back, and it seemed that even the tied-up black was watching with bated breath to see what his decision would be.

An-Shai the bishop knew what the decision should be, if he didn't want to imperil his argument. But An-Shai the horse had his nostrils full of the sweet, hot scent of the creosote bushes; his flinty hooves danced over the fiery sand; his willful spirit took command. Flinging up his head and his tail, An-Shai galloped away from comfort and care and into danger and privation as hard as he could go.

CHAPTER 12

An-Shai pulled himself up from the narrow bench and looked around. He had never had so vivid an experience in the overmind. It had taken weeks, subjectively, but the candle in its holder was only half burned away. Across the room, Tsu-Linn was stirring and groaning.

"Now will you believe me when I tell you that these outlanders are dangerous and should be destroyed?" said Tsu-Linn.

"I didn't expect such an elaborate scenario, nor one that had such power to draw the players into it, from novices," An-Shai answered with a groan.

"Perhaps this will teach you to expect the unexpected. These people are not as our peasants. You were a fool to run away at the end. You gave the woman the victory."

"I couldn't help myself. It was what the horse would have done, and by that time, I had nearly forgotten that I was An-Shai. But they haven't won yet. I'll have my chance to devise a scenario, and it won't be a simple one, easily mastered. It will be subtle and seductive, appealing to the wants and needs of such a woman as Adelinda. She cannot be frightened into obedience. We'll see if she can't be lured into it."

Tsu-Linn snorted. "Watch that you don't fall into your own traps."

Both were a little reassured to find that they had to help the two outlanders to find their way out of their drama; real experts would have kept track of their physical bodies.

"Well?" challenged Adelinda, when she had been brought

back to the physical world. "I noticed that you chose freedom over comfortable servitude."

"The horse I was, which you had a great part in creating,
did. Wait until you've been in my scenario before you
judge."

Len, who was still shaking his head, groaned. "Not tonight, surely."

"Your Grace, could Len have a little more to eat, please?
He's fading away," Adelinda requested.

They looked at the young man, who was as slight as a
twelve-year-old boy. His cheeks were hollow and his collar-
bones jutted out against his skin. "Very well, since you ask,"
said An-Shai. "He can have a double ration of vegetables."

Karel had been fortunate in finding a retired donkey-
packer who had traveled extensively in Godsland and was
garrulous enough to be willing to share his experiences. He
had no maps and wouldn't have recognized one if he saw it,
but Karel was able to draw one from his descriptions. He
gave all distances in days of travel, which Karel estimated
for a loaded pack train of donkeys as being about fifteen
miles.

"To the west, there's nothing but desert. We didn't go
there very often," the old man said. "Once I was with a train
that took a load of supplies to one of the frontier forts. It was
terrible. It was dry and cold and the wind blew all the time.
We lost half our donkeys and three of the packers."

"From thirst?" Karel asked.

"No, mirage wraiths." The packer shuddered. "They'd
build an illusion that looked like whatever you wanted most.
Even fooled the donkeys. Then, when you went running to
get it, the picture would disappear and these tall—shapes,
sort of—would close around you. When they went away,
there wasn't anything left but dried meat and old bones.
They suck out the water, you know. I was too smart for
them, though."

Karel sighed. Old Ku-Tse was full of gory stories about
the supernatural creatures he had narrowly escaped. "Can
you tell me where the watering places were?"

"Well, there was one the first night we camped. Wasn't

any the next night. The third night we had to go about an hour's travel off the trail to the north to find water—nasty bitter stuff it was, too. Then we had to come back the same way the next morning. . . ."

Karel was able to spend several days with the old packer and when he had pumped that well of information dry, he had a crude map of the area for about two hundred miles around. But how they were to get across the ocean without access to ships, he could not imagine.

It was Tobin who gave him the clue he needed to devise a plan to get the two prisoners out. "These people have no idea what the greathorses can do," he complained. "I found the bunch from Pink Spring Village borrowing Two Fountains Village's horses and harnessing all four of them to a tiny little cartload of hay that one could have managed without working up a sweat. They told me they always used four donkeys."

"That's it!" exclaimed Karel.

"Huh?" said Tobin.

"We'll hitch a team of horses to those pillars underneath and yank that whole wall of the palace right off. Adelinda and Len can just walk out. We'll be standing by with the riding horses all loaded and ready to go. Can you ride postilion?"

"I've seen it done," Tobin admitted cautiously.

"We'll get thirty or so of the greathorses here—we'll tell them it's for a lesson on driving large teams. With four of us on the leaders and swing teams and good long traces, it'll be a cinch."

"Won't they stop us when they see we're hooking the traces to the palace?"

"They won't see us. We'll fix up some kind of a big load and lay rigging for that out from the palace. We'll have fixed the real traces to the pillars the night before and buried them in the grass parallel to the fake traces. When we hook up the team, we'll do a quick switch, telling everybody to stand back because of flying fragments. The next thing they'll know, the south wall of the palace will be lying all over the lawn and we'll be riding out of the Vale sweet as you please. What do you think?"

"I think too much imagination is a dangerous thing."

An-Shai was kept very busy the next few days—too busy to bother with his prisoners. Anyway, it suited his purposes to let them stew. He didn't connect the outlanders with the sudden epidemic of imps that were pestering the priests nearly to distraction or the sprites whose pranks were offset by the dozens of delightful minor favors they did for those who left them a little treat of cakes or cheese. However popular the invisible beings were with harried housewives and farmers who could never quite get all the chores done, it was undeniable that they caused a lot of chaos, luring otherwise serious farmers and even their browbeaten wives to moonlit carousing and sunlit daydreams. None of these supernaturals were dangerous, but they had to be dealt with, and that took a lot of the bishop's time.

He did hear that the brawl that broke out one evening was due to a rivalry over Ina's attentions, but he didn't believe it. He had seen Ina (though not in the last few days) and could see no reason anyone would fight over her. Even when the incident was repeated the next evening in another village, he still couldn't fathom the cause. The unrest that was rapidly developing among the farmers was more worrisome to him. Not only were they grumbling, they were organizing, and the whole situation was developing quite beyond his understanding of the peasants' capabilities.

Tobin had taken his job as labor organizer to heart. He was convinced that the abuses he pointed out to the peasants were real ones, and his sincerity was more persuasive than any oratorical skill would have been. He put more effort into this work than he had ever done anything before, spending long hours riding from village to village, holding meetings and helping the villagers to set up committees.

Ina, too, was enjoying her role as disrupter. She made certain that any jealousies that already existed were exacerbated. If she went for a walk with a young man from one faction in a village, she made certain that she ate lunch with a party of another faction, and she made them both believe that he was the most important man in her life and that if he were any kind of man at all, he would protect her from the unwelcome advances of the others.

Orvet spent most of the hours of darkness roaming about, undoing An-Shai's efforts to control the plague of nuisancy supernaturals that was infecting the Vale. He also subtly altered and strengthened the bishop's own defenses against the direr sort. Even An-Shai would have had great difficulty in admitting night stalkers or the even deadlier werewolves if he had chosen to do so. As it happened, An-Shai was happy enough that Tsu-Linn, gone about his duties in the other dioceses under his jurisdiction, had been distracted from his plans to reduce the population of the Vale. He spent a lot of effort collaborating unwittingly with Orvet's efforts to rid the Vale of incubi, bone limpets, and several other kinds of dangerous supernaturals.

An-Shai was uncomfortably aware that, even with Tsu-Linn gone, there was another power in the Vale. The age-old balance was being disturbed; tolerances between certain kinds of supernaturals and the Church that had existed for generations were being upset. Thre was a great ferment in the overmind, as powers were unleashed in the physical world which unsettled the collective unconscious. It seemed to be a very real possibility that there was some very powerful and completely unknown influence abroad in the land, one that had no fear of the light of day and had no hesitation in pitting itself against the Vale's rightful protector. It was only more confusing that many of the activities of this unknown entity were positively beneficial to the folk of the Vale.

An-Shai failed to attribute the disturbance to a human agency. His thinking was limited by the preconception that the clergy were the only people in Godsland who received the kind of training it took to deal familiarly with the supernatural. He spent a great deal of time and energy trying unsuccessfully to track the unknown new power to its source. In this he was hampered by a growing fear that time was short. Tsu-Linn had left him directions for finding the Hall of the Initiates and instructions to report there as soon as he had cleared up things in his diocese, but he couldn't hope that the invitation would be held open forever.

At last he felt driven to turn his attention to his two prisoners. His desire to master the outland woman had developed into an obsession as she balked him again and again. He didn't realize himself how very much he needed to win the struggle that he had so lighty instigated, much less how important Adelinda had become to him.

He came into their prison carrying the bottle of liquor and the two little cups. Even he was shocked to see how emaciated Len had grown, and with what a lethargy he raised himself from his bed-shelf. Adelinda was in better condition, but she, too, was pale and listless. The "health" diet An-Shai had prescribed for his captives was having its desired effect, and the bishop was shocked and even a little saddened to see what havoc he had wrought. He was coming to respect the courage and tenacity of the two, but if a momentary fleeting wish that their enmity might be ended crossed his mind, it was sternly repressed.

He put the bottle and cups on the table. "Are you ready to take your turn at the scenario I've designed?"

Adelinda pushed back her heavy, tangled hair. "I suppose we have to be. We're certainly well rested." The three days since their last encounter with the Bishop had been days of unrelieved boredom. Too weak from hunger to exercise much, they had spent hours sitting or lying lost in their own thoughts. Their conversation had consisted mostly of reminiscences of home and the mouth-watering feasts they had attended there. In Adelinda's case, these had taken place at parties she had thought were excruciatingly boring at the time, but Len's were mostly the simple feasts at the Festival of Sunreturn and the Midsummer Games. Adelinda was more than a little shocked to find how scanty the meals that Len remembered with such longing were. And the fact that he always ended the recitals with "and everybody could eat until they were full" gave her more insight into the terrible poverty in which the farmer folk lived than all of Orvet's lectures.

An-Shai examined the captives with interest. They were ready, he judged. Their physical weakness would carry over into the overmind as a lethargy of will. "If you find that my view of the proper relationship between people like you and those like myself is correct, I can only hope that you will be willing to concede the point." He poured the doses.

"You weren't willing to concede," objected Adelinda.

"I'm willing to concede that for some people, a small minority, it is perhaps better to be free than to be cared for. But no woman is included in that category, nor any peasant. The vast majority of people are content to have their decisions made for them and their actions guided by a greater wisdom. In fact, most people, if guidance isn't provided by the society in which they live, will actively seek it out. From what Li-Mun tells me of your own society, its people are only too eager to ally themselves with strange cults, follow some self-appointed religious leader, or otherwise seek to throw away this freedom you're so determined to retain. Isn't this true?"

"Some people do that. Not everyone. Not all women and not all of the farmer folk or the city dwellers, whom I suppose you're equating with your peasants."

"We won't argue the point now. Swallow the liquor and see how you feel at the end of my scenario. Will you cooperate with mine as I cooperated with yours?"

Adelinda glanced at Len. "We'll try. I'm making no promises. Len's pretty weak. If I think he's threatened, I'll do my best to yank both of us out."

"You've just illustrated my point. You automatically assume the responsibility for Len's welfare, and he's pleased to let you. Haven't you just done the same thing to him that you claim is so intolerable for me to do to you?"

Adelinda blinked. "No, it's different. I can't exactly explain how, but it is. Ask Len."

"I don't know whether it is," said Len wearily. "Let's just get on with it." He took the cup and drank the liquor down.

"Very well. Remember that things that happen in the overmind can affect the body that remains in the physical world, and don't be too confident that you can just leave." He handed Adelinda her cup and watched her drink.

* * *

It was dark and cold. The heavy air reeked of smoke and the smell of death. The thin sound of a child's hopeless crying wove itself through the crackle of the dying flames. A little girl, a blond child of six or seven, dragged herself out of the brush pile where she had lain concealed for hours. She pushed the tangled hair out of her face and peered around through the darkness.

"Lenny," she squeaked anxiously. "Lenny, where are you?" She cocked her head to listen to the crying. "Lenny, please come out. It's Addie. We have to get away."

The crying paused and resolved itself into hiccups. "Addie, is that you?"

"It's me, Lenny. Where are you?"

"I'm under the box, Addie. I can't get out."

The girl scrambled out of the brush into a scene of desolation. Six dead onagers were still hitched to the smouldering remains of what must once have been an ornate traveling coach. She averted her eyes from the sprawled human bodies that lay about, stinking of blood and exposed guts, and scurried to a small crate that was overturned at the side of the clearing. A staring corpse lay draped across it, its weight making the crate an effective prison for the childish strength within.

Addie circled about the gruesome tableau. "Lenny? Are you in there?"

"Yes, Addie, get me out! I want to go home!" The crying began again.

Shuddering, the girl put her little hands against the cold, stiff body and shoved with all her feeble strength. It was fortunate that the thing was balanced precariously; it flopped over grotesquely, turning the crate on its side. A thin, dark little boy of about four scrambled from beneath it, wiping his runny nose on his sleeve.

"I want to go home, Addie. Where's Mama?"

"Mama's dead, Lenny," the girl said, with a child's brutal directness. "Uncle Orris brought his soldiers and came and killed everybody. We have to run away or he'll come back and kill us."

The boy began to wail loudly. "It isn't so. You're lying to me. Mama isn't dead. Mama, Mama! Addie's being mean to me!" He looked bewilderedly around. At least under the box, he had been spared witnessing the brutal massacre of his mother and her few loyal retainers; his sister had not been so lucky.

"Look over here, Lenny. That's Mama. I told you. She's dead." She pointed to one of the distorted corpses, the hacked and haggled body of a once beautiful and pampered young woman. Lenny stopped crying and stood staring, shocked. "Now come on. We have to run away. If you don't come on, I'll pinch you." She took the little boy's hand in her own and tugged him into the darkness at right angles to the road.

They stumbled through the darkness, shivering in the cold. It was too dark to see much, and as soon as they were a few steps away from the sullen light cast by the embers of the coach, they began to blunder into the thorny bushes, scratching their hands and faces. Addie hurried them on their way, though, and Lenny struggled bravely along as best he could.

They were long out of sight of the smouldering coach when Lenny stumbled and fell, rolling down a little declivity that neither of them saw. In reaching to grab him, Addie fell too, and both bruised themselves and tore their clothing. Lenny was too exhausted to do more than whimper, and Addie lay in a heap where she had fallen. When the baying of the hounds trickled into her consciousness, she raised herself suddenly and listened.

"Lenny, do you hear that?"

The whimpering stopped. "Yes, I hear it. What is it?"

"Uncle Orris's killhounds. Come on. We've got to run."

"I can't run any more. I want to go home."

"We can't go home. Uncle Orris is there. He wants to kill us. Come on."

With a small child's assurance that if he harps upon something long enough he'll get it, Lenny insisted, "I want to go home. I don't want Uncle Orris to be there. I want to go home now."

Addie abruptly changed her tactics. "All right. Go home.

Good-bye." She set out determinedly, listening behind her. Sure enough, stumbling footsteps soon came pattering up.

They trudged on for hours. The cold grew more intense, and neither of the children was dressed in more than the simple shift and pantaloons they usually wore under their elaborate costumes. An icy drizzling rain began to fall. At times the hounds seemed to draw near, but then the baying would fade away, and at last, as the eastern sky began to gray, the sound went away altogether.

The children were exhausted. When Addie spied a hollowed cavity under a fallen tree, she pulled Lenny into it, burrowing into the drift of fallen leaves.

"Are we going to rest?" asked the boy.

"Yes. Lie down and let me pile some of these leaves over you."

The children huddled together for warmth. Lenny fell asleep at once, but the girl was too tired to sleep, and too frightened. She was too young for the terrible responsibility that had fallen upon her, too young and too lost to know what they were to do.

The sun was high when they awoke. It was a dismal scene that met their gaze when they scrambled stiffly out of the leaves and looked about. The icy rainwater dripped off every naked branch and twig. The autumn's fallen leaves lay sodden on the ground. Even as far as they were from the site of the massacre, a scorched smell hung in the air, making breathing difficult. Their little fingers were stiff with cold, and Lenny's lips were blue. Both were shivering helplessly.

"Addie, I'm hungry."

"Me, too. We'll have to find something to eat."

"Where?" The two children gazed about the winter-dead forest. There was nothing that resembled food in the black trunks of the trees, the brown soil, or the gray sky. A single raven flew over; the forest was so still they could hear the beat of its wings.

"Well, come on, Lenny. Maybe there's something to eat over there." Hand in hand, they trudged wearily through the forest, angling away from the direction they had followed the night before. A leaden weariness weighted down their limbs, but they knew by some dumb instinct that to quit and

lie down was to die, and weak as they were, the will to live
pulsed as strongly in those tiny bodies as in the mighty
frame of some great warrior.

On and on they walked, sometimes stumbling in a daze,
sometimes looking about or even stopping to examine some
fungus or withered berry. Once Lenny even tasted a bit of
some white substance growing from the side of a tree, but he
spit it out in haste. They were both beyond tears now, and
the little boy seemed to have matured in the night beyond his
childish petulance.

When the light began to wane again, Addie was nearly at
the end of her strength, and Lenny was pinched and staring,
head lolling as she pulled him along. The air was growing
even colder; there would be a frost that night, and unprotected as they were, no covering of leaves would save the
children from death by exposure—no doubt what their uncle
was counting on, for the baying of killhounds had not disturbed the day.

Their feet had fallen naturally into a path they had come
across. The walking was easier there and the bare branches
were thick and tangled on either side, herding them along
the track. They were too far gone now to care where they
went anyway, and they were only kept moving, mechani-
cally, by Addie's fear.

When the shadow fell across them, they halted, as animals will halt when they find their way unaccountably
blocked. "Why, what's this?" The voice was deep and resonant, and when Addie raised her eyes, she had to look up
nearly forever, before her gaze finally reached the face of the
tall man standing astonished before them. It was a kindly
face, if an amazed one. "Children, in this forest, and all
alone, without even coats!" He sounded like a man used to
talking to himself. "Where are your mother and father, little
girl?"

Addie had to moisten her lips with her tongue before she
could answer. "They're dead, sir. Uncle Orris killed them,
and we had to run away so he wouldn't kill us, too. But
we're lost and—and Lenny's hungry."

The man smiled. "And you're not, I suppose. What's your
name?"

"Addie, sir."

"Well, Addie, if you would like to come home with me you may. There's a nice warm fire and a pot of soup that should just about be ready and a couple of cozy inglenook beds that would be just right for children about your size. Would you like that?"

The man seemed kind and friendly, and there was nothing in the world, except to have her mother alive again, that Addie wanted more than the promised warmth and food. The man meant well, she knew. The feeling of concern radiated from him the way light radiated from a candle. But Addie recoiled. She couldn't help herself. Without really knowing why, she felt that they would be better off to keep going, trusting to their own meager resources. The man observed her hesitation.

"Only if you want to come, mind. You can do anything you want," he said, more sharply, perhaps a little hurt.

Lenny too had seen his sister's indecision. He tugged on her hand. "Please, Addie, please?" he whispered. She looked at him. His dark eyes were pleading up at her.

Addie sighed and gave in. She was nearly at the end of her resources, anyway. "We'd like very much to come with you," she said, with a seven-year-old's grave dignity.

"Well, that's fine. Come on, then; my house is down this trail."

As young as she was, she knew better than to give a stranger their House name and rank. "My brother is Lenny."

"You may call me Shai, Addie. Lenny, would you mind if I carried you?"

The little boy stretched his arms up trustingly and the man picked him up, settling him in the crook of his arm. He offered his free hand to Addie, who hesitated for a moment but took it, grateful for the support. They had not walked fifty yards down the trail before Lenny was limply asleep, his head pillowed in the hollow of Shai's neck.

Shai accommodated his long strides to Addie's shorter legs. The child was almost dazed with relief at having the responsibility for their two lives removed from her frail shoulders, and followed the man trustfully, not even watching the trail. Before long, the forest opened up into a winter-brown meadow. Tucked under the spreading great trees at the back of the meadow was a little cabin, neatly fenced with rails. It was a comforting, welcoming little place, and Addie, used all her short life to the austere stone halls of her father's fortress-palace, felt as though at last she had come home. Releasing her hand, Shai pulled on the latch, kicking open the door.

They were in a sort of all-purpose room. A fire crackled cheerfully on the hearth of the great stone fireplace where a big soup pot simmered, giving off a delicious aroma. On each side of the fireplace, inglenooks contained little beds, made up with crisp white sheets and lots of fluffy pillows. Beneath a side window giving a view down the dappled aisles of the forest, a hand-hewn table and four chairs were placed, with sturdy crockery on shelves to the left and a sink and pump and food safe to the right. Comfortable chairs were drawn up before the fireplace and a door in the corner led to what was obviously the forester's bedroom behind the fireplace.

Lenny stirred and wakened as Shai put him down on the left-hand inglenook bed, and looked around wide-eyed. "Are we home?" he asked simply.

Shai laughed. "Yes, Lenny, we're home. Do you want a bowl of soup now?"

Lenny scrambled off the bed. "Oh, yes, please!" He trotted over to the table and climbed into one of the chairs.

Shai took two deep bowls off the shelf and put them on the table. Moving with swift and economical movements, he fetched fresh crusty bread and golden cheese from the food safe, then stepped outside and came back with a brown pitcher full of cold, foamy milk, a plate of yellow butter, and a bowl of crisp apples. Ladling each bowl full of the fragrant soup, he placed the bowls and spoons on the table. Taking his place at the table's head, he began to carve off great slices of bread and pieces of golden cheese. But he paused in his task, turning to look at Addie, who still stood in the middle of the floor. "Aren't you hungry, Addie?" he asked kindly.

Addie was hungry. Her mouth was so full of saliva that

she had to swallow before answering. "Yes, sir, I am, but I don't want to eat your children's supper."

"I haven't any family, Addie. There's plenty for you."

Addie walked over to him and looked up, her gray eyes questioning. "If you don't have any children, sir, why are there little beds, just right for children, all made up? Why is there such a big pot of soup?"

For the first time, Shai showed a little unease. Lenny had stopped spooning soup into his mouth as fast as he could blow it cool and was listening intently for the answer, spoon clutched in his little fist. Addie looked up into Shai's face and waited. "Well, Addie," he said at last, "I knew last night that something was disturbing the peace of the forest. The forest is my domain, and its dwellers often bring me news of happenings far away. I had a feeling I might have company today, and that they might be two children about your size and that they might be hungry and cold and tired. So I got ready, just in case. And as you see, my feeling was right."

Still Addie looked into his face, waiting, her own face grave. Shai made a little exasperated gesture. "Please trust me, Addie. I promise to take good care of you and your brother. Come and eat your soup."

Addie was not quite satisfied, but she was very hungry. She climbed into her chair and began dipping the bread, still warm from the oven, into the rich broth. Lenny's spoon clattered in his bowl.

Their meal finished, Shai took them outside and to a smaller cabin, built into the earth and heavily chinked. When he opened the door, warm steam wafted out. Within, a spout gushed water from a hot mineral spring into a bathing basin almost big enough to swim in. Shai efficiently stripped off their bloody, filthy, torn clothing and popped them into the constantly refreshed hot water. Briskly but gently he scrubbed Lenny clean. (Addie took the soap and cloth from him and retired with dignity to the far side of the basin, where she washed herself.) Drying them with huge towels that had been left on a shelf over the hot water inlet to warm, he laid out clothes that just fit, a soft gray-green dress for Addie with a woven design of silky butterflies and soft gray shoes to match, and for Lenny, a small forester's costume like the one he wore, trousers and smock and thick-soled boots with soft tops.

When Addie found that the clothing fitted exactly, she looked long and searchingly into the man's eyes, but this time he was ready for her, and met her gaze squarely with just a hint of a friendly grin. "My feelings are often more detailed than other people's feelings," he said.

He wrapped them in warm furry coats and ushered them outside. After the steamy warmth of the bathhouse, the outside air was chilling, and a few flakes of snow were starting to swirl lazily through the darkening forest. As they crossed to the house, Shai threw up his head. Muttering something, he listened. Thus alerted, Addie listened, too, and was horrified to hear the killhounds, near and drawing rapidly nearer, making the forest ring and echo with their hunting song. There was a sound of men's voices, too, shouting and laughing.

As they paused in the open between bathhouse and cabin, a baying mass of huge, brindled, heavy-shouldered war dogs erupted from the forest, followed by a group of men in fur-trimmed leather hunting costumes. They were joking and calling to one another. "Gone to ground!" one of them yelled when he saw the cabin, and the others laughed at his jest. Hunting children through the winter woods was obviously a fine and amusing sport.

Shai, still muttering, turned, stepping between the children and the pack. When they reached him, he spoke only one word, and in a soft voice and an almost conversational tone. But the air vibrated and the ground shuddered with the power of that word. "Stop," he said.

The killhounds piled up on themselves stopping. Panting, slavering, whining, they milled about uncertainly—but none of their movements took them any closer to the children. Orris himself stepped forward, magnificently dressed in sable-trimmed russet leather. "Woodsman, those children are mine. Give them to me," he said, arrogantly.

Shai looked at the hard-faced, beautiful young man mildly. "By what right do you claim Addie and Lenny?"

"They're my dead brother's children. Stand aside, and

perhaps I'll let you live." Orris stepped forward, confident of having his path cleared.

Again, quietly, Shai said, "Stop." The air shivered and the sky darkened. Orris halted as suddenly as if he had encountered a brick wall. "What do you intend to do with them?"

Orris tossed his gleaming head, baffled. His arrogance was undiminished, but the sudden check had made him perhaps a little warier. He laughed, a chillingly cruel sound with nothing of humor or merriment in it. "I just want to play a little game with them. Shall we play huntsman and hunted, little Addie?"

Addie shivered with sudden terror and shrank closer to the forester. His big hand fell reassuringly on her shoulder. Softly, Shai said, "These children are under my protection. Isn't that so, Addie?"

Addie looked up at him. He glanced down and smiled reassuringly. "Yes," she said, as loudly and as clearly as she could. "We belong to Shai."

Orris snarled, his beautiful face distorted by rage and hate and greed into an ugliness that reflected his warped and violent soul. Drawing his sword, he stepped forward. "The woodsrunner can't save you," he sneered. "He can keep you company in death, though."

Shai made a motion as though gathering some invisible substance into his hands. The air around him seethed and crackled. As Orris lunged forward, he flung his hands open again. Orris screamed, dropped his sword, and clawed frantically at his chest. The dogs howled and ran off into the forest. The men of Orris's retinue drew back, fascinated eyes on their writhing prince, who fell to the earth, convulsing, and then lay still.

Shai turned to the men, gathering the power into his hands again, looking steadily at them. They shifted, whispered among themselves, and drew back. Shai held up his cupped hands. They were clotted about with some shimmering substance that hummed faintly. "Do you want to take up where your master left off?" he asked, mildly. The men shook their heads nervously. "Then take him up and carry him away. I don't want him littering my front yard. You may tell those who are interested that I can and will protect the children against any who try to harm them. Tell them also that this forest is my domain and that I will tolerate no trespass within its borders—and I have the means to enforce that, too."

One of the men cleared his throat. "We want no arguments with sorcerers. We'll deliver your messages." Gathering up Orris—Addie couldn't tell whether he was dead or merely unconscious—the men slunk away.

Shai took a deep breath. Slowly he opened his hands as if letting something gradually trickle through his fingers. Addie noticed that he was suddenly pale. "Are you all right, sir?" she asked anxiously.

"Yes, Addie, I'm all right. Just a little tired. Gathering and throwing the power takes a lot of energy. Let's get inside. Those men won't be back to bother you." He held out a hand to each of the children and they walked together into the house. Moving with an unaccustomed lethargy, Shai gave them each a nightgown and helped Lenny into his, tucking him into bed and giving him a comforting goodnight hug and kiss before he pulled the blankets up around his chin. The exhausted little boy was asleep instantly.

Addie, seeing that her little brother was safely asleep in his warm, clean bed, went to the fire and sat on the hearthrug, spreading her long, heavy hair to the warmth to dry. Shai picked up a hairbrush and sank wearily into one of the chairs. "Come here and I'll brush your hair," he said softly, and without thinking, Addie went and sat on his lap. Gently, the forester brushed the golden mass, separating the tangles with his fingers so as not to pull, fluffing it out as it dried and letting the curls run riot through his hands.

Her hair was soon dry with this treatment. Addie turned to face Shai. "What will we do tomorrow?" she asked directly.

"I thought we'd start lessons," said Shai.

"Lessons!" said Addie indignantly. She hated lessons.

"Yes, you both have a lot to learn. Languages, for one. You must learn to understand and speak the language of the ravens and the foxes, because ravens are the wisest of the forest creatures and the foxes know what's going on from one end to the other. And the language of the trees, if you like. Their patience is well worth knowing and something I think you lack, little Addie."

She looked at him with wide eyes. "Trees have a language?"

"Oh, yes. But it's very slow. It may take a tree a month to say a single sentence, and then it's usually about the wind and rain and the rich earth. You have to go back again and again and remember what the conversation was about all summer. The trees mostly don't believe in us, you know."

"They don't believe in us?"

"No, we move too fast for them to perceive, and our lives are too short for them to really get to know one of us. To a being that may live a thousand years, we're regrettably short-lived creatures, like mayflies are to us."

Addie was fascinated. "What else are we to learn?"

"Lenny must learn about people and how to make good men love him and evil ones fear him. He must learn stewardship of the land and its people. He'll be a king one day, you know."

"What about me?" she said shyly.

"That depends on what you want, little Addie. I can teach you all the things a woman needs to know to be a good wife and mother, cooking and sewing and taking care of children. Then when you're grown up, I can find a good, kind man and give you to him to be his wife and live together with him all of your days, if that's what you want."

"But what if that's not what I want?"

"Then you can stay with me and be my apprentice and I'll teach you the healing arts and how to gather the power and throw it and how to bend men and animals to your will and how to use the beings of the supernatural to shepherd the people and to protect them. Then when you have learned your lessons—but it takes many years, Addie, and the work is very hard and often dangerous—I will go out of this forest and take up my place in the world of men in their halls of power. With you to help me and support me, I can make a real difference in the battle against evil and pain and cruelty." The lethargy had sloughed away; Shai was lit from within by the power of his vision.

Addie felt the power of it and the glory and her child's

spirit caught fire. "Oh, yes, Shai!" she cried. "That's what I want to do!"

He looked at her shining face and laughed for joy. "I hoped you'd say that," he said, and held out his arms. Gladly she came to him, clasping him around the neck with her thin little arms and snuggling her little body against his broad chest. He cradled her gently in his strong arms. Laying her head against his shoulder, the little girl could feel the powerful beat of his heart and see, out of the corner of her eye, the ruddily flickering flames in the fireplace, and she sighed with the deep happiness of one who has at last come home.

CHAPTER 13

Adelinda's first sensation upon regaining the real world was of warmth and comfort. She sighed and stirred, and the comfortable warmness stirred too. She became aware that she was being held in someone's arms, her head lying on a strong shoulder as if it belonged there, a warm breath ruffling hair on her temple as if it had a right. For a dreamy while she thought she was at home, lying in Dep's arms as she had done two or three times, moments as precious in her memory as they had been in life. She sighed and nestled closer, and the arms around her tightened responsively.

Then she remembered. Dep was far away. Then with whom did she lie? It certainly wasn't Len, as it had been once before when she surfaced from the overmind. The broad shoulder against which her head lay, the deep chest that supported her upper body, the powerful arms that held her snugly, most assuredly did not belong to slight and wiry Len.

It occurred to her that she might open her eyes and look, though somehow she was reluctant to find out for sure who held her, as if the knowledge would bring the comfortable moment to an end. But it was necessary. She found herself looking into An-Shai's compelling dark eyes, only inches from her own.

Indignation flooded her. She wrenched herself out of his hold, striking frantically out at him with her clenched fists. Instinctively, he clung to her, and she battered at his hands. When he released her, she flung herself halfway across the room, where she crouched, panting with fury and panic.

"What do you think you're doing?" she spat defiantly, though if the truth were known, her anger was due more to her own response to that comforting embrace than to anything An-Shai had done. "You keep your filthy hands to yourself, you damned hypocrite!"

An-Shai had meant no harm. The emotional moment at the end of his scenario had affected him as much as it had Adelinda. He had escaped the overmind sooner than she had and come to her prison room, his usual cool aloofness overwhelmed with a powerful protective feeling. The little girl snuggling trustfully into his arms had touched a deep need to nurture that he was unaware of in himself, and the feeling had spilled over onto the real-life Adelinda. Without thinking that the adult Adelinda had far less reason to trust him than the child Addie, he had gathered her into his arms. He had, in fact, been holding her for several minutes before she awoke, much to Len's amazement.

An-Shai was not a man who offered his friendship easily. If he had been asked to describe himself, he would have said that he was a cold man, unemotional, neither needing affection from others nor able to give it. In fact, never before in all his austere life had he opened himself to another with such unthinking sincerity. To have his tentative overture flung back into his face with such violent contempt lacerated his pride and exacerbated the sexual self-doubts that he had never given himself an opportunity to overcome since his adolescence.

He drew himself up and smoothed out the wrinkles in his robe. Without deigning to answer her question, he said haughtily, "You turned to me for aid quickly enough when you really needed it."

Adelinda straightened. The icy arrogance that An-Shai had assumed to cover hurt feelings inflamed her indignation even farther. "A child turned to an adult for protection. But I'm no child, and you're certainly not Shai."

"The perils you face as an adult are more deadly than the perils Addie faced. You need a more powerful protector, as much more powerful as I am than Shai. Admit it, woman, you're beaten. You were beaten when you agreed to go home with Shai. You knew what was at stake when you accepted his protection, even if Addie didn't."

Adelinda turned white with rage. "I face deadly perils, all right, and every one of them has been created by you. Do something about evil and cruelty and pain, you said to Addie. But in the Vale, who summons all the evil and causes the pain? Who has the power to stop the cruelty with a word, and chooses to let it go on? If Shai and Addie could fight together against the world's evils, you're what they'd be fighting against! You're condemned out of your own mouth!"

It was An-Shai's turn to pale with rage. Adelinda's blow had landed too close the mark for comfort. "You," he said with icy calm, "don't know the first thing about pain or cruelty. But you're going to find out." He wheeled and strode out of the room, the bars crashing into place behind him.

Len let out his breath in a long whistling sigh. "I really wish you hadn't provoked him like that. Before you woke up he was holding you like a father holds a daughter. Why did you have to act like he was trying to rape you? If you'd handled him right, we'd be walking out of here free and clear right now."

Adelinda gave him an agonized look, then sank onto the sleeping bench and buried her face in her arms. She had been far more shaken by An-Shai's scenario than she was willing to admit. Len stared. He had never imagined that Adelinda could be so powerfully affected.

"I'm sorry," he said simply.

Adelinda wiped her face on a corner of her blanket. "Don't be. You're right. I didn't handle him well. I haven't handled him well from the day I met him. He sets my hackles up somehow and then I do something stupid."

Len hesitated and looked at Adelinda. Her expression was full of sorrow and misery. "In a way I don't blame him for being angry. You must have really hurt his feelings. What happened after I fell asleep?"

"We were talking about the future. He told me what Lenny would have to learn to be a good king—you were the crown prince, did you know that?"

"I knew it but I didn't think about it. I was pretty young."

"Then we talked about what I would be when I grew up. He gave me a choice, to go on and lead an ordinary woman's life or to learn his magic and be his assistant. He was so good, so full of excitement, I couldn't turn him down! I wanted to be his apprentice." She bowed her head to hide the tears starting in her eyes again.

"There's nothing wrong with that. He offered you a choice and you took the one that seemed best to you. Not everyone can be the leader. There's no shame in being a worthy man's assistant."

She was silent for a while. Len paced restlessly around the room. Something strange was happening to him. He could almost feel the distress that Adelinda was feeling, could almost feel An-Shai's raging, angry hurt. "What happened then?" he asked.

Embarrassment lanced through Adelinda, and Len winced with the impact of it. "He—he put his arms around me, and I laid my head on his shoulder, and he held me. I thought to myself that I had found where I belonged at last." The last word was half choked into a sob.

"That doesn't seem so bad to me. What is there in that to make you act like he'd turned into a poisonous snake?"

Adelinda writhed. "When I woke up, I thought for a moment that he was Dep. I was so happy! Then I looked at him and he was An-Shai." Then she cried out as a terrible blaze of confused resentment flared from Len. Linked as they were from their experience together in the overmind, the power of his bitter anger scored her sensitivities like hot acid. "Ah," she gasped in pain, "don't!" She threw up her arm as if to ward a blow.

No blow fell. She looked up, to see Len standing in the middle of the room, staring at her in silent, sullen rage. "You don't know about Dep," she began, almost timidly, fearing to provoke another emotional blow. "He was a—friend—of mine a long time ago." Len stared stonily at her. "No," she said, compelled to honesty by the smouldering eyes. "He was more than a friend, he was my lover. He was of the farmer folk, and I—I—" She stopped and choked and at last admitted to herself more than to Len, "I loved him very much. He was kind and gentle and good and I miss him every day. I never loved anyone before him and I've never loved anyone since. I had to send him away. They found out about him, my brother and his friends, and they would have killed him." She looked up at Len. The resentment was slowly being replaced with bewilderment.

"Why didn't you go with him?"

It was Adelinda's turn to feel bewildered. "Go with him? Where would we have gone? How could I have married him with nothing to bring to him? He had his own life to live and I had kept him from it too long. It was the right thing to do for both of us."

"The right thing to do?" Len's resentment flared again. "So you could get back to your parties and your fancy clothes and your friends? You said you loved him? You don't know the meaning of the word. If you'd loved him you'd have gone with him." He took a menacing step toward her. The bitter words spilled jerkily from his lips. "Dep was my uncle. I was fifteen when you destroyed him, old enough to know what you did. He loved you. He'd have stood up to your brother and all his friends for you. He'd have broken his back to make a living for you. He lived to be with you, and you sent him away without a thought."

"It's not true," whispered Adelinda, cowering against the wall. She held up a hand to stop him, but he would not be stopped.

"You killed him. You broke his heart and cast him out and he wandered away. A few years later we got word that he'd drunk himself to death in a gutter in Eastend." Len paused, breathing harshly. "There wasn't anything any of us could do about it. You went on your merry way, and never even cared enough to ask about him."

"I thought he'd gotten married. I thought he was happy. I thought the best thing I could do for him would be to leave him alone," Adelinda moaned, beyond tears. She thought her heart would burst. She hoped it would, and that she would fall down dead in that instant and not have to hear what Len was going to say.

"You couldn't be that much of a fool. He must have told you he loved you. You must have seen how happy he was with you. He was always so quiet, almost sad, except when he knew he was going to see you soon, and then he laughed and joked until he was like a different man."

"I thought he was always like that. He had the kindest, most loving nature of any man I ever knew. Oh, please, Len . . ."

"He asked you to have his baby. Do you think a man asks that of a woman he doesn't love with all his heart? He asked you to have his baby, and you laughed at him. That was when his heart broke, when he realized he wasn't anything to you but a few moments' pleasure. But he made excuses for you. 'She doesn't understand what I meant, Len,' he told me. 'She's too young. She's not ready to make a permanent commitment yet. I can wait. I've got forever.' That's what he told me, and the next day you sent him away. I only saw him once after that. He was gray and crushed and all the light in the world had gone out for him. You'd have been kinder to have killed him with your own hand. You'd do as much for a dog. But you left him to suffer until he died."

Adelinda bowed her head beneath the lash of Len's contempt. She deserved what he said. Young and heedless, she had used Dep and cast him aside, and had made herself believe that he was well and happy and that she had done the right thing to send him away. The bitter truth was that she had sent him away, not for his good, but because, infected by the prejudices of her class, she had been ashamed to love a farmer lad and too cowardly to trust him with her future. And the bitterest betrayal of all was that for years she had persuaded herself that he had been no more to her than a casual affair, one among many, denying to herself that he could have loved her or that she had loved him.

She had killed him. What Len said was the truth, she never doubted it, for she could feel his blazing sincerity. She had done a great wrong for which there could never be any atonement, for he to whom the wrong had been done was beyond the reach of any reparations. She would carry the guilt and shame of what she had done to the end of her days. She groaned aloud in her agony.

She felt Len touch her shoulder. She winced beneath that feather touch as if it had been a mighty blow. His voice was changed from the voice of the bitter tirade. "Adelinda," he said, "I'm sorry. I didn't realize that you loved him too. I was wrong to tell you what happened to him." He sat down next to her. "I never meant to tell you. I was glad to get the job you offered and determined to put the past behind me. He never blamed you for what happened; he knew you better than I did, and he said, 'They made her send me away, Len, and she can't stand against her whole family.' I thought I knew better, but I see that he was right. You hurt yourself as much as you hurt him, didn't you?"

She was unable to answer his question; there was too much bitter truth in it that she had never understood. After a moment, he went on, "For his sake, you can count on me as a friend. I think he'd have wanted that. He never stopped loving you. I think he'd have been sad to know that I caused you such pain." He touched her again, just a brushing of fingertips, and this time she didn't flinch, but endured the kindness that was more painful than angry words. Len had been purged of his resentment. It would be a long lifetime before she would be purged of guilt.

In his library, An-Shai, linked to the two outlanders by their shared experiences in the overmind, clutched at his chest as Adelinda's terrible pain seared through his own heart. For a moment, he thought he was suffering a heart attack, and his panic intensified Adelinda's guilt and Len's remorse, but then he recognized the source of the feeling, and an expression of cruel triumph wiped out the rage and disappointment on his face. Now was the time! Now, when she was reeling from the blow Len had dealt her, he could crush her free spirit and reduce her pride to submission. But he had to move quickly.

He thought furiously. Then he dashed to the palace kitchen and snatched half a dozen sharp knives from a drawer, ordered a powerfully built palace servant to come with him. In his bedroom, he gathered some of the soft, thick ropes used to belt a bishop's robes. As he strode through the library, he brusquely ordered Li-Mun to follow him.

He burst into the prison room, throwing the knives and ropes down on the sleeping bench by the door. Adelinda was turned sideways on the bed-shelf, her feet drawn up, her face hidden on her upraised knees. Len sat near her, his hand on her shoulder, speaking comfortingly to her. Crossing the room in two giant strides, An-Shai grabbed the front of Len's shirt and yanked him to his feet with enough force to snap his head on his shoulders. Spinning the young man around, he caught his head in the crook of his arm chokingly.

Adelinda raised an astounded face and came to her feet. "What are you doing?" she cried protestingly.

An-Shai ignored the woman. "Strip him," he snapped. Li-Mun, confused but obedient, moved to obey. Len kicked weakly at him and was choked nearly to unconsciousness for his efforts.

Adelinda came forward. "Please, Your Grace, you're hurting him!" She grabbed his arm imploringly.

She was shaken off with enough force to send her staggering. "Hold her," he ordered, and the servant grabbed her elbows from behind, twisting them and forcing her to watch the action in the middle of the room. When Len's clothing was removed, An-Shai flung him onto the table with enough force to send it skidding across the room under its burden. Regaining his grip on Len's windpipe with one hand, and pinning him cruelly to the table, An-Shai, immensely powerful in his rage, used the other hand to wrench Len's arm down and hold it next to the table leg. "Tie him," he snapped at Li-Mun. "Tie him tightly. He's going to be thrashing around."

"The circulation will be cut off," protested Li-Mun.

"It won't matter," said An-Shai, his voice as deadly as a viper's sting. "It may even be better. Tighter!"

Mouth set, Li-Mun did so, and repeated the procedure on the other three limbs. The small table only supported Len's body from his knees to his shoulders; with his wrists and ankles tied to the legs, his head lolled uncomfortably off the edge.

"Bring her here," said An-Shai, when the tying was done and he had gotten the knives from the bench and returned to the table. Li-Mun shoved Adelinda forward, until she faced An-Shai across Len's helplessly sprawled body. Deliberately, watching her horrified face, An-Shai placed one of the knives under Len's chin, pierced the skin with a quick jab, and drew the blade down his stretched throat, down the center of his chest, and down his hollowed belly. The skin parted neatly in the knife's wake, showing the membranes beneath. An-Shai contemplated his handiwork, made a quick second cut at a place where he had not quite cut through the skin. Len was laid open as if prepared for skinning. There was surprisingly little blood from the shallow gash. The bishop had been careful to avoid cutting deeply enough to do any real damage.

An-Shai took another knife and looked up into Adelinda's dilated gray eyes. "Let me describe to you what I intend to do," he said with the same deadly evenness. "I won't kill him. I'll just cut off a few bits that he doesn't really need. Ears are really unnecessary, and noses, and fingers and toes. Without fingers and toes, hands and feet aren't much use. I wouldn't want him to suffer from seeing his ugliness, so his eyes will have to go. He won't have much to say to anyone, so his teeth and tongue will no longer be necessary. The sound of his own screaming might distress him, so bursting his eardrums will be a real kindness. What priest, however compassionate, will give a marriageable girl to a hulk like that? His genitals will only be a burden to him, so they'll have to be removed." He paused to see what effect his words were having. Adelinda was breathing in gasps, perspiration beading on her wax-pale skin. "And then I'll let you go, just as you've asked. Freedom was what you wanted, and if the price is a little high, well, anything worth having is worth paying for. You can even take your friend with you, although what use he'll be, blind, deaf, mute, crippled, and castrate, I don't know. But he'll be free."

"No," said Adelinda. "No, please."

"No? But I thought freedom was precious to you."

Adelinda looked wildly around the room. Her eye fell on Li-Mun's face. The secretary looked horrified and revolted, but there was not a shred of doubt on his face that the bishop would do what he said he'd do. Len moaned, whether in pain or terror, she couldn't tell. Using the new sensitivity that had developed in the overmind, Adelinda reached out desperately to An-Shai with her mind. She encountered only boiling rage and implacable purpose. Her gaze fell to Len's agonized body. Bitter defeat welled into her shuddering soul. She could not let An-Shai do those things to Len, not at the cost of her pride or her soul or even her very selfness. "No," she said dully. "Not that precious. Please, don't hurt him."

An-Shai straightened. Triumph blazed from him like a great white-hot light. Adelinda cowered from the impact of his victorious exultation, and Len whimpered. She groped for the words to express her final capitulation, while An-Shai waited, a grim anticipatory smile upon his lips. It was not easy to find the words; her surrender must be total, for he was quite capable of carrying out his threats if he thought she was withholding any crumb of heart or mind or soul.

Then one of Orvet's supernatural allies entered into the room. There was a high keening wail, and An-Shai jerked around in astonishment to find himself facing a specter of a kind completely unknown to him. It was a female figure, draped in flowing robes, flickering eerily. Its hand was raised and the clawed forefinger pointed accusingly at him. The face was a mask of sorrow, but what sent An-Shai reeling back was that the thing wore his face, mournful, feminized, but recognizable. "An-Shai!" the specter mouthed. "Ah-Shai, I have come for you. You will never be free of me again. I am Erinys, who comes to those who willfully do great evil."

An-Shai recovered from his astonishment. He gathered energy into his hands and flung a small clot of it at the apparition. "Begone!" he commanded. "Go back to wherever you come from. I do no willful evil."

The clot of raw power passed harmlessly through the specter and dissipated. "No," it wailed. "I will never go from you. You have chosen the wrong when you well knew the right. Wherever you go, I will be. Whatever you do, look beside you and I will be there. In your waking and sleeping, in going out and coming in, in illness and health, I will be, for I am An-Shai."

An-Shai bowed his head for a moment, as if gathering his thoughts, then, raising it and looking directly at the specter, spoke one word. The word had no meaning that any of those present knew, but the walls quivered when he spoke it and little gray flecks danced for a moment in the air. The specter ignored his efforts. The accusing outstretched forefinger did not waver in its steady inclination.

Adelinda wrenched away from the paralyzed servant and began to untie the bonds that held Len and help him into his clothing. An-Shai saw her out of the corner of his eye. "That won't help you. It will be easy enough to tie him up again." The Erinys gave such a mournful shriek of sorrow at his words that he shied like a startled colt.

"Are you going to follow me around and scream whenever I try to say something?" he inquired, with irritation.

"Oh, evil, evil," mourned the specter. "Shame and sorrow, for evil knowingly done."

"I have done no evil! Whatever I have done has been for the best interests of everyone concerned," he said vehemently. "Shriek as much as you like, or go back to whatever hell you came from. I don't care. I will do what I must however much you scream." He turned and strode across the room to where Adelinda was supporting a trembling Len. He wrenched them apart and cast the wobbly-kneed Len aside as if he were a bit of trash. He took Adelinda's upper arms in a firm grip. "We have business to finish, we two," he said grimly. "You were about to decide how many pieces of Len's person your freedom was worth."

"Oh, sorrow, sorrow, for destruction of souls and goodness turned to evil," cried the specter.

Even more sensitive to him now that he was touching her, Adelinda reached out again to contact An-Shai. He had been startled and upset by the Erinys; the shield of cold implacability slipped for an instant and Adelinda perceived with amazement that there was no hatred in him, either for her or Len. In fact, she caught a glimpse then of the image An-Shai had been so careful to hide, even from himself, of Adelinda turning to him in joy and gratitude and himself taking her gently in his arms to comfort and protect. Then the curtain snapped back into place.

Adelinda realized that An-Shai failed to understand his own feelings. It would be easy to force him into a position where he would think he had to carry out his threats against

Len. She knew that he would regret it; she had caught the merest glimpse of the shuddering distaste his own intentions aroused in him. She looked into his implacable face and opened her mouth. And then the world disintegrated. Or so it seemed for a moment. There was an ear-shattering groan, a creak, and a snapping sound. The floor lurched under their feet and fell, sliding sideways as it did so. The walls leaned crazily and cracked right across, and chunks of lath and plaster plummeted from the ceiling. The whole room bumped and slid, stuck and slid again, lurching downward with a mad staggering. The occupants of the room were sent sprawling, except for the Erinys, which never deviated its pointing forefinger from the bishop, no matter where he was thrown.

The south wall of the room split open like a melon, and the movement stopped except for the rain of displaced plaster and settling snaps and creaks. There was a confused shouting, a clattering of hooves, and then Tobin was peering in the crack in the wall. "Here they are," he shouted. Scrambling through the crack, he pulled Adelinda to her feet, shoved her toward the opening, and turned to help Len.

As Li-Mun pulled himself waveringly to his feet and rushed over to help the groaning An-Shai, Orvet's head popped into the crack. Adelinda came staggering dazedly into his arms, and he caught her and supported her, pausing for an instant to look at the Erinys, surprised comprehension on his face. Tobin scooped up Len and carried him to the crack, maneuvering him through the narrow opening with Ina's help.

Adelinda could have wept with joy when Orvet half supported her to the side of a familiar red-brown horse, saddled and packed. "Can you ride?" he asked her, and Red Hawk whuffled a greeting.

"I can, but look to Len. He's weak." Orvet boosted her into the saddle and turned away to Tobin, still carrying Len in his arms.

"What's the matter with him?" Orvet asked.

"I don't know. He doesn't weigh any more than a new calf. Look at this." Tobin held the limp body so that Orvet could see the cut inside the partly open shirt.

An-Shai came staggering out of the crack in the south wall of his palace, bellowing for his servants, accompanied by the Erinys, dim and insubstantial in the sunlight. Orvet glanced at the ruin, assessing the enemy's condition. Karel's plan had succeeded beyond their wildest dreams. Cantilevers were not used in the Kingdom, and without realizing it, Tobin had fastened the trace chains to the projecting ends of those great beams that supported the south wing. When thirty greathorses had lunged against their collars, the cantilevers had acted like enormous skids, and the whole wing of the palace had been jerked down the slope like a titanic stone boat. Now it was disposed crazily on the grass, drunkenly leaning in a dozen different directions.

"He has to ride. The bishop's going to get everything organized in a few minutes. Let's get him onto his horse. Len, hold on to the saddle. Can you hear me?"

Len moaned. Karel came galloping up on Dusty. "Everyone get mounted! We've got to ride now!"

Orvet scrambled onto his own mount, and guided it alongside Len's mare, reaching out to steady him on her back. Tobin took the reins, and the cavalcade wheeled out of the meadow before the palace and headed for the eastern trail to the ocean. Karel came galloping back again. "Not that way!" he yelled. "The way's blocked by the farmers who came to see the demonstration. We'd have to cut our way out with sabers and lances."

"Where, then?" shouted Orvet.

"The west trail. We can turn north and bypass the head of the Vale once we're clear." He spun Dusty on his hocks and led the way at a reaching canter for the trail they had followed when they hunted down the night stalkers.

CHAPTER 14

It was cold, and dry, and the grit-laden wind blew eternally. Len had to be helped to mount and dismount, though he clung doggedly to his saddle. His wound refused to heal, subjected to the constant chafing of the many layers of clothing they all wore against the paralyzing chill. Time and again they turned to the east, only to be balked by An-Shai and the twenty soldiers he had hastily mounted on greathorses. He knew where they were and even had a general idea of what thier plans might be, since he was in constant contact with Adelinda through the overmind. He could not discern her thoughts, but he felt her feelings as if they were his own, and it was less of an advantage to the outlanders, struggling through unknown territory, limited in their choices of action, that Adelinda was also aware of An-Shai's feelings. In any case, all she picked up from him in those desperate days were deep-burning anger and implacable determination.

Len, too, was aware of the feelings of the other two, but he was so sunk in misery and weakness that he was only distantly conscious of his surroundings much of the time.

The outlanders had one real advantage: their horses. Tough, enduring, their wiry mounts kept going day after day through hardships that would have killed lesser animals. Subsisting on the bleached scattered grasses, often thirsty, their once-glossy coats dulled with privation and their proud heads carried low, the mountain horses kept up their ground-eating walk hour after hour and day after day.

Each night in their comfortless camps, the first care of

each rider was for his horse's well-being. If the horses were lost, the riders were doomed, and they all knew it. Even Len, burning with fever, did what he could for his mare. The others walked, leading the horses to spare the animals' strength.

An-Shai's greathorses suffered terribly. The soldiers who rode them knew nothing of the care of horses. Ignorant as they were, they assumed that the greathorses, being bigger, must be faster and more enduring. They spent their mounts lavishly at first, only to find the outlanders melting away like mist before them, as elusive and as untouchable as any specter. An-Shai himself knew better; his brief experience as a horse had given him a unique appreciation for the huge creatures' limitations, but his knowledge was not equal to the task of caring for them.

But even the amazing endurance of the mountain horses was nearly at an end when the outlanders made a dry camp in a little swale that offered partial protection from the searingly cold wind. They had been turned back once again from an attempt to ride east to the ocean, and worse yet, had found a guard placed upon the only water hole they knew of for many miles. They were thirsty, and near exhaustion as they huddled together like sheep for the warmth, Len in the favored center. Discouragement was as much a burden to their spirits as their physical ills. (An-Shai, some miles away, exulted to feel how near his adversary was to surrendering to despair.)

"What are we going to do?" asked Tobin, at last. "We can't get past them to the ocean and we can't get to the water."

"We'll have to fight our way out," said Karel, but not as one offering a real hope.

"What, the six of us against all of Godsland? We might as well have stayed in the Vale and learned to be good little serfs."

Through cracked and bleeding lips, Len, his eyes bright with fever, said, "You don't know what you're saying. We're better off out here if we all die. I say we ride west."

"Into the desert? We don't know the routes or where the water is to be found. Winter's coming on, and we don't have supplies to last another week, much less until spring," said Tobin. Ina began quietly to cry.

"No," said Adelinda, decisively. "If I turn myself over to An-Shai, he'll let the rest of you go. This is my fault. I'm the one who has to do something about it."

"Don't be silly," said Karel, sharply. "First of all, he wouldn't let the rest of us go. And secondly, what he'd do to you doesn't bear thinking about. He's gone mad. He must have, to have chased us so long."

"He wouldn't hurt her," said Len, drawing the stares of the rest of the group. Manifestly none of them believed him. Adelinda stared pensively at the ground. "It's too important to him to break her spirit. He'd use the rest of us to do it without a thought, just like he tried to use me."

"Len's right," said Orvet. "Adelinda turning herself over to him wouldn't help us. I think we have to turn west. The desert can't go on forever, and we can swing to the north in the spring. We're off the edge of the maps Karel made already; we must be at the farthest western edge of the known part of Godsland."

"That's right," concurred Karel, grimly. "An-Shai won't be able to follow us, either."

"What makes you think that?" challenged Tobin.

Karel gestured at the huddled little herd of horses that loomed against the starlight, too tired even to eat the sere grasses. "Our horses are almost spent. His must be nearly dead. He can't follow us into unknown wasteland on foot."

"He will, though," said Adelinda. She well knew the quality of his determination.

Karel looked at her for a moment. "Well, if he does he can't catch us in a straight chase. He's only been able to keep in contact with us this long because we keep doubling back and trying to get past his forces."

"Don't forget," cautioned Orvet, "that he's a powerful sorcerer, and may send some of his creatures after us."

"Can you protect us against such things?"

"Only if the sendings involve supernatural beings. I'm an exorcist, not a wizard, and I know as little about the energy he throws or the overmind as you do."

Ina, wiping her violet eyes, asked rhetorically, "Why does he persecute us so? We've never done him any harm?"

Surprisingly, Adelinda chose to answer the question. "He isn't an evil man. He really believes that he's doing the right thing. He has been taught that only the upper ranks of the clergy are wise and benevolent enough to run things and that the common people are really better off being cared for and shepherded. We outraged his ideas of propriety and he took measures to restore things to order."

"I think things have gone beyond that. The battle is something personal between you and him now," said Karel, dryly.

"Yes, because I symbolize all the disorder he's fighting against. Religion does that to people—it makes them think they know the right answers for everybody. They may do the most horrendous things in the name of goodness and mercy. I'm not without fault myself. If I had sat down with him when we first got to the Vale, and calmly and rationally discussed our different ways of looking at the world, I think we could have worked things out."

"You can't discuss things rationally with a religious fanatic," said Karel. "They're beyond the reach of reason."

"That's true, but An-Shai isn't a fanatic. He believes in his religion because it's a tool he can use."

"I've got to say that I'm surprised to hear you defending him."

"I'm not defending him. The only chance we have to ever see home again is to understand our enemy. We've underestimated him all along, and this is where it's gotten us." She gestured at the bleak campsite, and the encompassing desert.

"Will we ever see home again?" asked Len. Silence followed, save for the unending whine of the wind and the rushing sound of the blowing grains of sand, as each waited for one of the others to say what none of them wished to hear.

At last, Orvet, more at ease with exile than the others, said slowly, "Maybe not. We never have had any idea of how to get back across the ocean without An-Shai's cooperation. Perhaps it's just as well we never did reach the ocean. We'd have been trapped between saltwater and An-Shai's forces."

Adelinda's gesture was eloquent of despair. "Then what can we do? If we can't reach home, where can we go? In all this continent, there is no place of safety for An-Shai's enemies."

"Surely," said Karel impatiently, "even An-Shai wouldn't follow us out into the desert. Somewhere there must be grass for the horses, game to hunt, land to plant crops. Maybe there are even other nations, more hospitable than Godsland, where we could live for a year or two. In time, we could find another way home or learn to live here."

"Live here, in this forsaken desert, among these religion-mad people? We'd be better off dead!" said Tobin, vehemently. "I want to go home. I didn't contract to spend the rest of my life wandering in the wilderness."

Adelinda sighed. "We all want to go home, but we certainly wouldn't be better off dead."

"You!" said Tobin, viciously. "Why should you care where you live? You don't have the dimmest notion what it's like to love someone or care about a home and family."

"Tobin, shut up. You don't know what you're talking about," said Len, wearily. Abashed, Tobin quieted.

"One thing's certain: we have to get away from An-Shai before we can plan anything else," said Karel. There was a low murmur of agreement. Adelinda's gaze rested on the ground in front of her crossed legs.

"Then in the morning, we head west. Agreed, Adelinda?" said Orvet.

"We won't escape An-Shai," she said quietly. "He'll follow us to the ends of the earth. But we have to go somewhere, and maybe it would be better for the final confrontation to take place on ground that's as strange to him as to us. West i   ."

An-Shai sat on his ragged greathorse staring out over the desert. His hugely elongated shadow stretched out before him onto the desert floor, pointing the way like some prophetic omen. He ground his teeth with rage and frustration. "She's headed west," he said to Tsu-Linn who had brought soldiers to help in the hunt. "She's given up trying to cut back to the sea and she's going to try to lose me out there in the wilderness."

"Give it up," the initiate answered. "You'll never catch her out there. It's never been explored. No one knows the trails or where the water's hidden."

An-Shai turned on his superior haunted eyes that glittered as if fevered. Indeed, haggard and strained as his face was, he looked ill, as if his consuming obsession was burning away his very flesh. The Erinys, wavery in the sunrise, pointed at him and wailed sorrowfully, unheeded. "No. If she can live out there, so can I. She'll never escape me. I will break her!" He drew a ragged breath.

"Forget her. Come with me to the Hall of the Initiates. You'll rise fast; already you're as powerful as at least half of the initiates."

"No. Come with me or not, just as you like. But I'm going to catch her."

Tsu-Linn sighed. "Don't be foolish, man. Look at your precious horses. Three dead already, and more will die before the day's out. You'll never catch her on these horses."

An-Shai raised his fists above his head, a gesture eloquent of rage and despair. "I must! I must!" Random energies popped and crackled in the air about his form.

Uneasily, Tsu-Linn drew a little away. Li-Mun spoke from the background, where he had been quietly observing the argument. "Yes, Your Grace, you must." He turned apologetically to Tsu-Linn. "He'd be no good to you in the Hall. This is what he has to do. But we won't take the horses. Return to the Vale, sir, and take the horses with you. We'll follow the outlanders on foot."

"You'll never catch up with them. Men on foot against those speedy horses!"

"We'll catch them," said An-Shai hoarsely. He dismounted and pulled at the saddlebags. "Len isn't well, and he's getting worse. They won't be able to travel fast."

Tsu-Linn snorted. "And when you do? Two of you against the six of them?"

For the first time An-shai looked directly at the initiate. "When I catch her," he said through gritted teeth, "I'll make her beg for mercy, and weep for joy to get a pat on the head.

She'll tremble if I frown, and if I care to smile upon her, she'll think the sun has risen. She'll plead for the chance to wash my feet or sweep my room, but I shall not indulge her often, for fear of spoiling her." This vision was so pleasing to the bishop that his gaunt features curved into a travesty of a smile.

Tsu-Linn shuddered and looked away. "Well, when you do catch her, bring her to the Initiates' Hall." He gave An-Shai a slip of bark paper with the directions to that mysterious place written upon it. "If both of you should survive the encounter." Raising a hand in sardonic farewell, he wheeled his horse back into the rising sun, the soldiers following after.

Shouldering their bags and their canteens, the two clerics followed their shadows out onto the desert floor.

Gathered about the bitter alkaline water, waiting for seepage to refill the shallow basin Tobin and Ina had scooped, Adelinda and Orvet did what they could to ease Len while Karel scouted ahead. In the days they had ridden and walked into the west, Len's condition had worsened, exacerbated by the exertions and privations of their trek. He was delirious much of the time now, and it was becoming increasingly clear that without rest and care and good food, his life was in grave danger.

Orvet looked up at Adelinda, who was supporting Len's wasted form while the exorcist coaxed him to drink a little of the bitter water. "Is An-Shai still following us?" he asked quietly.

Adelinda raised her head as if listening to the wind, though she sought with an inner sense. "Yes," she said at last. "But he's farther behind. He's getting desperate. He's beginning to think we may get away, and he can't bear the thought. The Erinys is distressing him more and more, too. It keeps him awake at night and disturbs his concentration during the days."

"Ah, good. I didn't hope for such a success when I summoned it."

"Why not?"

"They only appear to those who act against their own consciences. If An-Shai were a truly evil man, he couldn't perceive it at all. Erinyes are only found on one small island offshore of the Republics—an island with exceptionally civilized inhabitants. I thought the appearance of an unknown supernatural might serve to distract the bishop for a while. It was beyond hope that it would actually fasten on him. It means that he knows, whether he will admit it to himself or not, that what he's doing is wrong."

Adelinda smiled. "I expect it would make you think twice before you did something wrong if you knew you were going to have to put up with one of those things pointing at you all the time. But it doesn't help us much."

"Possibly not. But then again, you never know. Here, Len, try to drink a little." He bent again to the task of coaxing a few drops of water through Len's parched lips.

Just then Karel rode over the crest of the nearest dunes. There was a broad grin on his face. "Mountains!" he yelled, as Dusty slid down amid cascading sand. "A huge range, bigger than the Black Mountains, I'd guess." He pulled his horse up and stepped off, some of the old fluidity of movement restored for the moment by his elation. "Fresh water, game, grass for the horses!"

"How far?" asked Adelinda breathlessly, as they all crowded around eagerly.

"Two days' ride. Easy days," he added, with a glance at the semiconscious Len.

"We've made it!" said Adelinda wonderingly. "Once we're in the mountains even An-Shai will never find us. Len's going to be all right. We made it!" She took a deep breath and laughed for joy, sweeping Karel and Orvet into an enormous hug, to find her own ribs being cracked in turn by Tobin and Ina. Freeing herself, she ran to Len and bent over him, willing him to share the rejoicing. "Len, Len," she called. "Len, there are mountains ahead, an enormous range. There's going to be a place you can rest and get better. We're going to be safe, Len!"

Len opened his eyes and looked into her smiling ones. "Mountains?" he whispered.

"Yes, mountains!" She gathered his bony hands into hers and felt, infinitely weakly, a returning pressure. "You're going to be well again!" Then she burst into absurd tears as she knelt there beside him.

An-Shai stopped so suddenly that Li-Mun, his eyes on the ground where he was placing his dogged footsteps, crashed into him. "What is it?" he asked, a suspicion of irritation in his voice.

"She's getting away! They've found something—somewhere to go that I can't follow. She's going to be safe from me!" An-Shai's voice crescendoed to a scream. "No! I won't let you get away!" Dropping his battered saddlebags to the ground, he flung himself down beside them and began to rummage feverishly through their contents. At last he drew forth a tattered scroll. Muttering with satisfaction, he opened it and scanned it intently. The sparks of energy that surrounded him constantly now sizzled and darkened to a sullen green. Finding what he sought, he rose to his feet.

The Erinys gave a sudden, bloodcurdling shriek as of unendurable pain. "No!" it cried, coalescing nearly into solidity, even in the full light of the desert sun. "Evil! Evil! Souls destroyed by willing evil!"

Li-Mun, fearing that madness had at last overtaken his superior, asked uneasily, "What are you going to do?" The Erinys sobbed and wailed.

Both were ignored. An-Shai began to gather the energy from the atmosphere around himself, clutching it into his clawing hands, kneading it into a denser and denser clot of lightning-shot, greenish-black fire. The crackling of sparks deepened to a hiss that rose to a roar. The power he held now between his outstretched hands was enough to blast the walls of a mighty keep, and if he had flung it at a living person, only rags and scraps would have remained. The terrible concentration required to control such an awesome charge distorted his face into a bare-teeth grimace. Li-Mun backed away.

Vibrating with the pulsations of the gathered and concentrated power he held, An-Shai flung his head back. "I, An-Shai, summon you, Supplililumalitlalumasulisimula!" he called, his voice a sonorous, full-throated chant as he carefully enunciated every one of the fourteen syllables of the name. The power between his hands melted and dripped away, leaving not a spark behind. An-Shai slumped to the pebble-strewn sand, his breath coming in heaving jerks.

Li-Mun, who recognized the name, was horrified. "Your Grace!" he cried, kneeling in the sand beside An-Shai's exhausted body. "What have you done? Why have you summoned a dragon? You can't control it; it will kill us all!"

An-Shai groaned and tried to lever himself to a sitting position. Li-Mun supported him with an arm around his shoulders. The two men found themselves facing the Erinys, only a slight flickering now betraying that this was an immaterial supernatural being. Its face, so like An-Shai's own that it even reflected the havoc of hardship and hatred, was twisted with pain and terror and something like disgust. "An-Shai!" it moaned. "An-Shai is destroyed! An-Shai is no more! In pride and hatred, An-Shai has chosen to destroy himself so that he may destroy that which has done him no harm. An-shai, oh, An-Shai! Weep for An-shai! An-Shai who has chosen to slay that which he was meant to cherish is damned forever!" Never had the thing's enunciations been so clear; its eternally pointing finger quivered right in the hierarch's face.

An-Shai was seized with a fit of trembling. He shrank back into Li-Mun's arms, staring at the Erinys with weak fascination. It shrieked with unearthly pain, and he flinched as if struck a cruel blow.

The atmosphere shuddered and the glaring sun dimmed. Overhead, great translucent wings with spidery claws at the wrist joints spread two hundred feet across the sky. Effortlessly, the dragon banked and turned, flapped its wings once with a sound like thunder, and stooped to alight on the sand. It was a bluish bronzy red, and its gracefully curved neck was enormously long and as flexible as a snake. Huge it was indeed, but incredibly attenuated, so delicate that it seemed likely to crumple in the dry wind. Perhaps a hundred and fifty feet long, it could have weighed no more than a ton, its legs so unbelievably slender that they hardly seemed sufficient to support it, its wing membranes as thin as tissue. The head was as big as one of the greathorses An-Shai had left behind, but dry and spare, all hollows and concavities, save for the great slotted eyes. It stretched its wings to the sky, supporting itself upon its two delicate legs and its serpentine tail. Then it placed the leading edge of one wing upon the ground, the wrist claws splayed to help support its weight, and spoke.

"Who summons me?" Its voice was like a chorus of sweet trumpets, brassy and yet melodious. "Often have I heard my name spoken in spells meant to drive me away, but never before has a human creature dared to call me. Who summons a dragon?"

An-Shai struggled to his feet, supported by his secretary. "I, An-Shai, summoned you. And now I conjure you to depart as you have come. Supplililumalitlalumasulisimula, begone!"

The dragon laughed, a symphony of bugles and horns playing a wild harmony of untamed mirth. "You, An-Shai, have not the power to send me away now. If you did not wish my presence, why did you call me?" It snaked its reptilian head down to look the two men in the eyes. Its breath was heavily sweet with a scent of crushed herbs. Its fangs were edged as well as pointed and fairly hummed with sharpness. "Was it because you and your companion wish to be a dragon's snack?" Its ropy tongue slithered out to flick over them in feathery little touches. "Pah. Old and dried out. I prefer the sweet-fleshed young of the human kind, milk-fed and no more than two years old, for my snacks. Are you perhaps a male and female of your kind? I have often thought of breeding up my own delicacies."

"No!" said An-Shai. "We are both males."

"Useless. But I perceive another herd of your kind a short way to the west. Perhaps there are females among them. Come along."

The dragon reared itself into the air, the enormous downdraft of its wings blasting the two hierarchs off their feet. Before they had even ceased tumbling, they were each snatched up in one of the talons and borne vertiginously away into the air.

The party of outlanders were just putting the finishing touches on a horse litter in which to carry Len to the mountains. Two long poles were slung from Dusty's stirrups in front to those on Len's mare behind, and a rope wound around them between the two horses to support a pad of blankets and Len's slight weight. They were unprepared for the sudden rush of dragon wings, the blotting of the sun, and the swoop upon them which left the two hierarchs sprawling in their midst. The dragon, having deposited its burden, circled once around the camp, setting the terrified horses milling, and settled itself upon the crest of the dune.

The awestruck outlanders stared at the towering creature, paralyzed in amazement. "A dragon!" breathed Orvet. "I've heard of them, but I never thought to see one!"

The dragon reared its snaky head against the sky and bugled one clear, piercing note. Then it lowered its head into the camp. "Are any of you female?" he asked.

"Yes," said Adelinda incautiously, too surprised at the creature's melodious voice to think what she was saying. "Two of us are."

"Good. Then I will keep you. What do you graze upon?"

"What does it want with us?" whispered Karel.

"It wants to breed us to provide snacks. It likes two-year-olds best," explained Li-Mun. The outlanders all looked at him, aware for the first time that their enemies were literally in their midst.

"Answer my question!" commanded the dragon. "What shall I feed you upon?"

"We can forage for ourselves if you will let us get to the mountains ahead," said Orvet.

The dragon cocked its head and considered. "Very well," it said at last. "You needn't think you can elude me. That one, An-Shai, has summoned me and I shall always be able to find him and through him, the rest of you."

"You aren't going to eat our children," said Karel, pugnaciously.

"Are you female?" said the dragon, snaking its head to stare him interestedly in the eye. "If not, have a care. I have extra males. I already know that those two are males, and if there are only two females, one male would surely be enough. When can I expect the first litter of young?"

"Humans only have one child at a time," said Adelinda.

"Disappointing," trumpeted the dragon. It turned its attention to Len. "This one is sick. I'll put it out of its misery."

"No!" said Adelinda, drawing her sword and leaping between the dragon's head and Len's recumbent form.

"Do you dare to threaten me, human?" the dragon blared, baring its fangs in reptilian menace.

"You'd better not hurt me. I'm female."

The dragon withdrew its head a few feet. "Ah, I see. And the sick one must be your child. Very well, female, I shall expect offspring from you immediately." Without warning or leave-taking, the dragon stretched its translucent wings and leaped into the sky, where it circled on the updrafts like some unthinkably huge vulture.

Karel drew his sword and turned to An-Shai, just pulling himself painfully to his feet. "You summoned that thing? Why?"

An-Shai ignored him. He turned, wavering with exhaustion, to Adelinda, who was still standing protectively in front of Len. "I was wrong," he said harshly. "I have no right to protect you and your people, and less than no right to force my protection on you."

Slowly Adelinda returned her sword to its scabbard and stood studying his ravaged face. He met her gaze squarely. "I would arrange for you and your folk to return to your homes, if I could. Unfortunately, in pride and anger I summoned the dragon. I thought it better that we all be destroyed than that you escape me. I was wrong in that, too."

Still Adelinda stood waiting. An-Shai's gaze fell to Len's recumbent body. "I was wrong to have hurt him, too. I wouldn't have done those things to him."

Adelinda broke her silence. "He believed you. So did Li-Mun. And I certainly believed you."

An-Shai smiled wryly. "We were still enough in touch in the overmind for me to enforce a feeling on you. Neither his fear nor yours were any more real than Addie's feelings of love and gratitude when Shai saved them from their uncle. Nor any more real than the determination to harm Len you read in me when you reached out through the overmind."

Adelinda looked at him skeptically. "The cut was real enough."

"Yes. But not serious. With proper care it would have healed in a week. The infection, the fever, the refusal to heal—all were the result of your determination to get away from me." He bent his proud head humbly. "Still, I was wrong to have done it or even to have threatened as I did. I don't understand myself why I felt driven to do those things, nor why I summoned the dragon. I never wished you or your folk harm. I only wanted to take care of you, and for you to be grateful to me for taking care of you." He made a gesture of bitter despair. "How can I expect you to understand? You've never harmed anyone inadvertently when all you meant was good."

It was Adelinda's turn to wince and avert her gaze. Unknowingly, he had struck her a keen blow! An-Shai, sensitive to Adelinda's reactions as he had never been sensitive to anyone before, saw and wondered, and Karel, scowling, took a step toward the hierarch. "What will you do now? Your servant there will kill me if you order him to," An-Shai said, watching her keenly.

"Karel doesn't kill people because I order him to."

"No, but occasionally I kill people who need killing," said Karel.

"Go right ahead and kill him," said Li-Mun, "if you want to spend the rest of your days breeding up babies for yonder snake to snack on."

All eyes swiveled to him. "What do you mean?" said Karel.

"An-Shai summoned the creature against its will. Only he can send it away."

An-Shai shook his head. "I already tried. It wouldn't go."

"I know of a charm used by the shamans of the Far Archipelago to send dragons away," said Orvet. "I'll admit that the breed of dragon they have there is smaller and less intelligent than this one, being a sort of overgrown sea snake. But it might work."

An-Shai looked startled. "Who is this servant of yours who possesses the lore of a hierarch?"

"He belongs to an order whose purpose is the control and eradication of the supernatural. We have almost no supernatural beings left in the Kingdom, and the Order of Exorcists is why." Adelinda thought it wiser not to mention that Orvet was a renegade member of that order.

The dragon made its presence known again. It swooped suddenly upon them, barking at them without bothering to land, "Why are you delaying? Proceed to the mountains and commence to breed at once!" It banked sharply, one wing tip brushing the sand, and flapped to gain altitude. It could be seen to be watching them carefully as it circled.

"We had best do as it says," said Li-Mun. "His Grace is spent and will not be able to make the attempt to control the thing for a day or two. As we travel, Orvet can tell us about this charm he knows of."

"It seems wisest," agreed Adelinda. "Put your sword away, Karel. Bloodshed won't help anything. I think maybe we can count on An-Shai to make what reparation he can." She held out a hand to the bishop. "Cry truce, Your Grace?"

He took her hand in his own. "Truce, yes. Or even armistice."

Chapter 15

Here in the foothills of the unnamed mountain range it was even colder than on the desert's windswept floor. The eight travelers huddled about the crackling fire they had built at sundown; at least here there was plenty of wood, resinous, burning quick and hot, from the aromatic low-growing junipers that covered the hills. Among the trees, the bleached grass was belly high to a horse, and much of it still bore dry seed heads; the horses were tearing ravenously at this bounty.

"The shamans always formed a group—they called it a web—before they worked the spell," explained Orvet. "They told me that the spell was too powerful to be handled by one shaman working alone. But they were not able to explain to me how they combined their powers."

"That's easy enough; they must have linked through the overmind," commented An-Shai. "I don't understand how they could have controlled the sea-dragons without knowing their names, though. It seems to me that the power of their spells must have dissipated harmlessly without a specific object to center upon."

"I don't think the sea-dragons have names," said Orvet. "They have no speech. And I have seen the spell work on a whole pack of the creatures."

"Are you sure they were supernatural beings?" asked Adelinda. "They sound more like some overgrown sea creature to me."

"In many ways they are, but when you see them cast their net of rainbow light to drive a school of fish or a pod of pilot whales into the jaws of their companions, or hear them sing up a terrible storm, you realize that they aren't just ordinary sea snakes."

"Adelinda and Len and I can link through the overmind easily enough, and I know the name of this dragon. But I know of no spell effective in sending dragons away for more than a few hours," said An-Shai. "Tell us about the spell they used."

"There are three parts to it," responded Orvet. "There's the web, and the weaving, and the casting. The web is the group of shamans and the linkages between them. The weaving is the dance and the song of the ritual. The casting I hardly know how to describe; the dance and the song completed, the shamans seem to sink into unconsciousness, and the sea-dragons just to float on the waves, but the atmosphere seethes with power. Then, for no reason the watchers can see, the dragons fall into a frenzy, churning the sea into white foam, and swim away."

"Dance? Song?" said An-shai. The mental picture of the cool and dignified bishop dancing and singing was too much for Adelinda; she tried to muffle a chuckle behind a cough, but An-Shai was too sensitive to her feelings to be fooled and gave her a haughty glance. Then, perhaps catching a glimpse of her mental image, he smiled. None of them had ever seen him smile in genuine amusement; the effect was startling, as if a statue carved in ice had suddenly flushed with the warm tones of living flesh. Unnoticed and unlamented, the Erinys gave a final weak flicker and vanished. "I've never danced or sung before, but I suppose I can learn. I expect the shamans used the ritual to put themselves into a trance and enter the overmind."

"Can we do that?" asked Adelinda.

"We shall have to, if we're to form a linkage. I haven't any of the drug used to induce a trance. It shouldn't be difficult, since the three of us are still in contact."

"Len can't. He's too weak," said Adelinda, firmly. They all looked at him. His wasted form was propped against a pile of saddles. They had been camped among the junipers for three days now, while Karel and Tobin hunted and the impatient dragon alternately perched on the rocky ridge that sheltered them from the desert's eternal wind and nagged at them to begin producing young at once. Rest and the broth Ina and Orvet made from the game the hunters brought in had done much to restore the invalid, but he was still terribly weak.

"I can if I have to," Len said spiritedly, but his brave words were belied by the pinched white face protruding from the blankets that wrapped him around.

"I'm afraid he must," said Li-Mun. "The dragon told me today that if we didn't start breeding soon, it would begin eating the males. Fortunately, it can't tell the difference between individuals yet, much less their sex. It's all that has kept it from weeding us out before now."

"Can the two of us handle the dragon?" Adelinda challenged An-Shai.

"Possibly. We can only try. Orvet, show us the dance and the song and the rest of the ritual and we will see what may be done." Automatically, An-Shai assumed command, placing himself at the center as the exorcist disposed the members of the party according to the ritual. The song was a simple one, a few repeated phrases, easy to learn even in a strange language. The dance was more elaborate, involving a complicated series of relationships among all the members of the group, and even as they practiced the smooth gliding steps and stately turns, they could feel the atmosphere charging itself with power, not the sullen greenish stuff that An-Shai's anger had summoned, but a paler glow giving off golden sparks that snapped and crackled in random arcs between the dancers.

Ready to begin, they paused for an instant, An-Shai and Adelinda gathering their courage before plunging into the deadly confrontation. "If we don't succeed in driving the dragon away," said An-Shai, looking about him at the members of the party, "it will doubtless destroy us all. Dragon lore is very specific on that point. They are vindictive creatures." The yellowish glow of the invoked power played on his gaunt features and made his eyes glitter.

"It'll have a fight on its hands—or claws," said Karel, cocking his crossbow and setting his heaviest bolt in the groove. Tobin silently picked up his lance and set the butt of it against the packed earth.

"Let's get on with it," said Adelinda tightly. Her hair crackled with static and sparkled with little flashes of light.

Uncertainly at first, the chorus began, and then steadied as the singers found their notes. The steps of the dancers followed the precise pattern evoked by the music. The sparks of energy began to leap only toward the center around which Adelinda and An-Shai revolved, thickening in the space between them, dancing to the rhythm of the song like a concatenation of fireflies caught in a whirlpool. The dragon suddenly shrieked like a thousand discordant trumpets and stretched its wings into the dark sky, obscuring the stars.

Instinctively, An-Shai and Adelinda turned toward each other, gathering the energy more and more tightly between their outstretched arms and bodies. Adelinda's face was rapt, her eyes open but unseeing; An-Shai's face was grim with terrible concentration. A last few sparks leaped from the faltering dancers to the pair in the center, and the inward flow of energy died, leaving a pulsing heart of raw power like a captive sun. Tobin sagged against the shaft of his lance; Karel's crippled leg buckled under him and he sank to the earth. But none of the fascinated watchers took their eyes from the two who struggled to contain and control the energy between them. Then, suddenly, the light died, the energy vanished soundlessly, and the insensate bodies of the two flopped bonelessly to the ground. Adelinda and An-Shai were gone, taking the power they had gathered with them. The dragon leaped into the sky with a thunder of wings and vanished.

They found themselves in the overmind, soaring on powerful wings, their long serpentine neck recurved in the habitual attitude of flight of the dragon kind. Their vast wings were edged with golden fire; their scales dripped raw energy from serrated edges. They opened their mouth and trumpeted a mighty challenge to the darker-colored specimen of their breed they could see struggling to gain altitude. To the entity they had become, the dragon that had held them in such contemptuous captivity seemed delicate and easily broken. They tilted their wings and stooped upon it as the falcon stoops upon its prey, casually knocking it tumbling through the sky of this place that was only sky. Spread wings cupped the air again, and they soared, watching as the dragon fluttered frantically to regain its equilibrium.

But the dragon was far from beaten; it was a canny creature, and as they stooped on it again it flipped over and struck at them with its extended claws. It had won its aerial battles, both in the material world and in the overmind, and they had been earthbound creatures two minutes ago.

All that saved them from being gutted like a cod was the cloak of lambent energy they had been gifted with by their companions. A spitting arc of fire knocked the dragon aside, squawking with outrage. Then it had the height advantage of them and was stooping on them with a rush of air. But they had learned caution; they spilled the air from their saillike wings, beat the air once, twice, and finding themselves again above their adversary, struck, missing with claws but battering with wings and, with a bolt of golden fire, flung with an awful will to blast and damage. The dragon tumbled, veered, and struggled to right itself. Then it fled. Another dragon it could face with a will, and even the two bold and determined wills that opposed it. But not the sorcerous fire.

Once they had been two, but only vestiges of separateness remained. Now they were one, a single savage, greedy purpose, all will and cruelty. When the dragon managed to steady its flight and began flapping its wings desperately to gain escape speed, they stooped upon it again and exulted in its terror as it fell.

Again it regained its balance and raced for escape. They hovered above it, preparing for the final blow, talons ready to grasp and rend, fangs keening with eagerness for blood. But deep within their savage heart, they hesitated and debated with themselves. —Let it go, urged the part that had been An-Shai. —Such mistakes are easy to make. It will not bother the travelers further. —Very well, send it away, agreed the part that had been Adelinda.

They opened their vast maw and roared at the scuttling

dragon. "Flee!" they trumpeted. "Nor bother humankind again. Fly, little insect!" They set the overmind resounding with cruel dragonish laughter as the dragon, heartened by the knowledge that it was not to be blasted into tatters, stretched out its neck and flapped its wings even harder. It dwindled into the perspectiveless distance of the overmind and was gone.

Power dripping from their wings like golden rain, they banked and soared, rejoicing in the freedom of flight and in the end of loneliness. How could they ever be lonely again? They who had been two were one. Together they had the power to break out of the overmind into the material world, to soar in sun-drenched skies, to stoop upon the helpless prey, crunching bones and drinking warm red blood. No hierarch or initiate could stop them, they exulted, for their name, Anadeshailinda, did not have the fourteen syllables that were traditional for dragon names and could never be discovered by the methods used by the clergy of the Quadrate God. They wheeled around the immaterial sky, mustered their wills, and broke out of the overmind, transported with dragonish glee and greed. Poet or peasant or bishop in his palace, all would be fodder for their consuming. Coruscating with yellow fire, they swooped and dived, stalled and pulled out of their stall. Below them smouldered the dim fire of the camp, a mere spark in comparison to their radiance. They could see white amazed faces turned up to them and steadied their flight to strike.

—Wait a minute, we aren't really a dragon. —We could be a real dragon. —Our duty is to protect, not to destroy. —We would be worse than any real dragon. —Our friends are counting on us.

The argument within themselves nearly brought them out of the sky, the rhythm of flight lost in their confused wrangling, part of them arguing now for dragonish pleasures, now for duty and honor against the other part and then switching sides again until neither part knew what the other part wanted. At last the part that had been An-Shai said sadly, in a voice like quiet flutes, "If we go back to our own bodies we'll be alone again. I never knew how much I hated being lonely."

"We can't ever be completely alone again. I'm partly you and you're partly me." Adelinda laughed a little, a sound like a distant fanfare. "Perhaps it's just as well Len didn't come with us; it's confusing enough being two people."

"I'm here," said Len. "I came to show you the way back. But you were too busy flying around and thinking gruesome thoughts to notice. Come on, your bodies are this way." As they abandoned it, the vast dragon figure thinned into the immaterial wind and faded with a final shower of liquid golden fire.

For three more days they rested, for all were drained and exhausted, as if the dance and the outpouring of energy they had given to Adelinda and An-Shai had spent all their resources. During all this time, An-Shai and Adelinda avoided each other, keeping the width of the camp always between them. They had been too close to be able to bear each other's company, a sharing of memories and thoughts and emotions that were almost too chaotic to comprehend, and a baring of weaknesses before each other that was deeply humiliating to the two proud spirits. They each had much sorting and thinking to do.

On the evening of the third day, An-Shai came walking purposefully across the camp to Adelinda's resting place, knowing, as he would always know her every feeling and she his, that she was ready to discuss with him what was to be done. Wordlessly, she shifted to the side to give him room, and silently he dropped onto the blanket. The others, aware that the time for decisions was at hand, gathered around.

"I'll send you and your people home, if you wish," he offered, knowing that for him at least, that was as impossible as to cut off a part of his body and send it away, but also knowing that the offer had to be made. To try to keep her against her will was now unthinkable.

Adelinda was no more able to contemplate separation from him than he from her. "For my people, I accept, if that's what they want," she said gravely.

They turned with an uncanny harmony of movement to the rest of the travelers. "I want to go home," said Tobin immediately. "There's someone waiting for me."

"Me, too," said Ina. "There isn't anyone waiting for me, but there will be." Her wicked smile promised a fair degree of havoc among the young men who had never noticed her before.

"I'd prefer to stay here and find out what the clergy of Godsland know about the supernatural," said Orvet. "Len, if it would please you to stay, your scholarly talents would be more useful here than in the Kingdom."

"I'd like to stay," said Len shyly.

"Oh, yes," said Adelinda. "Please stay, Len. I need you." Then she turned to An-Shai, jolted by the sudden surge of jealousy he felt and almost as quickly mastered. "I owe Len," she explained, though it wasn't really necessary; An-Shai knew her feelings as well as she did. He reached out and gently touched her arm, soothing a little the familiar guilty sadness of Dep's loss.

"I think I'll head for home," said Karel, when they all turned to him. "I've had enough of adventuring for a while. That little cottage in the cottonwood grove looks pretty good to me. I have it in mind to marry and raise a family."

"A wife could be found for you here," offered Li-Mun. "I hope to have some influence with the new bishop of the Vale, and I could see to it that you got a pretty one."

"Thanks," said Karel dryly, "but I prefer to choose my own wife, and it won't be one who's been so downtrodden from birth that she's afraid of her shadow. I want a woman with a bit of spirit. The women of Godsland are pretty, I'll grant you, but they've got no character."

"Things are going to change in Godsland," said An-Shai quietly. "The practice of using supernatural predators to control the population is going to stop. Schools are going to be opened to the children of peasants and nobles—girls as well as boys. The clergy are going to teach as well as protect and comfort the people."

"I hope you realize that you're talking about reforming your entire society," said Orvet interestedly. "Just educating the children is going to rock your religion to its foundations."

"It needs to be rocked," said Li-Mun heatedly.

"There is no religion," said An-Shai bitterly. "It's all a

fraud, designed to control the people and backed up with magic and the supernatural."

"What do you intend to do, tell everybody that?" asked Adelinda.

"No, the people need the crutch—until they've learned how to cope without it. It may take generations. For now, just stopping the use of supernatural predators like the night stalkers and starting schools for everyone should be enough."

"You've changed a lot since we arrived."

"No, I haven't. I always felt that the duty of the clergy was to protect the people. I became a novice because I wanted to help." His glance fell. "Children do things for reasons like that. I learned ambition later, as I rose through the ranks, and forgot or put aside my first reasons for accepting the religious life." It was Adelinda's turn to give him a comforting touch.

"How do you intend to accomplish all these things?" asked Li-Mun. "I hardly think the initiates are going to welcome your revolutionary ideas with open arms."

"There's only one way. I'll have to rise through the ranks of the initiates as fast as possible and make myself the highest of all. It means facing and mastering every initiate from the lowest right up to the highest in tests of will, of control in the overmind, of handling the supernatural, and from what Tsu-Linn tells me, of skill in cards and dice." His face was grim.

"That could be quite a task," commented Orvet.

"I can't do it alone," said An-Shai bluntly. "If you will come with me and lend me your knowledge of the supernatural, and if Len will help me with the research I'll need to do and won't have the leisure for, that would help. But you would have to come to the Hall as my servants. I don't like to ask that of you." He paused, searching for the right words. Everyone looked uncomfortably away; they didn't have to have been in contact with him through the overmind to know that it was cruelly hard for him to say what he must say.

"Adelinda, if you will come with me and support me in the overmind, and with your will and courage, and I have reason to know that you're more than amply supplied with both, I might have a slim chance of succeeding. But there's only one way a woman would be permitted at the Hall." He stopped again and took a deep breath. "That's as my wife." He faltered again, aware of her sudden inner rebellion. The impulse toward freedom was very strong in her. If she had loved him as a man, her choice would have been easy, but her heart had been given long ago. Even though Dep was long dead, he was only recently dead to her, and she had not yet grieved properly for him nor come to terms with her own guilt. He felt these things even though he didn't understand. "I know that I've given you plenty of reason to hate and fear me, and I don't know how to behave toward a wife. I wouldn't ask you to—well, be a real wife—have children, and all those things."

If he failed to understand her, she was uncomfortably aware of his feelings. She understood too well that the sexual escapades of her youth, mere adventures to her, were loathsome to him, and that the thought of taking a real wife was at best confusing and upsetting. His youth and young adulthood had been spent denying and repressing all natural feelings in those directions. It would be very long before he would be able to establish a natural sexual relationship with any woman, if he ever could, and she was probably the least likely woman on the face of the earth to inspire affection or desire in this proud, cold man. The only way he could be touched, she thought, was through his strong protective instinct, and she had taught him well that she neither needed nor wanted his protection. Nor did he appeal to her; a man more unlike the warm, loving, merry Dep would be hard to imagine. He could never respond to her need for affection and gentle kindness.

The others were silent, waiting for her decision; she knew that if she refused to go with An-Shai that both Orvet and Len would follow her lead.

But in the last analysis, was there really any choice? The experiences in the overmind had melded An-Shai and Adelinda into something more than two individuals. They were two halves of a whole. Could they flourish or even survive for long if they parted? Would the breadth of two continents and an ocean sever the bond that had formed between them? She rather thought not, and she knew without quite knowing how she knew that so wide a separation would become in time a nagging pain that would draw them inevitably together. Even before they had merged to become a dragon they had been acutely aware of each other.

Sensitive to the trend of her thoughts, if not their exact content, An-Shai said, "I need you, Adelinda. If you leave me, I'll never be able to change the things that need to be changed, or even to live content with my limitations." He held out his hand for her to take.

She hesitated for only a moment. Then she sighed and laid her hand in his. "I need you, too, An-Shai. It seems our destinies are linked and we have a role to play in Godsland. I'll stay."